"Stop tryi~~ng~~

~~...~~ me."

Mark Taylor had to admit a grudging respect for the woman in front of him. But he wasn't about to let her see his feelings. "That's out of the question, Ms. Black."

"Do you have any idea what this will do to the child? Do you even care?"

"Of course I care," Mark said, leaning forward. "I'm his father."

"How long have you known about him, Mr. Taylor?"

"A little over three weeks."

"Well, I've been his mother for two years. Ever since his birth mother asked me to raise him. I've bathed him, fed him, changed his diaper. I've comforted him when he was sick, stayed up nights with him, bandaged his little knees, kissed his tears away, tucked him into bed at night. In other words, loved him. What have you done?"

"I'd have done every one of those things if I'd been given a chance."

"Why weren't you given a chance?"

Mark pushed aside another flash of respect and told himself he didn't owe her an explanation. "All that matters now is that I'm his father."

"On paper."

"On paper. In the eyes of the law. *In my heart.*"

Dear Reader,

A few years ago, my wonderful editor at Superromance and I had a brief discussion about the timelessness of the marriage-of-convenience theme in romance fiction. For months afterward, I found myself thinking about the idea of marrying a stranger and wondering what would possibly compel any woman in today's society to take such a drastic step.

It's not as if women today need a man to provide for them, or to save them from scandal. Money alone wouldn't be a compelling enough reason for me, nor would it be for most of the women I know. So *why* would a modern woman step into an unknown future with a complete stranger?

I could come up with only one reason I'd personally take such a step, and that was if someone was going to take away my child. If that threat were hanging over me, and if it appeared I had no legal recourse, I might do anything.

With that realization came the creation of Dionne Black and her son, Jared. Shortly afterward, a very determined Mark Taylor strode onto my imaginary stage, and I knew I'd found a match for Dionne. A man just as resolute in his decision to find his son and bring him home as she is to keep her child.

But that still didn't answer one basic question: Can a marriage based only on love for a child succeed?

I hope you enjoy meeting Dionne, Mark and Jared as much as I did and that their story warms your heart as it did mine.

Sherry Lewis

P.S. I'd love to hear from you. Write to me at P.O. Box 540542, North Salt Lake, UT 84054-0542.

FOR THE BABY'S SAKE
Sherry
Lewis

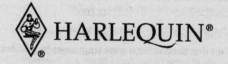

HARLEQUIN®

TORONTO • NEW YORK • LONDON
AMSTERDAM • PARIS • SYDNEY • HAMBURG
STOCKHOLM • ATHENS • TOKYO • MILAN • MADRID
PRAGUE • WARSAW • BUDAPEST • AUCKLAND

ISBN 0-373-70883-1

FOR THE BABY'S SAKE

This edition published by arrangement with Harlequin Books S.A.

® and TM are trademarks of the publisher. Trademarks indicated with
® are registered in the United States Patent and Trademark Office, the
Canadian Trade Marks Office and in other countries.

Visit us at www.romance.net

Printed in U.S.A.

To Valerie and Vanessa
who continually amaze me
And fill me with wonder.

CHAPTER ONE

IT WAS ALREADY early evening as Mark Taylor rode the elevator from his office on the twentieth floor to the mall far below. His briefcase was full, and his mind reeled with discovery, exhibits and testimony for his upcoming trial—the trial that would be a turning point in his career.

He paid scant attention to the people around him. He didn't have time for distractions. But when the woman standing in front of the jewelry store caught his eye, his feet stopped moving and his mind lost its train of thought.

Marianne?

He stared, wondering if he could possibly be imagining her. Marianne Holt had disappeared from Boston without a word three years earlier and taken Mark's dream of a home and family with her. He hadn't heard a word from her in all this time, and he'd long ago learned to ignore thoughts of her when they surfaced.

As he watched, the woman turned and gave him a better view of her face. She looked slightly different—her hair had grown from the short cut he remembered—but he'd have recognized her anywhere.

His heart picked up its pace while he hesitated, trying to decide whether to approach her. Mark had never been one to run from a confrontation, and the one he deserved with Marianne was no exception.

He made his way through the crowd and came to a stop behind her. "Picking out an engagement ring?"

She whirled to face him. "Mark," she said, eyes wide.

"Surprised?"

"A little."

Mark didn't know why she should be. He'd worked in this building the entire six months they'd been together, and she knew firsthand about the long hours required to move up in a large law firm.

She glanced away, then met his gaze again. "Actually, I'm here for a conference with an attorney from McAllister and Carter. I thought you'd have gone home by now."

He checked his watch automatically; it was later than he'd thought. "I see. And you figured you'd be safe."

"Something like that. This is late even for you." She laughed uncomfortably, looked behind her as if searching for an escape route, then pulled herself together. "Are you still working your way up the ladder at Jamison and Spritzer?"

"One rung at a time," Mark admitted. "I have a chance to make partner if I can just keep my feet to the fire. And without a home and family, that should be easy enough." He ignored the bitter twist of her mouth and asked, "And what about you? Still practicing law? Or did you give that up along with everything else?"

If his barb found its mark, she didn't show it. "I'm still practicing. I can't imagine not being a litigator."

Her devotion to her career had always been a sore spot between them. Not that Mark had wanted her to give it up. But while he'd indulged in fantasies about a future with a home and children, she'd been planning a life that didn't include those things.

Even after she'd made her feelings clear, Mark had clung to the hope that she'd change her mind…until she'd suddenly ended their relationship by disappearing without a word.

"Well," he said, "as long as you're happy."

"I am, and obviously so are you." She sidled a step away. "It was nice to see you again, Mark, but—"

Resentment Mark had kept buried rushed to the surface. "Don't you think I deserve a few answers before you disappear again?"

Her gaze flew to his. "Answers?"

"Sure." He lifted his shoulders in a deceptively casual shrug. "How about telling me where you went when you left here?"

Marianne took her time responding. Annoyingly cheerful music and chatter of passersby filled the silence, and when her answer finally came, he could barely hear her.

"I went to Idaho."

"Idaho?" He rocked back on his heels, trying and failing to picture Marianne in the rural setting. "Why there?"

"I have family there."

Mark turned his attention to the window display and tried to digest that bit of news. Something didn't feel right. Marianne had never been overly attached to her family. In fact, she'd hardly mentioned them. "I thought your parents lived in Florida?"

A flicker of a smile teased her lips. "I have a second cousin in Boise."

"A second cousin." He said the words slowly, turning them over in his mouth as if that might suddenly help him understand. But it made no sense at all. She'd turned up her nose more than once at the thought of spending birthdays and holidays with his lively bunch of relatives. He couldn't imagine her suddenly developing a yen for family ties. "What made you decide to run off to see this cousin of yours?"

She shrugged as if it didn't matter. "Everything."

He held her gaze, almost daring her to look away. "Don't you think I deserve a better answer than that?"

"It's the only one I can give you." She sounded defiant, but her gaze faltered ever so slightly.

Another man might not have noticed, but Mark had spent years learning to recognize when a witness was trying to hide something. He also knew how to drag out the truth when it was necessary—and it was necessary now, if only for his own peace of mind. "So, you just woke up one morning and realized it was time to go to Idaho."

"Something like that."

"And have you been in Boise all this time?"

"No." She lifted her chin slightly. "I left there two years ago and went to San Francisco."

That sounded more like the Marianne he'd known. "Is that where you live now?"

"Does it matter?"

"Chalk it up to morbid curiosity," he said with a bitter smile. "You know how I hate loose ends. Are you married?"

"No. Are you?"

"No."

Her expression faltered for a moment. "I'm sorry."

"Yeah? Well, so am I." He took a chance and touched her arm lightly. "I loved you, Marianne. And I believed that you loved me. I thought we were building a future together. It took a while to come to terms with losing you, but I managed. Now I just want to know why."

She drew away from his touch. "I had some things I needed to deal with."

"What things?"

"Things." She laced her fingers together and waited while a young couple looked longingly at a ring in the window. "Personal things," she said when they moved away again.

"We were talking about getting married," he reminded her. "What was so personal you couldn't share it with me?"

"You wanted a different life than I did, Mark," she said softly. "Talking to you wouldn't have helped. It would have made everything more difficult."

"Thanks for the vote of confidence." He ran his fingers through his hair, putting three years of frustration into the action. "It's interesting that you'd turn *away* from the man you claimed to love and *to* the family you never saw. What could they do for you that I couldn't?"

Her eyes darkened with anger. "This all happened a long time ago. I don't see any point in talking about it." She took another step away.

Mark knew she intended to walk out on him again.

He made an effort to pull himself together, to hide the anger, hurt and overwhelming sense of waste. "I don't want to get back together with you, if that's what you're worried about. I'm just curious about what made you leave, and why you chose Idaho of all places. It's been three years. What can it hurt to tell me now?"

She sent him a wary glance. "I had things to think about."

"Like what?"

"Like us."

He shook his head quickly. "Don't give me that, Marianne. I might believe taking a month to think things through. I might even understand two or three. But thirty-six? And what about letting me know what you decided...or are you still thinking?"

"I don't need your sarcasm," she warned.

Mark made an effort to drop it. "Look," he said carefully, "I just want a few answers. You ran out and left me completely in the dark. We were fine one day, and you were gone the next. So, what happened?"

She sighed heavily and glanced away again. "You haven't changed at all, have you?"

That stung, but he didn't want her to know that it did. "I guess not. Put yourself in my shoes for a minute. What if I'd been the one to disappear without a word. Wouldn't you want an explanation?"

She remained silent for so long, he began to give up hope. Just when he was ready to forget about trying to tie up loose ends, she turned a troubled gaze in his direction. "If I tell you, will you leave me alone?"

"Yes, of course."

"You won't like it."

"What difference can it make now, other than to fill in the blanks I've been carrying around with me?" He tried to soften everything about his expression—his eyes, his mouth, the set of his jaw.

"Okay." She took a steadying breath and studied his face for another moment, then seemed to come to a decision. "I was pregnant."

The music faded and the people around them disappeared. Disbelief, joy, anger, excitement and bitterness all corkscrewed together in his stomach. But outrage rose to obliterate everything else. "You were pregnant?"

She nodded without looking at him and lifted one hand to pluck nervously at the shoulder of her blouse. "Yes."

"Was it my baby?" He could barely get the words out.

"Of course."

"Then why did you disappear?"

"I had to think," she said in a near whisper. "I had to decide what to do."

What to *do?* What choices were there? Only two— one of which Mark found utterly unthinkable. And he knew without being told which one she'd made. Consumed by outrage, he looked into the eyes of the woman who'd killed his child.

Somehow, he managed to find his voice. "Shouldn't that have been a choice we made together?"

"*You* weren't pregnant."

"It was my child."

"And my body." She met his gaze steadily. "My choice to make."

"We're talking about a life, Marianne. A human being, not a possession you can get rid of because it doesn't fit the color scheme of your apartment."

Anger flashed in her eyes. "I know you don't think much of me, Mark. But I can't believe you're so willing to assume I decided on an abortion."

The roaring in his ears quieted and hope took the place of blind fury. "You didn't?"

"I decided not to. I carried the baby to term." She rested her hand on the narrow ledge outside the store and half smiled at him. "It was a boy."

He had a son. Hope pushed aside every other emotion and made his hands tremble. Tears of joy burned his eyes. "When can I see him?"

"You can't. I don't have him."

The spark of hope died. "You gave my son away?"

"I thought it would be best for everyone."

"Did it ever occur to you that it might not be best for me, or for him? That *I* might want to raise him?"

"With *your* career?" Marianne laughed and brushed a lock of hair away from her face. "Get real, Mark. You wouldn't have had time for him, either. No matter what you say, you're as married to your career as I am to mine, and I thought he deserved a life with parents who would put him first. Besides, I didn't want to see you."

"You wouldn't have had to see me," he said, clenching his fists until the stubs of his nails bit into his palms. "Where is he? What agency did you use?"

Marianne's eyes narrowed. "Why?"

"Because I'm going to find him, and I'm going to get him back."

"Oh, no." She shook her head and backed away. "You can't."

"If you think that, you don't know me at all."

"You can't raise a child alone. Not with the hours you work."

"He's my son, Marianne. Maybe you don't want him, but I do."

"He's been with my cousin for more than two years," she argued. "As far as he knows, she and her husband are his parents. *I* haven't even seen him."

"Is that supposed to make me change my mind?" He laughed harshly. "I don't care where he's been. I don't care who he's been with. You've stolen two years from me, and that's time I can't ever get back no matter what happens now."

Marianne drew herself up and faced him, no longer an ex-girlfriend but the attorney he'd always respected. "You can't take him from them. It wouldn't be right."

"Was it right for you to give him away without even discussing it with me?"

"Maybe not, but I can't turn back the clock and change that. What's done is done—"

He cut her off. "Is the adoption final?"

She hesitated just long enough to give him hope. *"Is it?"*

"I shouldn't have told you," she muttered. "I should have known you'd act like this."

Mark had gone beyond caring what she thought of him. "Tell me now," he said coldly, "or I'll take you to court to find out. It's up to you. I want every detail—his date of birth, the name of the hospital where he was born. Everything."

She looked as if she could cheerfully kill him, but he knew that he'd worried her. He hoped she'd want to avoid a messy personal lawsuit—especially one that was sure to get media attention. That the same love for her career that had made her decide to give his baby away would convince her to cooperate.

Instead, she checked her watch and shook her head. "I'm late. They'll be waiting for me upstairs." She turned to walk away, then added, "I've told you all you need to know, Mark. For all our sakes, leave it alone."

This time Mark let her go, but he wasn't about to take her advice. He had right on his side. He also had connections and training. The law no longer turned a blind eye on the rights of a child's birth father, and he intended to take full advantage of that. If Marianne wouldn't tell him what he needed to know, he'd track down her cousin and see what she could tell him. One way or another, he'd find his son and get him back.

EXHAUSTED AFTER a full workweek, Dionne Black stopped the stroller and unfastened the harness that barely contained Jared's squirming little body. August heat shimmered on the distant foothills, now golden-brown with drying wild grasses. A slight breeze stirred the tops of the cottonwood trees along the riverbank and made it more pleasant here than inside Dionne's tiny apartment with its woefully inadequate air conditioner.

The faint sounds of nearby traffic mingled with the cries of children clambering over playground equipment. Joggers passed her on the trail, huffing slightly, and she caught snatches of conversation as walkers in groups passed. She loved bringing Jared to the park in the evenings. It gave her a good excuse to slow down for an hour or two.

Lifting her excited son from the stroller, she started to wrap her arms around him for a hug, but he wriggled away. She smiled, telling herself she should know better than to expect cuddles from the energy-packed two-year-old before bedtime. Jared had more vigor and curiosity than she and Brent could ever have imagined.

She pushed away the sadness that always came when she let herself think about Brent. "All right, Jared," she said, setting the toddler down, "get moving. Let's work those wiggles out."

Jared started across the grass like a windup toy with wheels spinning. Dionne had always loved living in the heart of Boise, but lately she'd begun to wonder if she should move to the suburbs. There she'd be able to let Jared run and play without worrying that he'd dart out into the busy streets.

Some days, like today, she wondered whether she'd be able to keep up with him. Brent was supposed to be here with her, helping, chasing, laughing, teaching Jared about being a boy. But the accident last year had taken Brent from them.

No amount of wishing could change that, and she'd made a vow to be happy, if only for Jared's sake. Besides, Brent wouldn't want her to mourn forever. She could almost see him scowling at her and the clouds in his clear blue eyes.

I'm fine, she told him silently. *I'm just tired.* Her work at the insurance agency often left her exhausted, physically as well as emotionally. Maybe one day she'd go back to school and get her degree so she could work with disadvantaged children as she'd always dreamed. But right now she had to bring in a steady income, and that meant doing the monotonous work she hated so much.

Tucking her keys into her pocket, she started after Jared. "Don't go too fast, cutie. Mommy can't keep up."

He giggled over his shoulder and ran a little faster on his unsteady legs. "Over there," he said, pointing toward the jungle gym.

Of course he wanted to climb. Jungle gyms, stairs, cabinets—Jared didn't care, as long as he could go up and then jump down again.

"How about the swings instead," she suggested, catching up to him and holding out a hand to help him over the low concrete barrier that separated the playground from the rest of the park.

Jared shook his determined little head and scowled up at her. "Me do it."

"All right, you do it."

The breeze stirred the air again, tousling his dark hair as he worked his chubby legs over the step. Finally successful, he beamed up at her. "Swing."

"Okay. Let's see if we can find one with a belt so you won't fall out."

He toddled across the sand, and she had to hurry to catch him before he moved too close to the flying feet of other swinging children.

Luckily, they found an empty chair complete with safety strap, and within just a few minutes she had him swinging gently.

"More," he cried. "Go high, Mommy."

"You are going high," she assured him. High enough, anyway. In protest, he arched his body, pushing against the harness that held him in place. "You have to sit still," she warned, "or Mommy won't push anymore."

When he bucked against the restraint again, she caught the swing and held it. "Sit still, Jared."

His face puckered into an unhappy scowl and for a moment she thought he'd cry. He tried to twist in the seat to see her. "I wanna... I wanna go high."

"You were going high," she said gently. "Now, sit still or you'll have to get out." She wondered if all two-year-olds were so determined to go higher and faster, or if he'd inherited the trait from one of his biological parents.

Jared folded his tiny arms and scowled at her. "High."

"Shall we get you out?"

"No."

"Will you sit still, then?"

"No."

He looked so serious, she had to bite back a smile. "Either you sit still, or Mommy will get you down. Those are your choices."

They indulged in a silent battle of wills for a few seconds until Jared eventually, reluctantly, gave in. He shifted back in his seat and held on to the front of the chair. "Push, Mommy."

"Good boy." She gave him a gentle shove and let her gaze travel to the benches facing the playground.

If anyone had asked, she couldn't have said what it was about the man sitting there that bothered her. He'd been here every evening for the past week or more. He looked innocent enough—just a kindly middle-aged gentleman taking a rest on a park bench—but every once in a while, when he didn't think she was watching, she could swear he was following Jared with his eyes. Tonight, he had someone with him. A younger man of about thirty wearing a dark suit.

Dionne tried to relax. Maybe the younger man was his son. Maybe they were here enjoying the park and the breeze, just as she was. But she couldn't shake the inexplicable apprehension that pumped through her veins with every heartbeat.

To the best of her knowledge, the man hadn't ever followed her home. She was probably overreacting, but she took every precaution to make sure she and Jared were safe. She never stayed late, always took a circuitous route to her apartment, and avoided deserted streets. She'd even started carrying a can of pepper spray.

And now there was a second man—

If anything, the younger one seemed even more menacing. She studied them circumspectly so she could describe the younger man in as much detail as the older one if the need arose. Dark hair. Thirty to thirty-five years old. And he looked tall. Even sitting, he towered over his companion, and his legs, stretched out in front of him, reached halfway across the sidewalk. She paid only slight attention to his clothing—that didn't matter as much as his features—but she was too far away to get a good look at his face.

Tonight instinct told her to get Jared out of the swing and take him home. Home, to the safety of their tiny apartment with its dead-bolt locks on the doors. She hated the idea of keeping Jared cooped up all day at the baby-sitter's and all evening, too.

But she couldn't bear the thought of anything happening to him.

Scarcely daring to breathe, she waited until a woman she recognized from her building started herding her children away from the playground. Ignoring Jared's protests, Dionne stopped the swing, unbuckled the restraints and managed to hold him close until they got back to the stroller.

She forced a friendly smile and started a conversation with the other woman, falling into step beside her as if it was the most natural thing in the world. Only then did she dare to send a surreptitious glance over her shoulder, hoping she'd find the men chatting casually or watching someone else.

But what she saw sent a finger of ice down her spine. The younger man had risen to his feet and had even taken a few steps after them. The older gentleman was speaking quickly, urgently, motioning him back to the bench, but both men had their eyes locked on Dionne as she took Jared home.

MARK WATCHED the petite blond woman disappear into the trees with his son. *His son.* It had been two weeks since Marianne dropped her bombshell, but he still hadn't gotten used to the idea that he had a child. Now it was even more difficult to believe that the active little boy he'd just watched was his flesh and blood.

"Don't frighten her," Saul Mason growled, tugging him back to the park bench.

Mark sat reluctantly, though every cell in his body urged him to go after them. Saul was right. He didn't want to tip his hand too soon.

He sent the private detective a sidelong glance. "You're absolutely certain that was him?"

"Positive." Saul rested both arms on the back of the wooden park bench. "He was easy to find, the adoption being a private placement and all. And it was pure, dumb luck that I found him and your girlfriend's cousin together. Two birds with one stone, so to speak."

"Tell me about her again."

"Her name's Dionne Black. Widowed. Husband was killed in a car accident about six months after the boy went to live with them. They were trying to get their ducks in a row, so to speak, so they could adopt him." Saul's lips curved in a tight smile. "The husband being gone might make your case easier to win."

Mark had a brief flurry of sympathy for the woman, but who was he kidding? He knew he'd do anything to get his son back—even use the woman's misfortune to his advantage. But he wasn't naive, either. Mr. Black's death might make the judge sympathetic to the widow. A vicious divorce would have served Mark better.

"What do we know about Mrs. Black?"

"She works at Intermountain Health Providers," Saul replied. "It's an insurance agency with an office in the Mead Building downtown. She's been there for a couple of years, working in the claims department. Looks like she went to work for them right after her husband died."

"At least she didn't sit back with her hand out waiting for someone else to take care of her and the boy." Mark stared at the trees again, remembering the way she'd looked back at them as she spirited his son away, wondering what kind of caregiver she was.

Saul crossed his legs and let his gaze travel toward the river. "She has no family to speak of. An uncle somewhere in California, but both parents are gone. Father deserted the family when she was little. Mother passed away when she was sixteen." He flicked a glance at Mark and added, "Her in-laws are still alive, but they live in Florida."

Mark thought that might work to his advantage, as well. He turned his gaze away from the trees. "Did you get financial records?"

Saul pulled a folded document from his shirt pocket and passed it over. "I have the rest here, too. Where the kid goes while she's working, her home address, the whole nine yards."

Mark scanned the paper quickly, noting that Dionne Black didn't have many resources to draw upon. While she earned a reasonable salary, and didn't have a lot of debt, she obviously wouldn't be able to afford a lengthy court case.

"So what's next?" Saul asked.

"Next," Mark said, tucking the woman's financial records into his own pocket, "I take a trip to the courthouse and get the ball rolling. The sooner I get the custody suit filed, the sooner I can take Jared home with me."

"You want me to keep watching them?"

"Absolutely. She looks stable enough on paper, but I don't want to take any chances on her bolting after the constable serves the complaint."

"You got it." Saul stood and spent a few seconds readjusting his shirttail inside the waistband of his polyester slacks. He glanced at Mark, then at the nearly empty playground. "Of course, she'll be more cautious now that you've drawn attention to us. I might need a little more for expenses..." Another quick glance. "In case I need to rent a car or take other precautions to keep a low profile."

Mark pulled out his checkbook and flipped it open. "How much?"

"A thousand?"

A small price to pay, considering what was at stake. Mark wrote the check and handed it to Saul with a warning. "Don't let her know you're watching."

"I got you this far, didn't I?" Saul said, stuffing the check into his pants pocket. "You've seen your kid. And if it hadn't been for the mistake *you* made, she wouldn't have even noticed me."

Mark stood to face him, but he had to look down to meet the man's eyes. "She must have noticed you before this or she wouldn't have taken off like that."

Saul drew himself up to his full height, which put him even with Mark's shoulders. "Maybe. But she's never gotten spooked before."

With effort, Mark bit back a defensive response. Much as he'd like to, he couldn't deny Saul's accusation. He *had* made a mistake by starting after her. He just hadn't been able to stop himself.

He muttered something about checking with the detective the following day and started toward the far entrance of the park—the opposite direction from the one Dionne Black had taken with his son. He turned his face into the slight breeze and hoped it would wipe away some of the tension that seemed to knot every muscle in his body. But it didn't help. He had to struggle against the urge to double back and find the address Saul had given him, just to see where his son lived.

Until he had the court documents on file, he'd be smart to ignore his heart and stay as far away from her and Jared as possible.

CHAPTER TWO

"IS HE STILL out there?"

Dionne shook her head without turning from the apartment window. This was the fourth day in a row she'd seen the man watching them, but just like those other times, he'd vanished into thin air. Evening shadows had already begun to pool beneath the trees and shrubs. Rush-hour traffic had thinned to nothing more than a few stragglers hurrying home. She couldn't see the man anywhere.

Her friend, Cicely Logan, tried to peer through the chink in the living-room curtains over Dionne's shoulder. "Are you sure it was the guy from the park?"

"Positive." Dionne turned away from the window and lowered herself into a chair. Her hands still trembled and her heart thudded as if she'd been running up stairs.

Cicely took her friend's place at the window, and the fading sunlight formed a halo of her curly, dark hair. "It was the older man? The one you've noticed in the park before?"

"Yes." Dionne had trouble getting the word out. "He's been lurking outside all weekend and was on the sidewalk in front of my office again yesterday."

Cicely's dark eyes narrowed with worry. "What about the younger guy?"

"I haven't seen him since that day at the park." Dionne rubbed the bridge of her nose gently, wondering if it really had been only four days ago. It felt like a lifetime.

"Have you called the police?"

"Of course." Dionne's head pounded in rhythm with her heart, the product of nearly sleepless nights and stress-filled days. "They can't do anything unless *he* does something. There's no law against sitting in the park, or being on the sidewalk outside my office, or even across the street from my apartment. I can't say for sure that he's watching me."

Cicely let the curtain drop and turned back to the room. Her expression tightened when she looked at Jared, who was content for the moment with a stack of brightly colored building blocks. "If anyone tries to hurt him, I'll kill them."

Bile rose in Dionne's throat at hearing her own fears voiced aloud. "You don't think—" The rest of the sentence caught on her almost tangible fear.

Cicely seemed to realize she'd made things worse and dropped a comforting hand to Dionne's shoulder. "Maybe it's nothing. Maybe he lives nearby. Or maybe he thinks you're attractive and wants to ask you out."

Dionne sent her a doubtful smile. "He's old enough to be my father."

"Maybe he is."

Dionne gave her head an emphatic shake. "No, he's not."

"How can you be certain? You were only Jared's age when your dad disappeared."

"He didn't disappear," Dionne said, her voice

sharp. "He walked out on us to live with another woman. There's a difference."

"Maybe he's come back again."

"He wouldn't. And if he has, it's too late. My mother killed herself working two and three jobs to support me while he never once looked back. I'll never forgive him for that."

Cicely dropped onto an ottoman near Dionne's feet and grabbed her ice-cold hands. "Forget I said anything. It's probably not him. It's probably nothing at all. But I'll stay here with you if you want me to."

Grateful tears filled Dionne's eyes. "What would I do without you?"

Cicely shrugged away the question. "That's what friends are for. Give me half an hour to get my things, and I'll be back."

Dionne blinked up at her and tried to smile. "You don't have to do that. The doors are deadbolted, the windows secure, and we're three floors up. We'll be fine. I just don't know what I'd do without you to talk to, that's all."

Cicely dropped Dionne's hands and craned to see out the window again. "I don't mind staying."

"Thanks, but it's not necessary. I'm sure I'm over-reacting. I've been alone every night since Brent's accident." As Dionne trailed one finger along the silver frame that held his picture, an unexpected twinge of anger darted through her. If he'd been here, she wouldn't have to worry.

Swallowing guilt, she stood and turned away from the picture. "Just do me a favor," she said to Cicely. "Watch for this guy when you leave. He was wearing brown pants, a green-striped short-sleeved shirt, and—"

When the doorbell cut her off, she shot a panicked look at Cicely and sent up a silent prayer of gratitude that her friend hadn't left yet.

Moving on tiptoe, she crossed to the door and checked the outside entrance through the peephole. To her surprise, a uniformed officer stood on the threshold.

"It's the police," she mouthed to Cicely, who'd moved to Jared's side.

"Good." Cicely scooped Jared from the floor. "Maybe they're going to do something, after all."

Dionne opened the door and took a long look at the man's badge and uniform. "Yes? Can I help you?"

"Dionne Black?" He didn't even bother removing his sunglasses.

"Yes."

Without another word, he held a thick manila envelope toward her. When she took it, he made a notation on a document attached to a clipboard, curved his lips in a facsimile of a smile and pivoted away.

Dionne watched until he reached the elevator, then she closed the door and leaned against it.

"What is it?" Cicely gave in to Jared's wriggling and set him back on the floor.

"I don't know." Trembling, Dionne tore open the envelope, pulled the document partway out and scanned the court heading. "I'm being sued by someone named Mark Taylor."

Cicely's expression grew even more sober. "Who is he?"

"I have no idea." Dionne could almost taste the apprehension now. "This couldn't have anything to do with Brent's accident, could it? It's been such a long time—''

"Read the rest," Cicely urged, closing the distance between them.

As Dionne took in the caption, she grew numb with disbelief.

"What is it?" Cicely prodded again.

"It's a Complaint for Custody of Minor Child." She managed to choke out the words, but every one ripped a piece from her heart. Her worst nightmare had come true. Someone wanted to take Jared away from her.

She let the document drop to the floor and covered her mouth with her hands. She saw her friend scramble for it and pick it up.

Cicely flipped pages, reading quickly. Her soft brown face hardened. Her eyes glinted. "This can't be real."

But it was. Horribly, frighteningly real.

Cicely touched Dionne's arm gently. "We'll call my cousin. He's a lawyer. I'm sure he'll help. But, Dionne, this can't be real. Your cousin, Jared's birth mother, wanted *you* to raise him."

With all her heart, Dionne wished she could believe Cicely, but the vague sense of foreboding that had been plaguing her finally had a shape—someone was coming for Jared. And he had a name.

Mark Taylor—Jared's father.

WITH TREMBLING FINGERS, Dionne dug the old address book from the bottom drawer of her dresser. She turned pages quickly, sustaining a paper cut and accidentally tearing a page in the process. She could hear Cicely in the other room, soothing Jared, urging him to sleep.

She had an old telephone number for Marianne somewhere, but she had no idea if it was still current. Marianne had made it abundantly clear that she had no room in her life for Jared. Her career came first. At the time, Marianne's promise to disappear from their lives had seemed like such a good idea. Dionne and Brent had thought they had plenty of time to gently tell Jared the truth about his birth and to give him a chance to choose whether or not he wanted to meet the woman who'd given him life.

Marianne had assured Dionne over and over again that Jared's birth father would never be an issue. He was, Marianne had told her, completely devoted to his career. She'd given Dionne the impression that the relationship had been short-lived and casual, but the affidavit attached to his complaint certainly didn't bear that out.

Taking one ragged breath after another, Dionne flipped a few more pages and scanned the cramped writing for Marianne's name. They didn't come from a close-knit family, and though they had a relationship of sorts, they really were more like casual acquaintances than cousins. That's why she'd been so surprised when Marianne first approached them about taking Jared.

Marianne hadn't told her parents about the pregnancy. They wouldn't have approved, and she hadn't wanted to deal with their disappointment along with everything else an unexpected pregnancy brought into her life. She'd wanted to make sure Jared was placed with a loving family, but her work in the legal field had left her leery of people in general, so she'd taken a chance with Dionne and Brent.

Though Dionne had never seriously considered adoption before, it had taken less than a minute for her to come to a decision. Brent had been equally thrilled with the idea. Jared had literally been the answer to their prayers and, it seemed, they were the answer to Marianne's.

But she hadn't been in contact with Marianne since the day Marianne had left Jared with them and driven away from Boise.

Now Dionne had to find her. She had to know more about Mark Taylor, and how he'd found her after all this time. She wanted Marianne to explain why the story she'd told two years ago didn't jibe with the affidavit sitting on Dionne's coffee table tonight.

Finally, after what felt like forever, she found the notation she'd made with Marianne's number, written in pencil that was now half rubbed away. She sat on the edge of the bed and pulled the phone onto her lap. Her hands were trembling and she was having difficulty drawing breath.

She turned on the bedside lamp and squinted to make out her writing, then dialed quickly and held her breath while the phone rang four times. When the answering machine clicked on—a generic computer-generated voice that announced the number she'd dialed and instructed her to leave a message— she let out her breath and closed her eyes.

"I have no idea if I've reached the right number," she said quietly, "but if Marianne Holt is at this number, or if you know where to reach her, please ask her to call her cousin Dionne." She left her own number, replaced the receiver slowly, and clutched the telephone.

"Any luck?" Cicely's voice caught her off guard and pulled her head up with a snap.

"I found a number," Dionne said, "but I don't know if she's still there."

"What about your uncle? Won't he know how to reach her?"

"Maybe." Dionne met Cicely's dark gaze slowly. "If I don't hear back from her tomorrow, I'll try to call him."

"You should call him tonight," Cicely urged. "It would make you feel better."

Dionne shook her head quickly. "Uncle Charlie doesn't know about Jared. Marianne wanted it that way." She didn't go into any further detail. Cicely wouldn't understand the stone walls that seemed to separate each individual in her family, the long periods of silence that all of them just accepted.

Sometimes, she envied families like Cicely's where the people seemed to care about one another deeply, where they shared confidences and visited often. But she couldn't change what was, and it did no good to dwell on it.

Cicely came to sit beside her. "Maybe you should call your uncle anyway, if only for your own peace of mind."

Dionne shook her head again and tried to change the subject. "Is Jared asleep?"

"Yes. Finally." Cicely pushed a lock of hair away from her face. "He knows something's wrong."

"I'd be surprised if he didn't pick up on it," Dionne admitted. A yawn overtook her, but she fought it. She'd already been without sleep for three nights in a row, and she doubted she'd get any to-night, either.

As if she could read Dionne's mind, Cicely stood and started toward the bathroom. "Do you have any-thing in here to help you sleep?"

"Probably. I never did use those pills they gave me after Brent died. But I don't want to take any-thing."

"You need something, girl. You'll be no good to Jared if you wear yourself out."

Dionne opened her mouth to protest, then clamped it shut again. "I'll try to rest," she promised, "but I don't want to drug myself to sleep. I don't dare."

"Even if I stay here and keep one eye open at all times?"

Dionne hesitated, then shook her head again. "I'll sleep," she promised. But she could tell by the way her friend's eyes narrowed and her mouth thinned that Cicely didn't believe her. "I just need to be alone for a while. I need to think."

"I'll be back in the morning to check on you," Cicely warned, "and you'd better look more rested than you do right now."

That would take a miracle, Dionne thought. And she wasn't going to hold her breath waiting.

DIONNE COULDN'T SIT STILL. She paced in front of the leather sofa, ignoring the receptionist's pitying smile. Dionne had waited three endless days for this appointment with the attorney Cicely's cousin had recommended, and now she had to wait again. She hadn't eaten much in days, hadn't been able to con-centrate at work, and couldn't remember the last time she had more than an hour or two of sleep at one stretch. All the waiting and uncertainty left Dionne feeling as if she was teetering on the edge of a cliff.

She'd finally succumbed and called Uncle Charlie, giving a vague excuse for needing to reach Marianne. He'd given her a phone number for Marianne at work—not that it had done her any good. Marianne's secretary had informed her that Marianne was out of town on business until the following week. The woman had taken Dionne's name and number but had seemed completely unmoved by Dionne's repeated pleas about the urgency of her call. Dionne didn't hold out much hope that Marianne would get the message before she returned.

The woman watched as Dionne strode to the end of the waiting area and started back again. "I'm sure Mr. Butler will be here soon," she said, her voice low and soothing.

It wouldn't be soon enough for Dionne. She didn't think she could wait another minute. Her nerves were stretched taut, her ability to cope with even the smallest provocation almost nonexistent.

"Would you like me to find some other magazines for you?" the receptionist asked. "The ones we have out here are pretty old."

Dionne shook her head quickly. "No, thanks. I wouldn't be able to concentrate." Her pacing was probably driving the poor woman batty, but she couldn't seem to stop.

When she'd talked with the attorney on the phone, he'd assured her they had plenty of time to file an official answer with the court. Her response to Mark Taylor's custody suit wasn't due for another seventeen days. Logically, she knew nothing could happen until then, but every minute she wasn't doing something to stop the man felt like time wasted.

Behind her, the outer door of the office opened and a short, heavyset man with thin, blond hair stepped inside. He smiled at the receptionist and checked an upright tray for messages, then turned to Dionne. "Are you Mrs. Black?"

Dionne nodded. "Rudy Butler?"

He held out his hand and engulfed hers for a quick shake. "Sorry to keep you waiting. My court hearing took a little longer than expected."

He motioned her toward a long corridor lined with wooden shelves of law books. "I took a look at the complaint you faxed me," he said as they walked. "Unfortunately, precedent has been set for the kind of case Taylor has filed, so even without complications, it's not going to be as easy to win as it might have been a few years ago."

Dionne's heart squeezed painfully. "Complications? What kind of complications?" When the lawyer didn't answer, she pressed. "We will win, won't we? The court won't let him take Jared away?"

Rudy closed the door to his office, and gestured toward one of his client chairs as he settled himself behind a cluttered desk. Between stacks of files on the credenza behind him were pictures of a woman and three smiling children. His family? Somehow the sight of them comforted her. At least he understood a parent's love.

He leaned back in his seat and linked his hands behind his head. "I have to be honest with you, Mr. Taylor has a strong case."

Her insides turned to ice. The world in front of her shifted and blurred as tears filled her eyes. She tried to make sense of what he'd said, but the words ran together in her ears.

The lawyer leaned his arms on the desk and waited until she got the tears under control. "The first thing we need to do is have you answer some questions for me."

"Yes. Of course." Her response came out as nothing more than a whisper.

"The child has been with you for how long?" Rudy asked, flipping through a document as if he didn't really expect her to answer.

"Jared," she choked out.

"Excuse me?"

"His name is Jared." She tried desperately to sound strong, to act as if she wasn't falling apart. Jared needed her now more than ever. "He's been living with me for the past two years since he was only a few days old. My husband and I had planned to adopt him."

"Yes, of course." He looked at her over the rims of his glasses. "But you never did?"

"No. His birth mother is my second cousin. I know she wanted me to have him, but I didn't feel right about pushing her too hard."

The truth was, she had been afraid that if she pressed, Marianne would change her mind. To this day, she couldn't understand how Marianne had been able to leave Jared and go on with her life.

Rudy's eyebrows furrowed and his dark eyes clouded. "So, she never signed a consent for adoption?"

"No, she—" Dionne broke off and took a ragged breath. "Marianne thought about having an abortion, but I guess all the religious training her parents gave her stopped her. She decided to put Jared up for adoption, but she was afraid he'd go to someone who wouldn't love him as much as he deserves. She told us that she felt better giving him to someone in the family, even if she and I weren't exactly close. I thought she'd eventually sign the consent, but Brent had his doubts. He wanted to go to court and prove that she'd abandoned Jared, but I didn't want to stir up trouble.''

"I see.'' Rudy linked his hands again. ''Well, there's no doubt you'd have a stronger case if you'd started the adoption process.'' He sent her an unreadable glance. ''Or even if your husband were still alive.''

Dionne rubbed her forehead gingerly and tamped down a flash of anger at the callous comment. ''That's not something I can change, Mr. Butler. I want to know how this Mark Taylor person can do this. He isn't even listed on the birth certificate as the father. How can a court of law take him seriously?''

Rudy lurched forward, pulled a large envelope from beneath a file, and held it out to her. ''You'd better take a look at this. I received it by courier this morning.''

Scarcely breathing, Dionne removed a thick document from inside but her mind refused to work and her eyes still didn't want to focus. ''What is it?''

''A transcript of a deposition given by your cousin. Apparently, she's admitted under oath that Mr. Taylor is the child's birth father.''

Dionne's sudden, unreasonable anger at Marianne was almost as strong as her fear. ''What does this mean?''

"This means," Rudy said gently, "that any judge will probably give him the right to take custody immediately."

No! The word echoed through her heart, her mind, her soul. "He's *not* Jared's father," she cried, standing so fast she nearly knocked over the heavy chair. "He hasn't even been around for the past two years. He's never even *seen* Jared. How can he claim to be a father?"

Rudy lifted an eyebrow. "Have you read the complaint thoroughly?"

"Yes, but…"

"Then you know that Mr. Taylor claims he only recently learned about the boy."

Jared, her mind insisted. The attorney's refusal to call Jared by name made her feel as if he saw him as a commodity instead of a person. Maybe she should find another attorney—one who would see Jared as a human being. One who could comprehend the seriousness of this threat to their lives. But she'd never find one who'd agree to work with her on a payment arrangement as a favor to Cicely's cousin.

As if he could read her mind, Rudy's face softened. "I know this is upsetting, Mrs. Black. Believe me, I wish I could offer you more hope."

He sounded so resigned, Dionne wanted to scream. "There has to be something we can do."

"We can try appealing to the court—"

"Then let's do it."

"—but all too often cases end up being about semantics rather than what's fair. Unfortunately, the judge we've drawn for this case is a real stickler for going by the book." Rudy sent her a thin smile. "A lot of us call her a pit bull in panty hose. Not exactly politically correct, but..." He lifted his shoulders in a gesture of helpless surrender.

Dionne refused to give up so easily. "We can find another judge, can't we?"

"I'm afraid not. Cases are assigned randomly. Litigants aren't allowed to go judge-shopping."

One after another, he was crushing her slim hopes. "Then what *can* we do?"

Rudy shrugged again. "You're aware that Mr. Taylor has petitioned the court for visitation until the matter of custody is settled?"

"Yes, but—"

"I think you should agree to let him see Jared."

Dionne shook her head emphatically. "No."

Rudy held up a hand to quiet her. "Hear me out, Mrs. Black. Right now, your best bet is to at least *appear* cooperative. We can agree to visitation, but request that the judge grant supervised visits, which means you could be there."

"But I don't *want* to be there," Dionne replied. "I don't want to see him. And I don't want him to see Jared."

Rudy linked his fingers together on his desk. "I'll bet my reputation that the judge will grant visitation, whether you agree or not."

"But what if he runs off with Jared? What if he disappears?"

"That's very unlikely. He's an attorney with a large firm in Boston and he has a reputation to protect. I think we can trust him."

"Trust?" The word came out too loud, too harsh. It echoed off the walls of his office for a second or two.

"I understand how difficult this is for you," Rudy

said again, "but I really don't see that you have much choice."

Never in her life had Dionne felt so helpless, not even after Brent's accident.

"In the course of the visits," Rudy went on, "you can try appealing to Mr. Taylor on a compassionate level. Maybe if he sees how deeply you love the boy, he'll change his mind."

At last, a flicker of hope. Small. Almost nonexistent. But it gave her something to cling to. "I'll try," she agreed in a whisper. "But can't we convince the judge to refuse his petition? Won't she understand that this will traumatize Jared?"

"I wouldn't count on it. Many people think two-year-olds are too young to understand what's happening around them. And that if they do have upsetting circumstances, they'll eventually forget."

"That's not true," she argued. "I have memories from when I was that age." Vague ones, to be sure, but she still had images of her mother's hysteria after her father walked out.

Rudy acknowledged her point with a nod. "I agree with you. I happen to believe that children that young can remember. But I don't get to make the decision here."

"We have to try something," she said again, more to herself than to the attorney. "This man has no right to take Jared."

"Unfortunately," Rudy said softly, holding her gaze with eyes that held a warning, "if what your cousin says under oath is true—and I have no reason to believe it's not—Mark Taylor has every right."

CHAPTER THREE

IT WAS ONLY a matter of time now, Mark thought with a smile as he sipped from a glass of wine and watched the waiter clear away the last of his dinner. Candlelight flickered across white-clothed tables, and strategically placed houseplants made most of the tables feel secluded. Soft music playing from well-hidden speakers relaxed him even further.

Everything was going like clockwork so far. Soon, he'd be on his way back to Boston with his son. *His son.* The words still sounded unbelievable to him.

Marianne hadn't liked answering his questions during the deposition in his office back in Boston. Her anger had been evident in every word and gesture. But she couldn't refuse the summons, and once there, she'd been put under oath. Her respect for the law hadn't allowed her to lie—in spite of her unexpected loyalty to her family. He had all the pieces now, the lawsuit was under way, and the woman who'd been raising Jared had been served with the legal documents.

He'd even arranged things so he'd never have to meet Dionne Black face-to-face. The local attorney he'd hired would act as go-between for the custody transfer. Not that Mark was afraid of facing her, but he'd rather avoid that unpleasantness and spare Jared as much emotional upheaval as possible.

All he had to do was wait.

The only thing he had left to worry about was how Jared would make the transition to his new home and family. When Mark called his parents at their home in New Hampshire to give them the good news, they'd been stunned at first that they had another grandchild, but their shock had given way to excitement. In fact, his mother had already started planning a family get-together so that everyone could meet Jared and welcome him home. After living alone with his foster mother for two years, being surrounded by grandparents, aunts, uncles and cousins might overwhelm Jared at first. But he was a Taylor. He'd adjust. And he and Mark could begin to develop a father-son relationship.

Mark sipped again, vaguely aware of a woman in a black dress moving through the restaurant toward him. Even from a distance he could see her murderous expression and he felt a twinge of pity for the poor sucker she was after.

The maître d' intercepted her, and Mark looked away. He let his mind play with the fantasy of holding his son for the first time. He imagined Jared older—the spitting image of Mark, himself—playing catch on his grandparents' shady lawn in Sunrise Notch, rowing with his dad on Sunrise Pond, learning to ride a bicycle...

"Mr. Taylor?"

He jerked out of his reverie and blinked up at the woman who'd stopped at his table. "Yes?" He straightened in his seat and found himself looking into the face of the last person in the world he wanted to see.

Out of long practice in court, Mark managed not

to show his surprise or dismay as Dionne Black stared at him with eyes so cold they sent a finger of ice up his spine.

"Can I help you?" he asked.

She stood facing him. Stiff. Unyielding. Still holding his gaze with a challenging one of her own. "I'm Dionne Black...Jared's mother."

"Yes, I know." He took in her thin angry lips and the slight color in her cheeks. Under other circumstances, he might have said she was an attractive woman, but the stony expression she wore overpowered everything else. He searched for some resemblance to Marianne, but found none except the determined way she faced him. "Please sit down."

She slid into the seat opposite him. "I'm not staying long," she said. Then, in spite of his efforts to keep his face impassive, she seemed to read his mind. "I'm sure you didn't expect to see me."

He shrugged and sent her a confident smile. Leaning back in his chair, he straightened his tie slowly— a gesture meant to show how little her presence bothered him. When he realized his hand shook slightly, he lowered it and said, "I'm curious how you found me."

"My attorney told me where to find you."

"I see." He'd make sure *his* attorney knew about this first thing in the morning. But since she was here, he might as well satisfy his curiosity. "What can I do for you?"

"You can stop trying to take Jared away from me."

He had to admit a grudging respect for her courage. But he wasn't about to reveal his feelings. "Out of the question."

"He's just a little boy. Do you have any idea what this will do to him?" The glow of the candlelight against the pale waves of hair made her look almost delicate, but there was nothing delicate about the set of her jaw or the dangerous glint in her eyes. "Do you even care?"

"Of course I care," he said, leaning slightly forward. Another intimidation technique from his days in court. "I'm his father."

"On paper only."

"On paper. In the eyes of the law. In my heart."

"How long have you known about him, Mr. Taylor?"

"A little over three weeks."

"And in that time, without ever once seeing him, you've grown to love him." The scorn didn't show on her face but it sure as hell came out in her voice.

"I've seen him," Mark said. "And even if I hadn't, he is my son."

"On paper," she said again. The words dropped like stones between them. "I've been his mother for two years. I'm the one who's bathed him, fed him, changed his diapers. I've comforted him when he was sick, stayed up nights with him, bandaged his little knees, held him, kissed his tears away, tucked him into bed at night. I'm the one he calls Mommy. What have you done?"

"I'd have done every one of those things," he said tersely, "if I'd been given a chance."

"Why *weren't* you given a chance, Mr. Taylor?" There was nothing soft in the question. The fierce anger in her eyes was that of a mother protecting her young.

He pushed aside another flash of respect and told

himself he didn't owe her an explanation. He could simply walk away and let the court deal with her. But something held him back. "It's a long story," he said.

"I have time."

He smiled without humor. "Maybe you do, Ms. Black, but I don't plan to share the intimate details of my life with you."

"But you're more than willing to dig through the intimate details of mine. I read your complaint again this afternoon, Mr. Taylor. Apparently, you've done your homework. Or did Marianne tell you all about me?"

He shook his head quickly. "Marianne didn't tell me anything willingly. She doesn't want to hurt you. And neither do I."

Skepticism filled her eyes and colored her cheeks. "You've used everything you can against me—my husband's death, my financial situation…"

"It's what I do," he said with a modest shrug.

She didn't look impressed. "And is that what you plan to teach Jared? To exploit other people's tragedies and problems to get what he wants?"

Anger curled like a fist in his stomach and spread its fingers into his heart, even though he knew logically she had every reason to feel the way she did. "I'll teach Jared what he needs to know to get by."

"I'm *so* relieved."

"Sarcasm doesn't become you."

"No more than fatherhood becomes you." She leaned closer now. "Do you have other children? Are you married?"

"No," he admitted, "to both questions."

"Then what can you give Jared that I can't?"

"Family. *His* family. And financial security."

"Not love?" Her lip curled. "What about emotional security, Mr. Taylor? I had hoped, for Jared's sake, that you might have a heart."

"Oh, I do have a heart, Ms. Black. But if you're trying to appeal to it, you're wasting your time."

"So I see." She stood, swayed slightly, and gripped the table for support. Her skin had turned waxy, even in the candlelight.

For some reason, the slight evidence of weakness touched a part of him that her hostility and sarcasm hadn't. He'd intimidated antagonistic witnesses and battled some of the best attorneys in the country, but nobody had ever faced him with such grim determination.

"Sit down, Ms. Black." He softened his voice and added, "Please."

She glanced behind her uncertainly, and the action made him think of a bird trapped in a net.

"We've gotten off to a bad start," he said gently. "Instead of charging into battle, let's try again."

"Will you change your mind?"

Never in a million years, he thought, but he said only, "As I said before, I have no desire to hurt you."

"*Hurt* me?" She laughed bitterly. "Taking Jared away won't hurt me, Mr. Taylor. It will *destroy* me. And I don't even want to think about what it will do to him."

He motioned toward the chair again and waited for her to sit. She hesitated, obviously fighting with herself, then finally gave in and perched on the chair's edge. When he felt reassured that she wouldn't topple over, he said, "Suppose I let Jared stay with you…'' He ignored the flicker of hope in her eyes and the unexpected jolt of remorse for causing it. ''…would you eventually tell him he was adopted?''

''Yes, when he's older.'' Her voice sounded slightly less brittle.

''Even if you get married again?''

''I won't be getting married again,'' she said sharply. ''I loved my husband. I can't imagine ever loving anyone else.''

''So, you'll tell Jared he's adopted.'' Mark leaned his arms on the table and held her gaze. ''How do you think that will affect him? Don't you think he'll have questions about the parents who gave him away? Do you really believe he won't hurt if he thinks I didn't want him?''

''I'd tell him about you,'' she assured him, but her eyes glimmered with unshed tears and he knew she'd made the promise out of desperation. ''I'd even let him get to know you when he's older.''

Mark cursed silently. A woman's tears always stirred a myriad of emotions in him, and Dionne Black's brought out the one he hated most—guilt. He tried to ignore it, but her honest grief touched something deep inside. He stiffened his voice and his shoulders before he went on. ''Unfortunately, that's not enough.''

''But—''

He didn't let her finish. ''If you were in my shoes, would it be enough for you?''

She shook her head slowly, reluctantly, and lifted her eyes to meet his. ''No. But I've raised him for the past two years. Please, Mr. Taylor. If you *do* have a heart, don't do this to him.''

"To him? Or to you?"

"To both of us." She brushed a tear from her cheek with one trembling hand. "I'm the only family he knows. He's the only family I have. If you insist on taking him away—" She broke off with a choked sob, took a moment to pull herself together, and tried again. "I understand that he's your biological son, but you've never even met him. You don't love *him,* you love the idea of him."

"I intend to rectify that."

"Yes, I know. You've asked for visitation." She took a deep, shaky breath. "I'm willing to agree to your request—as long as you'll let me be there when you see him."

It heartened Mark to know that the woman who'd been raising Jared had such a fierce, protective love for him. He inclined his head slightly. "In spite of the fact that you'd probably rather kill me than sit at this table with me, you seem like a caring woman." He let himself smile, hoped he looked reassuring. "And it's obvious that you're concerned about doing what's best for Jared."

"I am. But I don't believe that letting you take him is what's best for him. You're trying to tear his world apart."

"I'm trying," Mark said patiently, "to give him the world."

"*Your* world."

"It's his world, too," he reminded her. "Whether you like it or not, I *am* his father. And if you push me too hard, I can turn into a real hard-hearted son of a bitch."

"*Turn into...?* You mean, this is you being *nice?*"

In spite of himself and the cloud of tension that filled the space between, he laughed. "*Touche,* Ms. Black." He let his smile fade. "So, when do I meet my son? Tonight? I'm through here. I could come with you now."

He watched her struggle with the decision and prayed silently that she'd agree.

After what felt like forever, she nodded, but the effort seemed to cost her dearly. "I have to ask you one other thing, Mr. Taylor. I need your promise that you won't confuse or frighten him by telling him who you are."

Mark could see some wisdom in the request, even though it disappointed him. "It's a deal. For the time being, at least."

Settling back in his seat, he savored the tiny victory. He'd come to Boise ready to pull out all the stops and the rest of the world be damned. But now, face-to-face with the woman who obviously cherished his son, he wondered for the first time about the wisdom of taking Jared away from her.

He shoved the doubts back and reassured himself quickly. She might love Jared, but she couldn't possibly give him what Mark could offer. Family. Roots. *A father.*

From here on out, he warned himself, he'd be smart to remember this woman was an adversary— and a formidable one at that.

THE SUN HAD long since set by the time Mark, driving his rental car, followed Dionne through the city streets from the restaurant toward her apartment. A summer thunderstorm had washed away the dirt and grime from the city and left everything clean. He could still smell the rain, the harsh scent of ozone, through his partially open window.

Of course, he'd seen Dionne's apartment from the outside already, but he'd deemed it prudent not to tell her at the restaurant. He'd had plenty of time during the week to drive the few blocks from the hotel and check out the home she'd been providing for his son.

In spite of his not wanting to be impressed, he'd been touched by the geraniums blooming in clay flowerpots on her two small balconies. She'd obviously made an effort to make a real home for his son. Her apartment was probably much more suitable for a two-year-old than his with all the antiques and objets d'art he'd accumulated over the years.

Dionne braked suddenly, catching him off guard and forcing him to swerve to avoid hitting her. When he came to a stop beside her car, she rolled down her window and almost smiled an apology. "This is the entrance to my parking lot. You'll have to leave your car wherever you can find a space. I'll meet you back here."

He nodded and pulled away again. He found an empty parking space two blocks away and jogged back along the rain-slick sidewalk.

She was still outside the parking structure when he drew up, breathless and light-headed. Gulping air, he motioned her to lead on.

She folded her arms and held her ground. "It's okay. You can take a minute to catch your breath."

"Must be the altitude," he gasped.

"I'm sure that's it." Her lips curved into a stiff smile.

He turned his gaze to the mountains standing sentinel over the city, let it travel to the sky. "This is a far cry from Boston."

"I've been to Boston," she told him, following the direction of his gaze. "But only once, and that was years ago." When she spoke again, her voice had softened, but not by much. "It's probably changed a lot since then."

Finally able to breathe again, he straightened and studied her in the fading light. She looked frightened. Vulnerable. Defenseless. And the guilt he'd felt in the restaurant returned. For the briefest of moments, he didn't want to take the chance of hurting her.

But in the next breath, everything about her hardened again. "If you want to see Jared, we'd better hurry. I don't want to keep him up too long past his bedtime or he'll be cranky all day tomorrow."

Mark laughed softly and muttered, "Sounds like me."

She stopped walking. "Excuse me?"

"I said, that sounds like me. If I don't get enough sleep, I'm a bear the next day. Always have been, to hear my mother talk."

Her face paled in the moonlight. She clutched the straps of her bag tighter and started walking again. "*All* two-year-olds are cranky if they don't get enough sleep."

Victory always left him feeling charitable, and tonight was no exception. He tried to lighten the moment. "Are you calling me a two-year-old?"

She flashed him a look that could have crumbled a mountain. "I'm simply stating a fact, Mr. Taylor."

"Look," he said, "you and I aren't ever going to be friends, but we don't have to be mortal enemies, do we? Considering that we have a child in common, why don't we at least move on to first names?''

"As long as you're planning to take away my son, you *are* my enemy, Mr. Taylor. And I don't intend to soothe your conscience by pretending to like you.''

"Not even for Jared's sake?''

Her step faltered and a deep frown creased her forehead, but she didn't soften. "Are you going to pretend that you're suddenly concerned about Jared?''

"I've always been concerned about Jared.''

"Always?'' She laughed harshly and stopped in front of the old building that housed her apartment. "For a whole three weeks?''

"Look—'' he began.

But she cut him off. "I've agreed to let you see him, but that doesn't mean I'm going to back down from the fight. I *won't* let you take him from me.''

Without thinking about the wisdom of his actions, he grasped her by the shoulders and pulled her around until their eyes met. "The chances of your winning in court are so remote, they're not even worth mentioning. The courts presume a child has the right to its parents, and no judge is going to let some distant relative keep a child whose parent is ready, willing and able to raise him. I'm a decent member of society, I make a good living, and I've never been in jail. If we went to court tomorrow, I could be on the way to Boston with him by nightfall. But for some reason, I'm willing to make this easier on you.''

"How kind.''

"Like it or not, you have to work with me if you don't want me to separate you from Jared forever."

She jerked away from his touch and put some distance between them, but some new emotion flickered in her eyes. "What do you mean? Your plan *is* to separate me from Jared, isn't it?"

"I mean, *Dionne,* that I'm not a heartless creature, no matter what you may want to believe about me. I can see how much you love Jared, and if you'll pull in your claws maybe we can come to some sort of agreement about letting you see him once in a while."

"Once in a while?" she repeated. "How generous of you. What do you expect me to do now, fall at your feet in gratitude?"

Something like that, he admitted silently. Aloud, he said, "No. But you could try ditching some of the hostility. To be perfectly honest, I don't see that you have much choice."

"That's where you're wrong," she snapped. "I have choices, including not letting you into my apartment tonight to see him."

"You'd only be shooting yourself in the foot," he warned, hoping his eyes didn't betray his sudden panic. He'd come this close, he didn't want to leave now without seeing Jared.

"Maybe," she admitted. "But it's my foot."

"And Jared's." He tossed her own argument into her lap and, with almost morbid satisfaction, watched her lips tighten and her eyes register the direct hit.

"Five minutes," she said, jamming her key into the lock and wrenching open the lobby door. "No more."

He sketched a bow and followed her into the

building. As they crossed the dimly lit foyer to the elevator, he stole another glance at her. For some reason, the stiff set of her shoulders disturbed him. And a small pang of regret inched up his spine.

DIONNE RODE the elevator with her back to the wall, keeping one eye on Mark as if she expected him to murder her inside the tiny box. Foolish, she knew, but the threat he posed was every bit as real as if he'd brandished a knife in front of her.

She didn't want to let him into her apartment. Didn't want to let him see Jared—especially since their features were so remarkably similar. She didn't want the resemblance to spark his paternal instincts. Only the hope that he'd change his mind after seeing how much Jared loved her kept her breathing.

And there was one small traitorous part of her that reacted to this man with something other than hostility. It was the part of her that recognized the curve of his lips when he smiled and the tiny ridge of flesh between his eyes when he scowled. In her heart, she knew she was looking at an older version of the person she loved most in the world. And that heart refused to let her completely hate him.

If not for him, she wouldn't have Jared. But neither would she be in danger of losing him now.

Mark kept his distance, hands locked behind his back, watching the lights on the elevator panel as they climbed slowly to the third floor. "Who's with Jared now?"

"A friend of mine." She almost smiled. If he thought Dionne was hostile, wait until he met Cicely. On the other hand, wait until Cicely saw what

Dionne had done. Dionne knew she'd have some tall explaining to do.

"Male or female?"

"Does it matter?"

"I suppose not…as long as Jared's safe."

The elevator door creaked open, and Mark put a hand against it while she stepped through. Such a gentleman, she thought bitterly, holding the door for her with one hand and snatching away her child with the other.

She watched him take in the narrow corridor, the faded roses in the carpet, the yellowed walls badly in need of new paint. She waited for him to curl his lip, but he turned a smile on her instead.

"Nice."

"Not really," she said, letting her own gaze travel over their surroundings. "I've been thinking of finding a house in the suburbs and moving out of city center."

"I suppose the middle of the city isn't the best place to raise a child."

"Not one as active as Jared." She drew to a stop outside her door and tried to calm the thundering of her heart. "Remember," she warned, "you are not to tell him who you are."

Surprisingly, Mark looked almost offended. "I gave my word."

She supposed that should make her feel better, but it didn't. He'd also given his word to win. With trembling hands, she tried to unlock the door. When she had trouble getting the key to fit, Mark gently took it from her and inserted it himself.

As he turned the knob, his eyes met hers. "Ready?" His voice had lost most of its hard edge.

She couldn't afford to lose hers. This kindness she saw now was probably nothing more than a tactic to put her off her guard. "I meant what I said downstairs. You can have five minutes, then you leave or I call the police."

FILLED WITH ANXIETY and anticipation, Mark didn't say a word. He pushed the door and waited for Dionne to lead the way.

Inside, a woman sat on the couch watching Jared drive his toy trucks across a mound of building blocks. Her face tightened, hardened, when she saw Mark, but Jared popped up and toddled across the room toward his mother.

Seeing the boy up close made Mark's breath catch. Tears of amazement stung his eyes. He still couldn't believe this boy was his son.

"Mommy. Mommy. Come see."

Dionne scooped Jared up and held him close. Mark ached to do the same but he stayed put, waiting for his chance.

Jared squirmed, protesting the too-tight hug, let his body go slack and tried to slide out of Dionne's arms. Slowly, reluctantly, she put him on the floor again. "I love you, Jared."

"Love you." He reached for her hand. "Come see, Mommy."

Mark was aware of the other woman's stony stare, but he avoided looking at her. This moment belonged to him and to Jared. He wasn't going to let anyone ruin it. He tracked Jared's progress across the room, taking in every unsteady step, every feature. Through the tears, he saw his mother in the boy's face. His father's nose. His own chin. It was a miracle, and Jared was the most beautiful person he'd ever seen.

He drew a ragged breath and caught Dionne watching him with an odd expression on her face.

"Who's this?" the other woman demanded, dragging Dionne's attention away.

"Cicely Logan...Mark Taylor."

Mark flicked a glance and a smile at her, but he didn't let his attention leave Jared for more than a second.

Cicely shot to her feet, grabbed Dionne's arm, and tugged her a few steps away. "What are you thinking, girl?" She kept her voice low, but Mark could hear every word. "Are you a fool, bringing him back here like this? Do you have any idea what this will do to your case in court?"

Dionne knew what she was doing, Mark thought. Letting him come here was the smartest thing she could have done. He wondered if she knew just how smart it was.

"We can talk about this later," Dionne whispered back, shrugging away from Cicely's grasp and lowering her purse to the coffee table. "He's only staying five minutes."

"Five minutes too long," Cicely warned.

Mark tore his gaze away from Jared and settled it on Cicely. "I'm not going to hurt either one of them, if that's what you're worried about."

"You've already done that," Cicely retorted.

He'd meant a different kind of harm, but he knew she was right. "Yes," he said softly, turning back to Jared again. "I suppose I have."

Dionne put an arm around Cicely's stiff shoulders and gave her a gentle squeeze. "I'll explain everything later. I promise. But I don't want to talk about it in front of Jared.''

The appeal got through to Cicely. She started toward the couch again, but Dionne stopped her. ''Why don't you go home. It's late, and you have to work tomorrow.'' And in answer to Cicely's worried scowl, ''We'll be all right.''

The assurance gave Mark hope, and Dionne's understanding of his need to see Jared without Cicely's hostile presence filled him with gratitude. While Cicely reluctantly gathered her things, he got down on the floor but still kept his distance from his son.

''Come see, Mommy,'' Jared demanded again. ''Truck's gonna crash.''

''In a minute, sweetheart. We need to say goodbye to Cicely.''

Jared sent Cicely an unconcerned glance and waved his chubby fingers. ''Bye-bye.''

Cicely crossed the room and gave Jared a quick hug. She turned tear-filled eyes on Mark, but she held her tongue.

Dionne gave her friend another reassuring squeeze, whispered a promise to call tomorrow, and let Cicely out the door. Then she turned back to watch.

Jared was blissfully unaware of the upheaval surrounding him. Mark picked up a stray block and held it for a moment, then offered it hesitantly to Jared.

Jared scuttled backward and looked to Dionne for reassurance. ''Mommy?''

Battling disappointment, Mark got to his feet and backed away to put some distance between them. When Jared relaxed enough to go back to his game,

Mark met Dionne's gaze again. "He's beautiful." A weak word to describe the absolute wonder he felt.

"Yes," she said softly, "he is."

"He looks like my mother. She's going to adore him." Mark let his gaze settle on Dionne's face, sharply aware of the roiling emotions that kept her silent. Guilt twisted through him again. "For what it's worth, Dionne, I'm sorry."

That tore a response from her. "Sorry?" She turned away, folding her arms and clutching them tightly. "If that were true, you wouldn't do this."

He looked away from her and drank in the sight of his son again. Maybe she was right. Maybe he was making a mistake.

He shook off the doubts and pulled himself together. There were many things about this situation he hadn't anticipated, many emotions he hadn't expected to feel. But that didn't make it wrong to fight for his son. Remembering his promise, he crossed to the door, cast one last longing glance at Jared, and let himself out.

DAMN. Mark paced the inside of the elevator as he rode down to the first floor and swore again, this time aloud. *"Damn!"*

He hadn't expected to feel sorry for her, but the pain in her eyes had been too deep to ignore. He hadn't expected to have doubts about his decision, but the bond between Jared and Dionne was too real to deny.

"Damn!" He jabbed at the first-floor button again.

He couldn't explain his reaction to the picture of Jared in Dionne's arms if he'd tried. Maybe he was just relieved to see that Jared had a mother who actually cared about him. She might be related to Marianne, but the similarities ended with their bloodlines. Even a fool could see that Dionne loved Jared as completely, as fully, as Mark's mother loved him. Only a heartless creature would rob a child of that kind of love.

"Damn," he said again as the elevator doors swished open. Jamming his hands into his pockets, he strode through the dimly lit lobby, glaring at the furniture. He pushed through the doors into the night, listening to the rhythm of his steps as they echoed on the wet, empty sidewalk.

Meeting Dionne Black had changed everything. Now what was he going to do?

CHAPTER FOUR

MORNING DAWNED gray and cloudy, the perfect background for the ache in Dionne's heart. She lay in bed, curled next to Jared, too hurt to move. She rarely let Jared climb into her bed unless bad dreams woke him. Even then, she usually comforted him and carried him back to his own room. But she'd needed to keep him close, to feel his small body beside her and know that she still had him with her.

Mark had been as good as his word last night. Five minutes, then he'd disappeared. But anything might happen today. He might show up at the door ready to take Jared. He might—though she held out only scant hope—even change his mind.

She supposed she should take some comfort in knowing that he seemed kind. That he seemed to genuinely care about Jared in his own way. That he seemed capable of loving Jared. But nothing lessened the fear that had lodged in her throat all night and kept her awake, tossing and turning and listening to the soft drumming of rain against her windows.

Blinking back tears, she touched Jared's cheek with her fingertips, softly so she wouldn't wake him, then rolled to her side and stared at the picture of Brent on the nightstand. For the past week, she'd fought against the anger. Today, she let it come.

If Brent hadn't been so reckless, he'd still be here

to fight with her and for her, she wouldn't be fighting the worst battle of her life alone. He'd have found some way to protect their tiny family. She *knew* he would.

She stared at the eyes that had once made her feel secure and the smile that had once given her faith, then slowly, resolutely, turned the picture facedown on the table.

Jared made a noise and shifted position. To keep from waking him, Dionne forced herself to get out of bed and walk on legs as unsteady as his tiny ones to the door of her bedroom. Clutching the frame for support, she looked back at him. Her arms ached to hold him, but she refused to let herself do it until he woke on his own.

She pulled on her robe and made her way into the cramped kitchen. Working automatically, she scooped coffee into a filter and filled the carafe with water, then sat at the table and waited while it brewed, staring with sightless eyes at the gray sky and the wash of moisture on the windows.

A few minutes later, a soft knock pulled her from her reverie. At first she thought it had come from the apartment next door, but the second time, she realized someone was at her door.

It had to be Cicely. Usually, Dionne welcomed her visits, but not today. She couldn't face her friend's questions this morning. She had no answers to give. But neither could she ignore her. Cicely would only knock louder and wake Jared.

Running her fingers through her hair, Dionne hurried to the door and pulled it open. But it wasn't Cicely standing on the threshold. Instead, she found herself looking into Mark's deep brown eyes.

Shock numbed her. Was this it, then? Had he come for Jared? How could she stop him? What could she say to convince him?

Her heart slowed and her mind raced. "What are you doing here?"

With his hair and shirt wet from the rain and shadows forming deep circles beneath his eyes, he looked almost as haggard as she felt. "We need to talk."

"Talk? About what?"

"About Jared. About what's best for him."

Hope that he'd come to say he'd changed his mind sprang to life. Fear that he hadn't shadowed it. She stepped aside and let him in, vaguely aware that she hadn't bothered to pick up Jared's toys last night.

Mark didn't seem to notice. He walked toward the couch and motioned for her to join him.

She perched on the edge nearest her bedroom, ready to fly toward the door if she had to. The splatter of rain against the windows mixed with the gurgle of the coffeemaker. The earthy scent of coffee filled the air, but it didn't soothe her as it usually did.

Mark studied her with agonizing slowness, letting his eyes roam across her hair, her face, and finally settle on her eyes. "Did you sleep at all?"

She shook her head, wondering why he asked. Why would he even care?

"Neither did I."

The confession surprised her, but she tried to keep her face from showing any expression at all.

"I've been doing a lot of thinking," he said, pushing to his feet again. "I've thought about what you said at the restaurant, and about the way you and Jared interacted last night. It's obvious you love him."

"Yes. With all my heart."

"And it's equally obvious that he loves you. But he's still my son..." Mark broke off and rubbed his face with both hands. "The fact that I've only known about him for a short time doesn't change that."

He reached a hand toward her, then seemed to think better of it. "Are you all right? Say something, so I know you're still alive in there."

"You're going to take him." Her voice rasped and her throat burned with the effort.

He studied her for a long moment. "I called my office this morning and asked for another two weeks here. That should give both you and Jared time to get to know me. Maybe then you won't worry about him so much when I take him back to Boston."

She stared at him, incredulous. "Two weeks won't change how I feel."

Mark rubbed his neck slowly, tilting his head to work out the kinks. "I believe you." He sent her a thin smile and lowered his hand. "I realized last night that I don't want to put Jared through a long, ugly custody battle. He's too innocent and trusting, and I don't want to change that. I'm hoping we can work out a compromise—a way for all of us to win."

Dionne eyed him warily, trying desperately not to get her hopes up. "How?"

"First, I think he should get to know me here in the setting he's used to. I don't want to frighten him by changing everything too fast."

"I think that's the best idea you've had so far."

"I'd like to be here while he eats breakfast, play with him in the park, read him bedtime stories. I'd like to do all those things you talked about last night."

Dionne hated the idea of him insinuating himself into their lives and robbing her of her precious time alone with Jared. But it was preferable to having him spirit Jared away. And maybe, once he saw how difficult life with a two-year-old could be, he'd change his mind about taking on the task.

"All right," she said reluctantly. "You can spend some time with us."

His quick, pleased smile seemed genuine. He closed some of the distance between them. "Good. When can we start? Today?"

Today? No! She held back her automatic response and remembered her attorney's advice. Refusing wouldn't accomplish anything except, perhaps, postpone the inevitable. She forced herself to nod and said again, "All right."

"Great." Another pleased smile curved his lips and excitement sparkled in his eyes. "I also think it would be a good idea for us to try to get along. Jared will pick up on the hostility and it won't be good for him."

Much as she hated to admit it, he was right. She forced herself to say, "I agree."

Mark visibly relaxed as if he'd been worried about her answer. "What time does Jared get up in the mornings?"

"On the weekends, I let him sleep until he wakes up. On weekdays, I get him up at seven and leave for work at seven-thirty. But I can't have you around on workdays. I'm always racing against the clock as it is."

"Then let me help. Let me feed him breakfast while you get ready. Let me take him to the sitter. Or, even better, let me watch him while you work."

She shook her head quickly. "I don't think that's a good idea."

"Why not?" His smile faded and his dark eyes clouded. "Are you afraid I'll abscond with him while you're at the office?"

That's exactly what she feared, and his perception caught her by surprise—just as the almost kind look in his eyes did.

He leaned closer, propping his elbows on his knees. "You don't have to worry about that, Dionne. I won't do that to Jared."

While that offered some small relief, it didn't completely allay her fears.

"I know you're afraid," he said, "and I can't say I blame you. I barged in here like a storm trooper ready to do battle. But you weren't exactly trying to make peace either, you know." His expression softened even more. "If you'll be honest with me, I'll be honest with you. I won't steal Jared while you're at work if you won't try to disappear with him while my back's turned. I really want to work out a compromise," he said. "For Jared's sake."

Dionne bit her lip and glanced at her son's door. For Jared's sake, he said. If he meant that, if he really wanted to do what was best for Jared, maybe he wasn't quite as bad as she'd first thought. She had to believe that. Like it or not, she had to trust him a little.

She just hoped she wasn't making the biggest mistake of her life.

MARK SAT on the faded carpet of Dionne's living room, trying not to be hurt by his son's continuing wariness. The overworked air conditioner in the window did little to relieve the afternoon's intense, dry heat. Sounds from neighboring apartments drifted through the thin walls and added to his frustration.

He didn't expect miracles. He'd known Jared would be apprehensive at first. But after nearly two days together, Jared was still wary. He behaved as if Mark was a stranger in spite of Dionne's introduction of Mark as a friend. But Dionne didn't treat him as a friend, and even a child could sense she was lying.

At least Dionne had finally left them alone for a few minutes. She'd been standing guard, watching every move Mark made, no doubt judging his performance. He knew they both needed time to get used to him, but time was the one thing he didn't have much of. He couldn't stay away from Boston and his career indefinitely.

Determined to break through Jared's wariness, Mark stacked a couple of blocks near Jared and watched his reaction. The boy studied them for a moment, then reached out one tentative finger to touch them.

Progress!

"Do you want these?" Mark asked gently.

Jared pulled his hand back quickly. "No."

Mark held back a frustrated sigh. He hated Marianne for putting them all through this and resented her bitterly for walking away unscathed and leaving three innocent people to deal with the fallout of her decision. Her body, her choice—those had been her words. Yet *her* life was the one least affected by the choice she'd made.

The clatter of dishes in the kitchen pulled him back to the moment and he caught Jared watching him, eyes round with distrust, a deep scowl on his face.

Mark sent him a reassuring smile and hoped he hadn't ruined everything by thinking about Marianne and letting his anger show. "Do you think Mommy dropped something?"

Jared backed a step away.

"Should we go see?"

Jared gave that some thought, then nodded. But when Mark reached out to pick him up, he threw himself onto the couch, face first, as if by hiding his eyes he could also make the rest of his body disappear.

Mark backed away and held up both hands. "All right, sport, you're safe. I won't pick you up. Why don't you show me where the kitchen is."

Jared peeked out from behind his hands, then scooted off the couch and pointed. "Over there."

"Do you want to lead the way? I'll follow."

Jared nodded and toddled off toward the door, checking behind him every few steps, either to make sure Mark was behind him or that he hadn't gotten too close.

Dionne looked up when they entered, smoothed her hands along the legs of her jeans, and frowned slightly. "Is something wrong?"

"No." Mark leaned against the door frame and hooked his thumbs in his pockets. "We heard a crash and got worried."

She glanced at the dishes on the counter. "I'm a little clumsy today for some reason."

Mark laughed. "Couldn't be that you're nervous, could it?"

She half smiled in response. "No, of course not."

Then, as if talking about herself made her uneasy, "How's Jared doing?"

"Still a little shy."

She riveted her attention on the casserole in front of her. "That's to be expected."

"Yes, I know. I have some experience with two-year-olds."

"Really?" She glanced quickly at him. "Who?"

"Nieces and nephews and cousins—lots of them."

"Oh." Moving stiffly, she pulled a carton of milk from the refrigerator. "How many?"

"Three nieces, three nephews, and two dozen cousins—most of whom have several children apiece. We're a close family, so I'm around the kids several times a month."

She looked back at him over her shoulder. "How nice for you."

Mark laughed. "I can tell you really mean that." He took another step into the kitchen. "So what's the matter? You sound disappointed."

"No." The answer came quickly—too quickly. "Not at all. Why should I be?"

He shrugged lazily. "I don't know. Maybe you were hoping to discourage me by letting me see what life with a two-year-old is really like."

"Don't be ridiculous," she said with a laugh, but color flamed into her cheeks and convinced him he'd hit the nail squarely on the head.

He shrugged again and let his gaze travel across the tiny kitchen. It couldn't even begin to compare with the spacious kitchen in his condo, but everything was clean and neat. "Okay. I won't read anything into the situation that's not there."

"Good." Her cheeks went from pink to red.

She looked small and fragile, but Mark had seen the steel in her backbone and knew what an illusion that was. "Do you mind if I make a suggestion?"

Her gaze flew to his. "About what?"

"It's not about Jared," he assured her, making himself even more comfortable against the door frame.

"Well, that's a relief."

He gave in to the urge to smile, surprised to find that he was enjoying himself. "It's just that I don't think you should ever try to play poker. Your face gives you away."

She opened her mouth to protest, then clamped it shut again and turned her back on him. "I'll keep that in mind."

Mark picked up a toy truck and pushed it close to Jared, then crossed to the counter and leaned on it to watch her. "Have you talked to Marianne?"

Her quick glance gave him the answer even before she spoke. "I've tried to reach her, but she's away from her office. Apparently *you* know where to find her, though." She wiped her hands on a towel and reached for a bowl in the cupboard. The material of her blouse stretched tight across her breasts and sparked an unexpected response inside him.

He looked away quickly. "She's staying at the Marriott in Boston," he said, his voice gruff, "I can give you the number if you'd like."

Her eyes narrowed. "Why?"

"Because I'm sure you have questions about me, and she's probably the only person you'd trust to answer them."

Dionne closed the cupboard and eyed him speculatively. Shadows tinted her eyes a deep blue, and he wondered if they always revealed her moods so clearly. "I'm not sure I'd trust her, either," she admitted softly. "I'm so furious I could hit something. I hate her for doing this to Jared."

"And to you."

"And to me," she admitted softly.

"She hurt me, too, you know. She knew how much I wanted children of my own, yet she hid Jared from me."

"Maybe she had reasons for keeping him from you."

"Oh, she did," he assured her. "She knew I'd never agree to give him up."

"Then I can't say I'm sorry she didn't tell you," she said quietly. "Having Jared in my life is the best thing that's ever happened to me."

"Even now?"

"Even now. I wouldn't trade the past two years for anything—not even to avoid this."

"Then maybe you can understand how I feel."

Dionne nodded reluctantly. "I guess I can in a way. But I also know that Marianne gave him to Brent and me because she wanted him to have a stable family life. Obviously, she didn't think you could give that to him."

For a second—and only that—Mark felt a twinge of guilt. After all, Marianne *had* known him well. With the hours he worked, could he really give Jared the security and stability he needed? Was he being fair to his son? To Dionne?

Of course he was. Jared deserved to know Mark and his family. He deserved the love of his father. And Dionne deserved...

Hell. Dionne *wasn't* Mark's responsibility. He had to remember that.

"You don't have to worry about Jared," he said. "He'll have everything he needs."

"Except his mother."

Mark was saved from having to respond when Jared tripped over a block, tumbled to the floor, and hit his head against the leg of a chair. Instantly, Mark started toward him, Dionne beat him. And she was the one Jared reached for.

She swooped Jared into her arms, checked him thoroughly, and cradled him against her. Jared's howls subsided and his tears slowed. He clutched the fabric of her blouse, and Mark's guilt increased.

He'd come to Boise determined to win, but with every passing hour he grew less certain about what winning would mean.

SOFTLY, so as not to wake her son, Dionne closed Jared's bedroom door and walked slowly back toward the couch. She curled into one corner and stared at the telephone, trying to work up the courage to pick up the receiver and make her phone call.

Earlier, she'd pleaded a headache to convince Mark to leave. And he'd gone, just as he had the first time, without argument.

Outside, the sounds of an occasional passing car stirred the stillness. Inside, the hum of the air conditioner working to cool the small rooms teased her already jangled nerves.

She needed answers. She needed to know what kind of person Mark was, what happened between him and Marianne, why Marianne had kept Jared hidden from him, and what had made her tell him after all this time. And Dionne desperately needed to release some of the anger that had been propelling her through each day and affecting her sleep at night.

Yes, she was angry with Mark for showing up and wanting to take Jared, but she was far more upset with Marianne. How could Marianne promise Dionne that she could have Jared and then tell Mark where they were. Marianne must have known Mark would come after his son. Marianne should have *some* loyalty toward her—shouldn't she? They were family, after all. Distant, to be sure, but family nonetheless.

Expelling a deep breath, Dionne picked up the receiver, dug the scrap of paper with the number Mark had given her from the pocket of her robe, and dialed before she could talk herself out of it. It seemed to take forever for the connection to go through and the phone to ring on the other end. Another eternity for Marianne to answer. When she did, her soft, rich voice caught Dionne off guard.

Dionne identified herself and found some small satisfaction in the silence before Marianne said, "I knew you'd probably be calling me. My dad told me you'd been looking for me. This must mean Mark's been in contact."

"In contact?" Dionne caught her voice rising and forced it to remain level. "He's filed a lawsuit for custody, Marianne."

"I'm not surprised."

"No? Well, I was. But, then, *I* didn't know about him." Dionne glanced at Jared's door and pulled her voice under control again. "Why didn't you warn me?"

"I guess I hoped he wouldn't actually follow

through,'' Marianne said. ''I honestly thought there was a chance he'd think about it and decide to leave things the way they were.''

Dionne brushed a lock of hair from her forehead. ''*Did* you? I hardly know him, and I can't imagine him backing down from anything. You certainly knew him better than I do. How could you ever have thought he'd change his mind?''

She could almost hear Marianne's shrug, casual and unhurried. ''Because he's so locked up in his career. He might think he wants a family, but I'm not sure he does. Not really.''

That gave Dionne a moment's hope, but it evaporated almost immediately. What if Mark didn't really want a family, but didn't realize it until *after* he'd taken Jared away? She took a steadying breath and tried to keep her agitation under control. ''I need the answers to some questions, Marianne.''

''Such as?''

''For one thing, why did you change your mind about telling him?''

''When I heard about Brent's death, I thought you might have second thoughts.''

''How can you say that?''

''It's just that things were different when your husband was alive. There were two of you to take care of Jared, someone else to help support him—''

''*I* can support him,'' Dionne snapped. ''I can give him everything he needs.''

''Yes, but there's more to life than just the basics,'' Marianne argued, her voice irritatingly smooth and unruffled. ''What about the extras? Can you send him to camp? Enroll him in sports programs? I hear people talking all the time about how expensive those things are. And what about a college education when he's older? Will you be able to provide one for him?''

Trembling with rage, Dionne fought back. ''There's more to life than material things. What about love? Security? I grew up without things, but I knew my mother loved me.''

''So did mine. And so will Mark. He's a decent man, Dionne.''

''Then why didn't you tell him about Jared in the first place?''

''I wasn't ready to do the family thing, and he was. I thought if he knew there was a baby, he'd try to convince me and that wasn't a battle I wanted to fight right then.'' Her voice softened. ''Maybe you need to think about whether you want the burden of caring for Jared all by yourself.''

''If you think raising Jared is a burden,'' Dionne said through clenched teeth, ignoring all the warning bells and whistles jarring inside her head, ''then it's a good thing you gave him up.''

It was only afterward—after she'd slammed down the receiver and stormed into the kitchen—that she began to wonder if antagonizing Marianne had been such a good idea.

CHAPTER FIVE

THREE DAYS LATER, Dionne sat on the park bench under the blazing afternoon sky and watched while Mark played with Jared. In just one short week, the child had adjusted to having him around. Jared seemed to like him—just as Mark had hoped. Just as Dionne had feared.

They looked so much alike, it hurt. Two dark heads bent together, two identical laughs, two terrifyingly similar faces. And they acted so much alike, Dionne felt a pang of jealousy. No matter how close she and Jared were, they didn't share physical attributes or mannerisms.

Mark helped Jared climb up the short plastic slide, then jumped down the steps and raced to catch him at the bottom. When Jared slid into Mark's arms, Mark whooped triumphantly and swung Jared high onto his shoulders.

Jared crowed with delight and pointed at the slide. "Again!"

"Are you sure?"

"Again!"

Mark tromped through the sand, obviously unaware of how out of place he looked in his starched white shirt and suit pants, and started the process all over again. The delight on his face was a far cry from the expression he'd worn when they'd first met. The warmth of his smile when he saw Jared each morning, the glow of love in his eyes, the softness on his face when he kissed Jared good-night at the end of the day all touched her deeply. And in spite of herself, she was beginning to believe Jared deserved a father—*his* father.

Under other circumstances, she might even have liked Mark. But she didn't, she reminded herself firmly. She couldn't afford to get softhearted just because he'd teased an occasional giggle from Jared, shown concern over a scraped knee, or continued to treat her with quiet respect. She couldn't let down her guard even though he seemed genuine about easing into Jared's life instead of bulldozing his way in.

The bottom line hadn't changed. He still intended to take Jared to Boston. Eventually, he'd marry and some other woman would take her place as Jared's mother. At most, Dionne would be left with occasional visits, playing the part of a doting aunt or close family friend.

Laughing at something Jared did, Mark settled the boy on his shoulders again and carried him toward her. "Look, you're bigger than Mommy."

Jared giggled with delight and leaned down to kiss her. "I'm big, Mommy."

Her heart constricted painfully. "Yes, sweetheart, you are. Very big." She reached for him, but he shook his head and pulled away again.

"No, Mommy. Me stay up here." He clapped his hands to Mark's head and held on to his hair, as if he thought she might force him down.

She swallowed the bitter taste of betrayal and reminded herself Jared was only a baby. He *couldn't* betray her.

As if he could read her thoughts, Mark held on to Jared with one hand and disentangled his hands with the other. ''You'd better get down, sport.''

Annoyance, sudden and unreasonable, flashed through her. ''Let him stay if he wants to.''

Mark ignored her and pulled Jared from his shoulders. Of course, the child set up a squall, and Dionne watched while Mark teased him into a better mood. He seemed to know how to handle a distressed two-year-old, and for Jared's sake, she was glad.

When he'd calmed Jared down again and had him happily digging in the sandbox, Mark dropped onto the park bench beside her, moving his suit jacket out of the way as he did. ''He's a great kid, Dionne. You've done a remarkable job with him.''

But now that job was over? She studied him intently, trying to read the expression in his eyes. ''It hasn't been a job,'' she assured him.

''I know.'' Mark shielded his eyes against the sun and watched Jared for a minute. ''I know how you feel about him, Dionne. Any fool can see that. And I know how he feels about you.'' He let out a heavy sigh and turned to face her. ''Any chance you're willing to relocate to Boston?''

The question caught her completely off guard, but she recovered quickly. ''What do you mean?''

He shrugged and leaned back against the seat. ''You have to admit, it'd make this easier if we lived in the same town.''

''Yes, it would.'' She spoke slowly, trying not to let the observation get her hopes up. ''Any chance *you're* willing to move to Boise?''

To her surprise, Mark laughed. It started out as a

low rumble deep in his chest and worked its way out. "Has anyone ever told you that you're stubborn?"

"Not recently." She bit back an unexpected smile and told herself she wasn't enjoying the banter. "Has anyone ever told you that you're pushy?"

"Every day." He leaned back and rested one arm on the bench behind her. His gaze settled on Jared protectively. "I'm serious, Dionne. If we lived in the same city, we could work out an easy arrangement."

"But we don't," she said unnecessarily.

"No, we don't. So what do we do?"

Dionne shook her head, surprised to find herself in this position, yet strangely comfortable with it as well. "Could you move here?"

"I can't leave my career in Boston. I've worked too long and too hard to get where I am."

"And your career is important to you."

"Of course it is." He glanced at her quickly. "Isn't yours?"

Dionne smiled halfheartedly. "Not especially."

Mark shifted toward her eagerly, his eyes glittering so that they looked almost black. "Then *would* you consider moving?"

"I don't know. It's not something I've ever thought about before."

"Maybe you should."

Suddenly her future looked a little brighter. But the idea of leaving everything familiar—home, job, Cicely—frightened her. She rubbed her forehead gently. "I—I don't know. I need some time to think—"

"We don't have much time," Mark warned. "I have to get back to Boston soon."

"But you'll be back for the court hearing."

He didn't speak for a long time. When he did, his voice came out hushed. "We could avoid a hearing if we could work out a compromise. Personally, I'd like to spare Jared all that. It's no kind of memory to give a kid."

Dionne shifted to look at him better. "You're really serious, aren't you?"

"Completely." He sent her a hopeful smile. "Just promise me you'll think about it."

She nodded slowly. "All right."

"I'll stay out of your way tonight so you can think without me around."

He really *was* serious, Dionne thought. But could she seriously consider such a proposition? Of course, if she won in court, she wouldn't have to take such a drastic step. But Rudy Butler wasn't offering much hope on that score.

She could almost hear Brent telling her to refuse. But Brent had never been good at compromising. Besides, he wasn't here. She'd have to make this decision on her own.

SEVERAL HOURS LATER, vaguely unsettled, Mark tugged off his shirt and tossed it onto the bed of his hotel room. He thought about his comfortable bed back in Boston, about his view of Boston Harbor, about the life he'd made for himself. No matter what happened now, it would never be the same.

He briefly considered calling his parents to give them an update, but he didn't know how to tell them that everything was less settled, less certain than it had been last week or the week before. The last time he'd talked to them, they'd been full of plans. Not that they wouldn't understand his confusion, but

Mark had always been the kind of guy who set his mind on something and then got it. He rarely wavered...until now.

He dropped onto the bed and turned on the television, scanning channels in an attempt to find something in the late-afternoon programming that would take his mind off Dionne and Jared. The ball was in her court tonight. All he could do was wait.

Finally settling on an episode of *Biography,* he dimmed the bedside lamp. Though he usually found the show fascinating, tonight it didn't hold his interest.

He turned up the volume and tried to pay attention to the story of Thomas Jefferson's life, but Dionne's image kept interfering. Her infrequent smile, her shaky laugh, the utter love on her face when she held Jared.

Mark blinked, and Jared's image joined hers. His laughter, his little-boy voice calling out to her, his chubby legs churning as he ran toward her.

Mark thought of his own childhood as he had a million times in the last few days and wondered what life would have been like if he'd been taken away from his own mother. What kind of heartless jerk would do something so devastating to a child? Or to the woman who'd been his mother for all of his short life.

After spending only one week with the boy, Mark was so attached to Jared he couldn't imagine life without him. But if *he* felt this way, how must Dionne feel? He might argue bloodlines in court, but he knew that families were made in the heart.

In the middle of a commercial, the telephone rang and startled him back to the moment. He dropped the remote on the floor, scrambled for it and muted the set, then grabbed the receiver. The voice that greeted him was the last one he'd expected.

"Mark? Royal Spritzer here."

Mark dropped onto the bed again. Why was his boss calling? He had no cases pending in court, no imminent trials, no depositions scheduled. He'd given his secretary the hotel's number in case of an emergency, but he certainly hadn't expected one— especially not on a Saturday afternoon.

Royal's voice boomed through the wire again. "Mark? Are you there?"

"Yes. Sorry. What can I do for you?"

"It's very simple, my boy. You can come back to Boston."

Mark turned off the television. "Now? But I have another week of leave."

"Change of plans." Ice clinked against a glass on the other end of the connection and Mark pictured Royal leaning back in his leather chair. "Oscar Nee- bling and I met with a new client yesterday, and after talking about it today, we've decided we want you in on the case."

"No problem," Mark assured him. "I'll review the file and get up to speed when I get back. Or Anna can fax me the pertinent documents here on Mon- day."

"Not good enough." Royal let out a sigh and set his glass on a hard surface near the telephone. "I don't want to fax anything. I don't want anyone to get wind of it. It's a precedent-setter, my boy. A real landmark case."

Mark reached for a notepad and pen from his briefcase. He could feel the adrenaline begin to rush through his body. He'd been waiting for a case like this. "Can you tell me anything about it over the phone?"

"A little, I suppose." Royal took another drink and let out another sigh. "Very little. We're filing suit against a major national company. Alleged malfeasance with their employee pension plan."

Mark let out a low whistle. "Who's our client?"

"It's a class action suit," Royal told him. He sounded pleased with himself. "A group of former employees who allege that the CEO knew of and condoned siphoning funds from the pension plan to get himself out of financial hot water elsewhere."

Interesting, but hardly a landmark case. Mark ran his fingers through his hair and paced as far as the short telephone cord would let him. "You said it would set precedent...?"

"That it will, my boy. And I'll fill you in on all the details when you get back here where you belong."

"Yes, but— Things still aren't settled here."

"That's unfortunate." Royal's voice sounded anything but sympathetic. "But you've already been there for two weeks. Can't you handle the rest from here? How tough can a simple custody matter be?"

"I'm afraid not. It's a little tougher than I expected."

"What's the holdup? I thought you had everything you needed to get the boy and come home again."

Everything but a clear conscience, Mark thought, but he couldn't admit that aloud. Royal wouldn't understand. "I thought I did."

"You need a little pressure from the firm?"

Hell, no. "Thanks, but I think I've got a handle on it."

"Give me the judge's name and let me make a phone call," Royal said with a laugh. "Put me in touch with opposing counsel. If you can't bring him around, I'll do it."

"I'm sure I can wrap it up if I can just have a few more days."

"How many?"

Mark pulled a number from thin air. "Until Wednesday? I can be back in the office on Thursday morning."

Royal's chair creaked again. "Do whatever it takes, but get yourself back to the office by Wednesday afternoon. We need you on this case."

"Yes, sir."

"Pull out all the stops and get what you went there for. You're an associate with Jamison and Spritzer, my boy, not some country-bumpkin attorney. You don't want me to start wondering if you have what it takes to be a partner here."

Mark had always taken pride in his association with the firm, but he resented the thinly veiled threat behind Royal's warning. When Royal disconnected, Mark replaced the receiver slowly and paced to the window. Shoving aside the curtain, he stared at the mountains and sighed heavily.

He'd postponed as long as he could. There was one solution to the problem. It was pretty radical, but maybe she'd go for it.

WHILE JARED PLAYED contentedly at her feet, Dionne put away groceries in her tiny kitchen. Even with the window cooler on high, the apartment was sweltering. She pulled a cold soda from the refrigerator and held it against her cheek. Emotional and physical exhaustion swamped her, scratched at her eyes, and made her almost light-headed. Worry kept her moving.

She should call Cicely. Mark had taken up so much of her time, she hadn't spoken to Cicely in days. Her friend was probably half out of her mind with worry. But Mark had given her an evening alone with Jared and she didn't want to lose a minute of it.

She glanced at the top of Jared's head and smiled. His resemblance to Mark still disturbed her, but it no longer filled her with terror. Nor did the similarities in their personalities.

There was something high-voltage about Mark. Something almost larger than life that drew her in even while it frightened her. Much as she hated to admit it, there were many things about him she liked—his sense of humor, his unselfish concern for Jared, his generosity—but she never completely lost that sensation of danger when he was around. And it wasn't only the danger of losing Jared. There were other things going on inside her as well, and those had nothing to do with Jared. But she didn't want to think about that. Even the briefest acknowledgment of it felt disloyal—to Brent, to Jared, and to herself.

Jared banged two blocks together and beamed up at her. His broad smile changed suddenly as a yawn puckered his mouth and put a deep scowl on his sweet face.

"You're sleepy, aren't you, big boy?"

Jared shook his head firmly. "No." Even though his eyes watered from the huge yawn and another soon distorted his face. He dropped the blocks and rubbed his ear.

"Silly me," Dionne said, closing the cupboard and picking him up. "Of course you're not tired. But what do you say we get you into your jammies, anyway?"

"No."

"I think we'd better." She pushed the blocks aside with one foot and started toward the living room. "We can read a story."

Jared's eyes lit. "Baby Blue Cat?"

"Sure." Stifling a yawn of her own, Dionne kissed his cheek. Not surprisingly, Jared's favorite story was *The Baby Blue Cat Who Said No.* He could listen to it over and over again. "And then we could read *Mama, Do You Love Me?* if you're still not sleepy."

Jared snuggled against her shoulder and worked his fingers into her hair. "Okay."

For once, Jared didn't struggle while she changed him into light summer pajamas. Instead, he cuddled up to her, put his tiny hand on her cheek, and yawned again.

Such love filled her, it seemed as if her heart would explode into a million tiny pieces. But the uneasiness that had been with her ever since Mark appeared on the scene and the nagging reminder that she needed to think seriously about his suggestion, still hovered nearby, just waiting to destroy the moment.

Doing her best to push that problem aside, she gathered Jared and his books and settled into her favorite armchair to read. But before they'd even reached the part where Baby Blue Cat refused to eat his supper, a knock on the door interrupted them.

Since Jared was nearly asleep, Dionne settled him in the chair and hurried to answer before another knock could wake him. But when she checked through the peephole and saw Mark standing there, she hesitated.

Then slowly she opened the door. "I thought we agreed that I'd have tonight alone with Jared."

"We did. But something's come up."

Dionne checked on Jared, pleased to see that he'd fallen into a deep sleep. His cheek rested against the arm of the chair and a lock of hair fell across his forehead. "Fine," she said with a resigned sigh. "Come in. Just give me a minute to get Jared into bed."

When Mark didn't ask to help, she knew something was bothering him. As she carried Jared into his bedroom, she heard Mark shut and lock the door behind him. While she arranged the covers over Jared, she heard Mark pacing the living room like a caged animal.

She kissed Jared and let her gaze linger on his face for a moment, then took a deep breath to steel herself and rejoined Mark in the living room. He'd stopped pacing and had made himself comfortable on the couch, but his expression was troubled.

"What is it?" she said. "What did you want to talk about?"

"We have a problem," he said, running his hand through his hair and leaving soft tufts in its wake. "I got a call from the senior partner in my firm this afternoon. I have to be back in Boston by Wednesday of next week. We have to make some decisions."

She froze. This was it, then. To her dismay, she realized that she'd started getting used to having

Mark around. Now he'd be leaving, and when he did, he'd expect to take Jared with him. He was suddenly, irrevocably, her enemy again.

He stood and crossed to Jared's door, pulling it shut with a soft click. "Have you given any more thought to moving to Boston?"

She watched him warily, her senses almost numb. "You want a decision now?"

"I need to be back in Boston," he said again. He came back to the couch and sat beside her. The light caught his hair and made it look almost black. "And I don't want to leave Jared behind when I go."

A knot curled in Dionne's stomach. "What will happen if I do move to Boston? Will Jared live with me or with you?"

"We could work out a visitation schedule."

"But he'd live with you."

Mark tilted his head to one side. "Yes, most of the time, but—"

She couldn't bear it. She couldn't. But what options did she have? "How do I know you won't lure me there just to get Jared closer and then take him away?"

"If the court grants me custody, I promise that you'll always have a place in his life. You're his mother, Dionne."

"Marianne is still his legal mother," she reminded him, hating the way the words sounded.

"Yes, but she doesn't want to raise him. She chose you to do that."

"But she's never signed the consent for adoption. Either of you could take Jared away from me any time you wanted. I can't live like that."

"If the court grants me custody—"

"So you say," she snapped, jerking to her feet. "But I'm not sure I can trust you."

He ran a hand across his chin. "What do you want from me, Dionne? I'm giving you all I can."

She shook her head, unable to voice her own needs.

"Do you want me to go away and pretend Jared doesn't exist? That none of this happened? I can't do that, Dionne. I won't."

"But you expect me to give him up and be happy seeing him only a few days a year?"

He remained silent for so long she began to worry. At long last, he spoke. "There is another solution. A way we can both have Jared in our lives."

"How?"

"It's kind of extreme," he warned.

"What is it?"

He held her gaze steadily for what felt like forever before he spoke again. "We could get married."

"Married?" She reeled as if he'd shot her and jerked her hand away. *"Married?"*

"I warned you it was extreme. But let me explain before you toss me out on my ear."

He was crazy. Unspeakably crazy. But a small voice told her not to reject the idea outright. "All right. Explain."

"As Jared's legal father, I can establish custody with the court and that would ensure that he would stay with me. As my wife, you'd be his legal step-mother."

Legal. The word seduced her, gave her hope, and made her want to hear the rest.

"You've already said you're not planning to get

married again," Mark went on. "You're still in love with your late husband, right?"

"Yes, but—"

"And I'm... Well, let's just say that I've been burned one too many times to have any romantic notions about finding true love." His mouth twisted bitterly, making her wonder what had happened between him and Marianne. He composed himself quickly. "But we both love Jared, and we both need him in our lives. More importantly, he needs both of us."

"Yes, he does," she admitted reluctantly. It was a hard admission to make, but like it or not, Jared did need his father.

Mark's eyes darkened with gratitude. "So, why should either of us have to give him up?"

She must be demented to even consider it. But his argument made a strange kind of sense.

He touched her softly, just a flicker of his fingers across her hand, but his touch affected her deeply. Its gentleness was strangely healing. "We'd keep the relationship purely platonic, of course. I don't want you to worry about that. We could find a house in the country, where Jared would have plenty of room to play. One with at least three bedrooms."

"But—"

"We'd need to live within commuting distance of Boston, though. As I said before, I'm not willing to abandon my career. But I'm more than willing to provide for my family and let you stay home with Jared—unless you *want* to work, of course. Full-time. Part-time. Nothing at all. That will be your decision. You'd be my wife in every sense of the word except one." He held her gaze again, almost pleading with her to agree. "And most importantly, you'd be Jared's mother."

How could she even consider saying yes? How could she refuse? He held all the cards, yet he was offering her an unbelievable chance. And if she married him, she could ensure that no other woman would ever take her place in Jared's life.

She let her gaze travel over his face, taking in every detail—the thin scar above his lip, the tiny smile lines around his eyes, the way his eyebrows arched when he laughed, just like Jared's. She closed her eyes for a moment, feeling instead of thinking, remembering everything Marianne had told her about him.

Brent had always chided her for making decisions with her heart instead of her head. But in some instances, there was no other way to choose.

She opened her eyes again slowly. "Why are you doing this?"

"I told you before I'm not an ogre." Mark smiled gently. "I'm a fairly decent guy. And I've realized that I don't want to take Jared away from his mother. I'd like to be able to look at myself in the mirror without hating who I see there."

Again, a tiny piece of her brain warned her to think. A sliver of logic made its way to her heart. She knew so little about this man. To even consider his proposition was insane, at best. She should refuse. But Jared chose that moment to toddle out of the bedroom door, his feet scuffing softly along the carpet as he walked, his tiny fists rubbing his eyes, the cupid's bow of a mouth open in a wide yawn. And she knew she was lost.

No matter how illogical, how foolish, how... frightening, there was only one decision she could possibly make.

CHAPTER SIX

"THIS IS INSANE," Cicely snapped as their waiter positioned salads in front of them the following day. "You can't do it."

In spite of the air-conditioning, Dionne could feel patches of perspiration beneath her arms. She'd chosen a neutral spot for this conversation, but even the crowded restaurant didn't inhibit Cicely. Dionne kept her attention on her plate and didn't speak until the waiter walked away.

"I *can* do this," she said softly, "and I'm going to. I won't give Jared up."

Cicely pushed her plate aside. "I can understand how you feel, but there has to be some other way."

"If there is, I'd like to know what it is."

"What about your job?"

"I told them this morning I'm quitting. Today's my last day."

"Without notice? That's great. What about all your things?"

"Our clothes and a few of Jared's toys will fit into suitcases. We'll ship what we can't carry, and Mark's paying a moving company to pack up the furniture and dishes and take them to storage."

"But this guy's a stranger. How do you know he's not psychotic or abusive or...or—" Cicely broke off and waved one hand to encompass all the other possibilities.

"I've talked to Marianne about him," Dionne reminded her, "and she had nothing bad to say about him. Considering what he's prepared to do, I'd say it's obvious that he has a kind heart." Dionne kept her voice low, hoping none of the other customers seated nearby could overhear. "He's offering me a way to keep Jared. How can I walk away from that?"

Cicely reached across the table and covered one of Dionne's hands with hers. "I'm just worried about you. I don't want to see you hurt."

Dionne gripped her friend's hand gratefully. "No matter what happens, I won't be hurt as much as I'd be if he took Jared away. Please, Cicely, don't make this harder than it already is. I need you on my side."

Cicely sighed and shook her head, but some of her reservations seemed to fade. "Maybe I wouldn't feel so bad if you were going to be close. But New England…"

"You can always come to visit."

"Oh, I will. I intend to see for myself that this guy doesn't hurt you." Cicely tried to smile and her fingers tightened on Dionne's. "So, when is the wedding?"

"Tomorrow."

"So soon?"

"Mark has to be back at work by Wednesday afternoon, and we'll need time to travel and get settled. And I don't want to leave here without a wedding. I'm not taking any chances."

"How are you going to explain this to Jared?"

"We'll tell him that we're getting married, of course."

"And that Mark's his father?"

Dionne nodded slowly. "He still knows Brent as 'Daddy' from pictures around the house, so we've agreed to tell him that Mark is his new daddy—at least for now. I have a few reservations, but telling Jared the truth is one of Mark's conditions. I suppose he's right. I can't expect him to be happy with Jared calling him 'Uncle Mark.'"

"I guess not," Cicely agreed grudgingly.

"I'm scared," Dionne admitted, "but I have to do this. Will you be there for me?"

"You know I will." Cicely made a visible effort to put her concerns behind her. "It's your wedding day."

"I've had my wedding day," Dionne reminded Cicely firmly, "with Brent. This is a business arrangement, that's all. Tomorrow is just the day we make the contract binding."

"There are a lot of things this is," Cicely argued, "but a business arrangement isn't one of them. You're committing to live with a stranger for the rest of your life."

The words sent a bolt of panic through Dionne, but she tried to ignore it and made a weak joke. "He won't be a stranger for long."

"You're right about that. The man is going to be your *husband*. What are you going to do when he wants to act like one?"

"That won't happen," Dionne insisted. "We've agreed to have separate bedrooms and keep the relationship platonic. But for Jared's sake we're not telling anyone else that, not even Mark's family. Everyone will believe we fell in love and got married."

"That ought to keep you safe," Cicely said sarcastically.

"Mark's no more interested in me than I am in him," Dionne insisted.

"Right." Cicely frowned, then waved a hand in front of her. "Assuming that's true—and for the record, I don't believe it for a minute—how will you explain your sleeping arrangement to Jared when he gets older?"

Dionne ran her fingers along the side of her water glass. "I don't know. We'll cross that bridge when we come to it."

"That bridge and a hundred more," Cicely predicted.

"Maybe. Probably." Dionne met Cicely's gaze steadily. "But no matter what problems we have, it will be worth it."

"What if *you* start liking *him?* Or what if you meet someone else in a year or two you fall in love with? What then?"

Dionne scowled at her. "That won't happen. I had my turn. Brent was my soul mate. No one could ever take his place."

"I know you feel that way now, but—"

"I won't change my mind."

"Okay, what if he finds someone else and falls in love?"

Dionne had had that thought herself. And she also had the answer. "If Mark has custody, I'll be Jared's legal stepmother. Nothing will change that."

Cicely studied her for a moment, then let out a heavy sigh. "You're so damned stubborn."

Dionne could feel the tide of the conversation turning, and let out a soft sigh of her own. "Yes, I know."

"It's not a compliment."

"Okay."

Cicely waved her hand again, this time in resignation. "All right. Fine. If you're determined to do this, I guess I won't argue with you anymore. But if you ever—*ever*—need me, promise you'll call."

Dionne sketched an X over her heart and smiled sadly. "I promise." She reached over to grasp her friend's hand. "Thank you, Cece. I feel a whole lot better having your support."

Cicely's eyes glittered with unshed tears. "I wish something would make *me* feel better."

"How about knowing that Jared and I will be together and happy?"

"Together, yes. But happy?" Cicely tossed her napkin onto the table. "We'll have to wait and see about that."

As IF IN A DREAM, Dionne followed Mark into the justice of the peace's office. Behind her, Cicely carried Jared, who wanted to get down and explore.

"Hush now," Cicely said softly. "Stay with me for just a few minutes. Look how pretty Mommy is."

"Down," Jared insisted. When Cicely didn't release him, he took a deep breath and prepared to let out a howl.

Mark stepped forward quickly, as if he'd been dealing with Jared his entire life. He pulled a colorful key chain from his pocket and handed it to the boy. "Hang on to these for me, will you, sport? See if you can make the light shine." He showed Jared where to push the mini-flashlight and ruffled his hair affectionately.

Dionne sent him a grateful smile, then looked around the bleak office that was so unlike the church where she'd married Brent. Instead of flowers, they were surrounded by file cabinets. Instead of organ music, the sounds of morning traffic filled the air.

But it was perfect for this occasion.

At her wedding to Brent, she'd been full of hope and dreams. Now she clung desperately to the hope that she wasn't making the biggest mistake of her life.

Her finger, without the ring Brent had placed on it, felt bare. Within minutes, she'd be wearing one of the matching gold bands Mark had shown her as they'd carried her bags to the car. He'd seemed almost eager for her approval of his choice, but she didn't care. That ring would symbolize none of the things Brent's had.

The justice of the peace, a middle-aged woman with a bad Doris Day haircut, smiled and stood to greet them. "Right on time. We should be able to get you to the airport with no problem." She shook Mark's hand and nodded toward a short, gray-haired man standing in the corner. "I've asked my husband to stand in as your other witness. I hope that's all right."

Mark left Dionne's side to shake the man's hand. "It's fine. I appreciate you taking time out of your schedule to accommodate us."

"Glad to do it," the man said, stepping forward to stand beside Cicely.

Dionne kept her smile in place and nodded in response to Mark's soft, "Ready?" She *was* ready.

Ready to seal the bargain they'd made. Ready to take the step that would allow her to remain in Jared's life. Ready to put the past behind her and move on.

Still, the brief ceremony passed in a blur. She scarcely heard the woman's short speech about the sanctity of marriage and the sacred nature of the vows they would soon exchange.

She responded with a whispered "I do" when the justice of the peace looked at her expectantly. A moment later, she heard Mark's identical response through the roaring in her ears. But her anxiety escalated when she heard the woman pronounce them man and wife and gave Mark permission to kiss the bride.

There really was no going back now.

When Mark hesitated, Dionne lifted her face to him, knowing she had to keep her end of the bargain. Except for Cicely, no one would ever know what a sham this marriage was.

He gingerly kissed her cheek, then stepped away again. She glanced at the simple gold band on her finger and tried to hold back the sudden tears that burned her eyes.

The justice of the peace looked concerned. "Are you all right, Mrs. Taylor?"

Mrs. Taylor.

The name sounded all wrong. Dionne blinked and sent the woman a tremulous smile. "Yes," she whispered. "I'm fine."

"Just overwhelmed, I'm sure." The woman touched her shoulder gently. "Weddings are such emotional times."

The poor woman would be shocked if she knew *which* emotions were racking Dionne at this moment.

Fear, guilt and disbelief mixed with faith and hope. Dionne reached for Cicely's hand, needing a lifeline to cling to if only for a moment. To her dismay, the hand she caught wasn't Cicely's. It was big and rough-skinned, and completely male.

If the contact surprised Mark, he didn't show it. Instead, he closed his hand around hers and gave it a gentle squeeze. Unexpected warmth began at her fingertips and radiated up her arm.

Stunned, she pulled her hand away and glanced at him quickly. She didn't *want* to be aware of Mark. She was, and always had been, in love with Brent and she owed it to his memory not to betray him.

"Well," Mark said, shoving his hands into his pockets. "I guess that's it. We'd better hurry if we're going to make our flight."

Dionne struggled to still her trembling fingers and turned toward Cicely.

Mark followed the direction of her gaze, then looked back at her again. "We have time for you to say goodbye."

Grateful for his understanding, she took Jared from Cicely and surrendered gratefully to her friend's warm embrace.

"Remember," Cicely spoke softly, "if things don't work out, all you have to do is call me."

"But they *will* work out," Dionne insisted. "They have to."

"I hope so," Cicely whispered. Releasing Dionne suddenly, she straightened her shoulders, propped her hands on her hips, and turned to Mark. "If you ever hurt either of them," she said, "you'll have to answer to me."

Mark nodded soberly. "I'll keep that in mind."

"Would you stop worrying?" Dionne said. "Everything's going to be just fine, you'll see."

But as she carried Jared out the door, firmly resisting the impulse to turn around and flee back to Cicely's side, she couldn't help wishing she was as confident as she'd managed to sound.

ONE OF THE THINGS Mark liked best about traveling was coming home to Boston. He always looked forward to getting back to his routine. But now his routine would never be the same. He had a child. And a wife.

A wife who didn't look happy at all.

She held Jared close, cradling him almost as if he was some kind of protective shield. She looked nervous. Pale. Her cheek still bore the imprint from the seat of the cab where she'd fallen asleep on their way from the airport.

Mark watched the cab pull away from the curb in front of his condo, then glanced at their bags on the sidewalk. Dionne shivered in spite of the warm night air and pulled Jared closer.

"Well," he said, shoving his hands into his pockets, trying to hide his own nervousness. He forced a weak smile. "Here we are."

"Yes."

Mark pulled his hands out of his pockets again and picked up their bags. "I think we should both get a good night's sleep," he said, nodding for her to walk in front of him. "We'll have to start looking for a place to live in the morning."

"Yes." She spoke so softly, he could barely hear her over the passing late-night traffic.

He juggled luggage and held the door for her. "I

know this is tough for you, Dionne. Hell, it's not going to be a piece of cake for me, either. But we're going to be together for a long time. We might as well try to be friends.''

She stopped inside the lobby and looked back at him. ''I'd like that. I know so little about you, about your family—'' She broke off and stared at the ornate ceiling, the rich marble floor and pillars. Mark knew she was comparing this building and the one she and Jared had called home in Boise, and for the first time he saw it as gaudy and ostentatious.

Suddenly embarrassed, he nodded toward the elevators. ''We're going to the twelfth floor.''

She made her way across the deserted lobby, but didn't speak again until the elevator doors closed. ''Can you believe this is happening?''

''You mean that we're married?''

''It keeps hitting me in waves,'' she confessed, leaning against the wall and adjusting her hold on Jared. ''Just when I think I've accepted it, something new happens, like realizing Jared and I are going to be living here.'' She ran a hand over Jared's head and sent Mark a weak smile. ''Or realizing that we'll be meeting your family soon.''

''My family?'' Talking about them put Mark back on firm ground. ''You don't have to worry about them. They're great.''

''I'm sure they are, but I've been alone for a long time. My mother died when I was sixteen, and I have no idea where my father is. Brent's been gone for a year. It may take me a while to get used to... everything.''

He appreciated her honesty. It was the first step in

closing the gap between them. "If it helps, I've lived alone most of my adult life."

"But not completely alone. Your family has obviously played a big part in your life." She watched the lights above the door for a moment. "Maybe you should tell me something about them."

He didn't know where to begin, but he welcomed the chance to fill the nervous space between them.

"I have three brothers," he said as the elevator doors swished open again. "David's the oldest, and I come between Jerry and Steve, who's the youngest." He motioned her toward the far end of the corridor and kept talking as they walked. "David's married. He and his wife, Kaye, have four kids. Jerry's divorced. He sees his two daughters twice a month on weekends. And Steve..." He smiled ruefully. "Well, Steve's a lot like me, I guess. He's twenty-seven and shows no signs of ever getting married."

Dionne glanced at him uneasily. "I wonder if I'll ever be able to keep them all straight."

"Sure you will. But that's not all." He stopped in front of his door and ran his finger between his neck and collar. The realization that she belonged inside brought on a fresh wave of apprehension. "There's Aunt Nonie and her husband, Bruce, Uncle Pete and Aunt Shirley, Aunt Pam and Uncle Carl, a couple dozen cousins, their spouses and kids."

Dionne's eyebrows knit. "They won't all be there at once, will they?"

He unlocked the door, pushed it open, and then stopped. Surely she wouldn't want him to carry her across the threshold. He glanced at her quickly, saw wariness etched on her face, and decided to let her walk in on her own. "My parents' house is like Grand Central Station," he went on. "It's where everybody gathers for any occasion—or no occasion at all. Every family has one."

A shadow passed across her eyes. "Mine didn't." She hitched Jared higher on her shoulder. "We won't be expected to spend every weekend with them, will we?"

"No, of course not. David and Kaye practically live at my parents' house, but they own a house in Sunrise Notch, so that's only natural. Jerry and Steve only show up every few weeks. And between my obligations at work and the things I'm sure you'll get involved with, we'll be too busy to go, even if we wanted to." He turned on the light for her and shut the door. "Well, here it is," he said. "Home sweet home." He found himself watching her, waiting for her reaction.

She gazed around slowly at the furniture, paintings, and sculptures, then took a ragged breath. "It's very nice."

He laughed, but it sounded jittery and tense. "Maybe. But it's no place for a two-year-old. I'll have to get rid of most of this stuff or put it in storage until Jared's older."

"Are you going to be okay with that? You must have spent a lot of money getting everything just right."

She looked so uncertain, he almost gave in to the urge to put his arm around her. But the memory of how quickly she'd dropped his hand after the wedding ceremony made him hold back.

"I'm fine with that," he assured her. "It's just stuff."

"Very expensive stuff."

"Maybe, but it's still stuff." He picked up her suitcase and started toward his bedroom. "I'll put your things and Jared's in here. I'll sleep on the couch."

Her eyes widened. "This huge place only has one bedroom?"

"Sad but true."

"You don't need to give up your bedroom for us. I don't mind sleeping on the couch, and I can make Jared a bed on the floor with some of the cushions—"

Mark shook his head quickly. "Sorry. I was raised to be a gentleman."

"A gentleman doesn't dictate to a lady." Her voice sounded almost teasing.

"A lady doesn't turn down a gentleman when he offers her his bed." The instant the words left his mouth, he regretted them. A sudden, sharp image of his sheets clinging to her body formed in his mind, and the air seemed charged with something that hadn't been there a moment before.

To his relief, Dionne didn't seem to notice. She laughed softly, but the warmth of her laugh and the light dancing in her eyes only made the image sharper. "Is that right?"

"That's right." He tried to block out the mental picture, but it wouldn't go away.

Great. He'd promised to keep their relationship platonic, but they hadn't even been married twelve hours and already his sex drive was threatening everything. Dionne would hate him again if she guessed the kinds of thoughts he was having. She'd probably think that he'd lured her here just to take advantage of her.

Maybe this marriage had been a mistake on both their parts. But it was too late now.

Cursing himself under his breath, he tried to keep his mind on the tasks at hand. The task of settling his new wife into his bedroom. The task of embarking on a life with a woman he hardly knew and a child he couldn't live without.

HEART POUNDING, Dionne woke with a start and sat bolt upright in bed. Sunlight streamed through the windows and burned her tired eyes. She'd overslept. She'd be late for work.

When she tossed back the covers, her hand brushed Jared on the bed beside her. In a rush, everything came flooding back—the emotional turmoil of the past three weeks, the wedding, the long flight. Blinking quickly to clear her eyes, she pulled her hand back and lowered it to her lap. And she watched Jared to make sure she hadn't woken him.

She'd slept hard almost from the moment her head touched the pillow, but she didn't feel rested. Judging from the way Jared slept, he'd been worn out by the long flight. Spending the night in a strange bedroom two thousand miles from home had certainly left her physically and emotionally exhausted.

This was home now, she corrected herself. This bedroom with the wheat-colored comforter and matching sheets, the polished hardwood floor and woven rugs, the Native American art and paintings of southwestern landscapes. And the man who owned it all was her husband.

Just when she'd started to relax around him last

night, he'd changed. He'd suddenly become remote and chilly, and had left her and Jared alone in the bedroom as if he couldn't get rid of them fast enough.

Maybe he'd been nervous. Heaven only knew *she'd* been on edge. But his inexplicable mood swing worried her. Her mother had been moody, and the shifts from one to the other without warning had always left Dionne anxious and uncertain.

Old emotions she'd thought long gone rushed to the surface and made her wary. After climbing off the bed gently, she crossed to the bedroom door and pressed her ear against it to listen. She couldn't hear Mark moving around, which was fine with her. She didn't mind a few minutes of solitude and a cup of fresh, strong coffee before she had to see him again. If she was careful, she could find the kitchen and make a pot without waking him.

After closing the bedroom door behind her, she waited for a few seconds to make absolutely certain Mark was still asleep on the couch. She couldn't see him, but she could make out a mound of blankets and the edge of his pillow.

Quietly, scarcely breathing, she tiptoed through the living room, taking in the furniture and obviously expensive paintings on the walls. Bookshelves flanked the fireplace but, unlike her own particle-board bookshelves in Boise that she'd filled with well-thumbed paperbacks, his books were hardbound and looked new.

She moved into the dining room still on tiptoe. There, a large oak table and matching chairs gleamed in bright morning sunlight. Green plants tumbled from baskets in the corners and curled along a sideboard against the far wall.

Nice. Much nicer than anything she'd ever owned. And she was suddenly glad she wouldn't have to protect Mark's valuables from Jared's quick little hands for long.

Sighing, she crossed to a door that she assumed led into the kitchen and pushed it open. But when she saw Mark standing there with his back to her, she froze in place.

Wearing only a pair of sweatpants, he scooped coffee into a filter. His hair was sleep-tousled, and his back and feet were bare. He looked young and vulnerable and strangely appealing. While she watched, he lowered the can to the counter and stretched. Muscles appeared out of nowhere on his shoulders and arms. The sweatpants slipped a little lower on his hips.

Something Dionne hadn't felt in a long time flickered deep within her. Desire? No, she told herself firmly. Not desire. It was just...just...

Trembling, she closed the door between them and leaned against the wall. This would never do. She didn't need this purely female reaction to the sight of a half-dressed man. She wasn't *supposed* to have that kind of reaction to him. Her heart still belonged to Brent.

She squeezed her eyes shut and tried to catch her breath. At least Mark hadn't seen her. She'd have been mortified if he'd noticed her reaction and misinterpreted it as something personal. Because whatever it had been, it *wasn't* personal. She couldn't allow it to be.

Shivering slightly, she pushed away from the wall,

raced back to the bedroom, and closed the door firmly. She started toward the bed, but she didn't want to wake Jared, and the idea of sitting on Mark's bed suddenly made her uncomfortable.

She hoisted her heavy suitcase onto a chair instead and pulled out jeans and a baggy T-shirt—sensible clothing that was decidedly *un*sexy.

Resolutely, she carried her overnight bag into the bathroom, locked the door behind her, and undressed quickly. Even with the door locked, the idea of Mark, bare-chested and undeniably sexy, only a room or two away made her uncomfortable.

She turned the shower to a heavy pulsing rhythm that should have pummeled some sense back into her. Instead, it seemed to make her body more fully aware. She turned it to a gentle spray and leaned her head against the shower wall.

Now that she knew she could feel desire again, she also realized she couldn't act on it. Mark had suggested this marriage because he felt sorry for her, not because he found her attractive. She'd agreed only because she was desperate.

If she'd been in Boise, she'd have picked up the phone and called Cicely. But even Cicely couldn't help her this time.

She'd have to solve this one on her own.

CHAPTER SEVEN

DIONNE STRUGGLED to keep her eyes open as Mark scooped the last bit of creamy chowder from his bowl and slid it into his mouth. Jared played contentedly with a small container of crayons and a coloring book provided by the restaurant. Both of the men in her life looked ready to hit the house-hunting trail again. Dionne would have given anything for a nice long nap.

Her eyes felt gritty from exhaustion and her muscles had long ago turned to gelatin, and all for nothing. After two days of house-hunting, they were no closer to finding a place than they'd been when they stepped off the plane at the airport.

They'd found charming houses with only two bedrooms, large houses located on busy streets, houses that were practically falling apart, and houses even Mark couldn't afford, but they hadn't found anything that would fit their needs. And she'd been so exhausted each evening when they got back to Mark's condo, she'd gone to bed almost the minute they walked in the door.

After that moment in the kitchen that first morning, avoiding time alone with him seemed like the wisest thing she could do. But some traitorous part of her was disappointed that he didn't seem to mind.

Sighing with contentment, Mark leaned back in his

chair. "If all the restaurants around here are this good, maybe we *should* buy that house."

"The two-bedroom one?"

"Don't worry," he assured her with a quick smile. "I'm only thinking about my stomach."

She let herself relax slightly, though she was determined not to let her guard down completely. Smoothing a lock of hair from Jared's forehead, she smiled at the serious look on his face as he colored a cartoon lobster bright blue. "The food is wonderful here," she agreed, glancing at the low-beamed ceiling and the huge fireplace across the crowded room. "But it's also expensive. I think they're charging for atmosphere."

Mark shrugged easily. "Probably. But it's worth it, don't you think?"

"You obviously live differently than Jared and I do."

"I'm not rolling in money," he said, "but I do okay. You don't need to worry."

She felt him watching her, waiting for her to look at him again. Slowly, hesitantly, she forced herself to do just that. "I'm not worried. I'm used to living on a pretty tight budget. I'm *not* used to relying on someone else to fund the budget."

"Did you work while you were married to Brent?"

She nodded. "I've worked since I was old enough to get a job."

"Doing what?"

"You name it," she said with a thin laugh, "I've done it. I've baby-sat, decorated Christmas trees, worked in a garden shop, and cashiered at a grocery store. I've slung burgers and waited tables... I could go on, but you get the general idea.''

He looked confused. ''Didn't you go to college?''

''No.''

''Not interested?''

''No. I would have loved to have gone. I just couldn't afford it.''

He looked almost embarrassed by her admission. ''If you had gone, what would you have studied?''

She smiled to set him at ease. It wasn't his fault she'd spent her entire life without money. ''I used to dream about being a counselor for troubled children. I wanted to help kids who grow up feeling unloved and disconnected because their parents are absent for one reason or another.''

His eyes glinted with approval. ''What made you decide on that?''

''I guess because that's how I felt when I was growing up. My father walked out on us when I was only two, and my mother worked herself into an early grave trying to support me. She wasn't ever home, even when she was alive.'' She still felt strange telling him something so personal, but they'd agreed to work on their friendship and he couldn't understand her unless he also understood her past.

Before she knew what he intended, he put a hand over hers. ''I'm sorry.''

She tried to ignore the sudden flush of heat that swept through her and struggled not to react to the concern in his voice.

''There's nothing to be sorry for,'' she said firmly and drew her hand away, resisting the urge to let it linger in the comfort of his. ''It's just how things were at my house.''

"But you dreamed about helping other kids in the same boat."

"For a while. But real life brought me back to earth in a hurry."

Something she couldn't read flashed in his eyes. "Do you still think about doing it?"

She shook her head and laughed away the idea. "I don't really have time to indulge in dreams."

"Maybe you should."

"No." She folded her napkin and set it on the table. "Life is much better when I keep my feet on the ground."

Mark let his gaze travel slowly across her face and settle on her eyes again. "I don't agree with you. Life goes nowhere when you're afraid to take risks. You could still get your degree if you want to."

She shook her head firmly. "No, I can't."

"Why not?"

"I've got Jared to think about. I wouldn't be able to put in the hours studying that I'd need to. Not to mention the cost of tuition."

Mark's mouth twisted slightly. "You're not the only one around to take care of Jared, you know. We could find a sitter for him while you're in class, you could study in the evenings while I spend time with him, and finding the money for tuition wouldn't be a problem."

Uneasy, Dionne scooted her chair away from the table and started to pick up the crayons from Jared's high chair. "I can't take that kind of money from you."

"Why not?"

"Because...because it wouldn't be right."

"I don't know why not. You *are* my wife."

"Technically, yes. But—"

Mark cut off her next argument. "Besides, I think you should give some thought to what you're going to do when Jared gets older and starts school himself."

"That won't be for a long time," she said almost desperately. She touched Jared's hand gently, suddenly afraid to see him grow older. "He's only two." And three years seemed like an eternity away.

She wondered briefly what their marriage would be like then. Would they still feel like strangers or would they have settled into a comfortable routine? Would she still feel this quickening of her pulse when Mark looked at her with those deep brown eyes, still tremble when he touched her.

"Three years will pass before you know it," he predicted, picking up the dessert menu. "At least think about going to school. Don't cross it off your list yet. I want you to be happy here."

She ignored the fluttering in her abdomen and managed a weak smile. "All right. I'll think about it." At least, she'd pretend to. "In the meantime, there are more important things to think about, like deciding how we're going to split the household chores."

Mark seemed reluctant to change the subject, but at least he didn't argue. "All right. What do you suggest?"

"We could each make a list, starting with the thing we enjoy most and working down to our least favorite. Maybe we'll discover that I don't mind cooking and you like scrubbing toilets."

"I can guarantee we won't discover that," he assured her with a warm laugh. "Do you like to cook?"

"I'm not a gourmet chef, but I enjoy making simple recipes."

"Then the cooking is all yours." He lowered the menu and rested his hands on the table. "I haven't mowed a lawn in years, but I don't mind doing the yard work."

"I like growing flowers," she said, "but I'll be thrilled to let you do the rest. Does your offer include weeding and trimming and edging?"

"Sure. And shoveling snow. What about dusting and vacuuming?"

"I can do those," she offered. "I'll have plenty of time on my hands." She glanced down at the strange gold band on her finger and added, "I think we should each do our own laundry. I'll do Jared's with mine."

"Good idea." Mark cleared his throat, then picked up the dessert menu again, and made a pretense of studying it. Color flooded his cheeks and she could see his pulse beating against his temple. "And it would probably be best if neither of us left our underthings drying in the bathroom."

He looked so ill at ease, Dionne nearly laughed aloud. "Of course."

"Okay." He shifted on the chair, but his eyes never left the menu. "The cheesecake looks good. Would you like some?"

Dionne shook her head and rested one hand on her stomach. "No, thanks. The chowder was too filling."

"Then let's get out of here." His voice came out gruff and hard-edged. He tossed his napkin onto the table, slipped more than enough money to cover the bill onto the table, and started to lift Jared. "Are you ready, sport?"

Jared leaned back toward the high chair, wriggling his fingers at the picture he'd been forced once again to abandon. "My picture."

"Mommy's got it," Dionne assured him, brushing a kiss to his forehead.

"I need to get to the office," Mark said as he started away again. "Do you want me to drop you two off somewhere, or do you want to go home?"

Dionne gathered her things, surprised but pleased by his reaction. "Jared needs a nap. I think we should just go back to your apartment."

"It's yours now, too," Mark said quickly. "At least until we find someplace else to live."

Dionne didn't argue, but she wondered if she could ever get used to calling his condo home. If she'd get used to calling *any* place home she shared with him.

Someday, perhaps. But not yet.

FOR THE FIRST TIME in weeks, Mark felt like himself again. His office with windows overlooking Boston Harbor, his files, the credenza loaded with work—all of it helped to ground him. He stood inside the doorway for a minute or two, then lowered his briefcase to the floor beside his desk, stripped off his jacket, and draped it over a chair.

Royal wanted a draft of the Young Technologies brief by the end of next week, and Mark wouldn't disappoint him. The case would require hours of research, but he'd never had trouble setting aside his personal life for his professional one. Of course, he hadn't had a wife and son before.

Settling himself in his comfortable leather chair, he pulled the file toward him. Just as Royal predicted, it was an interesting dispute, one that could be a landmark decision if the court ruled the way the firm wanted it to. And maybe, if Mark could immerse himself in the case, he could put Dionne out of his mind for a while.

He hadn't planned to be so damned attracted to her, but every moment he spent in her company only made the attraction stronger. The way she rubbed her forehead when something worried her. The way her eyes changed from ice to slate to sky blue when her moods shifted. The soft swell of her breasts and the curve of her hip...

Scrubbing his face with his hand, Mark told himself to think about work. Exhibits. Testimony. Legal research. There was nothing particularly sexy about any of those things.

He opened the file and spent a few minutes skimming the documents inside, but when a soft knock sounded on the door and his secretary of three years, Anna, peeked inside, he abandoned the case eagerly.

"Hey there." Anna stepped into his office and closed the door behind her. "Welcome back. How did it go?"

Seeing Anna's familiar face, her wild red hair and trademark huge round glasses grounded him a bit further. Grinning, he leaned back in his chair and motioned her inside. "It went fine. Great, as a matter of fact."

"Then you were able to bring back your little boy?"

"I sure did."

"Oh, Mark, that's wonderful." Anna's curls

burned in the sunlight—a nice contrast to the blond ones that kept intruding into his thoughts. "When do we get to see him?"

"Soon. After he's had some time to settle in."

Anna dropped into the empty chair in front of his desk and made herself comfortable. "How's he doing? Does he miss his mother?"

Mark tried to keep his gaze steady, but he couldn't do it. He glanced down at his hands and hesitated over his response.

"Mark?" Anna prodded gently. "What is it? What have you done?"

"What makes you think I've done anything?"

"I know you."

She had him there. They'd been friends as well as co-workers for a long time. Anna had provided a listening ear after Marianne disappeared, and he owed her a lot. But he couldn't tell her the truth about his relationship with Dionne. "It's a long story," he said at last.

"I have time."

"Unfortunately, I don't." He made a face and gestured toward the mess on his desk. "Royal wants this complaint by the end of next week, and I haven't even started on it."

Anna's eyes fastened on the new ring on his left hand and her eyebrows knit. She crossed her legs as if she intended to stay for a while and nodded toward his finger. "What's this?"

He glanced at his hand as if he'd never seen the ring before and tried to joke. "This? I don't know. How'd that get there?"

"What did you do?" she asked again.

He lifted both shoulders in a casual shrug. "I got married."

"To—?"

"To Jared's mother."

Anna scowled at him. "You married Marianne?"

"No." He smiled and leaned back in his chair. "His other mother."

Suspicion turned Anna's eyes almost green. "Really. Do you mind telling me why?"

"Not at all. We wanted to get married."

"Why-y-y?" She dragged out the word and tilted her head to one side, as if she could see through him from that angle. And she knew him so well, she probably could.

"Because we fell in love the instant we met." This was only the second time he'd tried saying it aloud, but the words fell easily off his tongue.

"You fell in love at first sight? *You?*"

He smoothed his tie and tried to look like a man head over heels in love. "Me."

"And it just *happened* to be with the woman who's been raising your son."

Her gaze disconcerted him. He shifted his attention to the file in front of him. "As luck would have it, yes."

He chanced a glance at her. The expression on her face told him she didn't believe a word he was saying. "Well, you know what they say." He laughed, but it came out sounding forced and unnatural. "Truth *is* stranger than fiction."

"I know what they say." Anna leaned forward. "But this is me you're talking to. I know you, and I *know* you didn't fall in love with her in three short weeks. What's the real story?"

"That *is* the real story, Anna. We met, we talked about Jared, and in the process we fell in love. Neither of us wanted to be separated by two thousand miles, so we decided to get married."

"And, by the merest coincidence, you both ended up with your little boy."

Mark had always prized Anna's ability to cut through the fog surrounding legal issues and get right to the heart of the question, but having her turn it on him was another matter entirely. "Don't you have work to do?"

She sent him a triumphant smile. "Yeah, I do. And you've got messages." She pulled a handful of pink slips from the pocket of her suit jacket and started creating a stack on his desk. "Alan Cracroft wants you to call him to discuss a settlement on the Patterson matter. Mrs. Billings called about the deposition next week. And your mother has called three times. She wants you to phone her back."

Mark scowled up at her as the light went on inside his head. No wonder Anna had noticed the ring so quickly. "You talked to my mother?"

"Three times."

"What did she say?"

"That she has something to discuss with you."

"Uh-huh." Mark sent her a resigned smile. "And let me guess... She told you about the wedding."

Anna leaned back in her chair again, looking smug. "She might have mentioned it."

"*Might?* My mother?" Mark laughed and set the messages aside. "Okay, spill it. What did she say?"

"The same thing you did, but I didn't believe her, either."

"You should have."

"Don't lie to me, Mark. I know how you felt after Marianne left, and I've spent three years listening to you say you won't ever fall in love or trust a woman again. Either you're lying, or this wife of yours is one hell of a woman."

"She is," he said, surprised to realize he meant it. She had courage and devotion and loyalty like nothing he'd ever seen before—at least to her son and Brent. He wondered if her husband had realized how lucky he was to be loved like that, then gave himself a mental shake and focused on Anna again. "I certainly hope you didn't mention your suspicions to my mother."

Anna waved one hand in the air. "Don't be silly. I'm completely loyal to you. And I figure you must have some reason for trying to pass off this marriage as the world's greatest romance."

He opened his mouth to set her straight again, then gave in to the temptation to tell her the truth. Anna *was* a trusted friend, and it would be nice to have one person he could be honest with. He rubbed the back of his neck and stretched to work out the knots of tension he could feel forming. "Okay, you're right. We got married for Jared's sake. But we don't ever want him to know that we got married for any reason other than love."

"No one will ever hear it from me," Anna promised. "But if you don't love each other, what makes you think you can make a marriage work?"

"We have to," he said, rubbing his neck a little harder. "Neither of us can stand the idea of being without Jared. When I left here, I didn't care about her. I was ready to fight to the death to take him away...until I saw them together."

"And now you do care?"

"I care about Jared. And, I care about her in a way. None of this is *her* fault. She shouldn't have to pay for what Marianne did."

Anna's smile softened. "In spite of your reputation in court, I always knew you were a decent guy. So tell me what she's like, this wife of yours."

"She's intelligent, warm, caring. She loves Jared with all her heart, and she's willing to cook. I can't ask for more than that."

"You could ask for someone who loved *you*."

He shook his head. "I did what I had to do to have my son with me and still be able to look at myself in the mirror. But love? That's not in the cards." He didn't like the sadness that worked its way through him when he said those words, and he didn't like the direction their conversation was going. "Maybe you don't approve, but what's done is done. And I really do have work to do."

Anna stood reluctantly. "I'll let you get to it then." She crossed to the door and paused. "Do you want me to spread the word about your marriage?"

"If you'd like to." He'd have to face the questions sooner or later. Might as well get it over with.

When Anna left him alone, he tried again to concentrate on the brief, but his telephone rang not five minutes later. And his mother's cheerful voice greeted him when he answered. "How's my newly married son?"

"I'm fine, Mom. What's up?"

"Your dad and I have had the most wonderful idea, but we need to check with you before we finalize our plans."

"What is it?"

"We want to give you and Dionne a reception."

Mark leaned back in his chair and rubbed his eyes. "Why?"

"Why?" His mother laughed. "Because you got *married*, Mark. And since we couldn't be there for the wedding, we'd like to do something."

Guilt at denying his mother the wedding she'd been waiting for pricked him. "I'm not sure Dionne will want you to do all that," he said warily.

"Nonsense. Honestly, sometimes you men can be so dense. Every woman wants her wedding to be something special. I don't want to be rude, dear, but getting married in a justice of the peace's office isn't very romantic."

She had a point. Their wedding hadn't been special or beautiful by any stretch of the imagination. And when it came to knowing what women wanted, his mother certainly knew better than Mark did.

"When do you want to do it?"

"How about this weekend? I'm assuming you and Dionne will be here for Labor Day, and the rest of the family is coming. It won't take much effort to add a few things to the menu, order a few flowers, and let friends and neighbors know."

The family always got together for holidays, but with everything that had been happening, Mark hadn't given Labor Day a moment's thought. "I don't know," he hedged, "Dionne's already overwhelmed by the idea of meeting the family."

"We won't go overboard," his mother promised. "Just a quiet barbecue with family and a few close friends. We're all dying to see Jared and meet Dionne. You aren't going to make us wait, are you?"

Mark couldn't ignore the pleading note in his

mother's voice, and he rationalized his decision by telling himself Dionne would have to meet everyone eventually. This way she could get it over with all at once. "Sure, Mom. That sounds fine. What do you want us to do?"

"Nothing at all. Just show up on Saturday. We'll plan to start about six, but you can come early so we have some time alone before the guests show up."

He smiled tiredly. "Okay, Mom."

"You won't be sorry, Mark. Really. This is something I'm sure your new bride will want."

Mark replaced the receiver slowly, hoping his mother was right. Dionne had given up a lot to come to Boston. Maybe this would make it up to her in some small way.

MARK CHECKED his watch and grimaced as he shut the car door. He hadn't intended to work so late, but one minute it had been early afternoon, the next, evening shadows had been drifting across his office and making it difficult to read.

Shifting his briefcase to the other hand, he tried to find the key as he walked through the parking lot toward the condo. He should have paid more attention to the time. Halfway home, he'd realized he should have called Dionne to let her know where he was.

The idea of having someone else around and a part of his life left him slightly off balance. He'd lived away from his family for years. Before Marianne, he'd had only casual relationships that didn't require a commitment from him. And Marianne certainly hadn't been demanding of his time. Their relationship had consisted entirely of late nights in bed and those few weekends when they both took time away from the office.

But Dionne was different. She wasn't married to her career. At the moment, she didn't even have one. She'd spent the entire afternoon alone with Jared, and they were probably both starving, waiting for him to come home. She deserved an apology.

And he was ready to give one as he put his key in the lock. But the aromas that hit him when he opened the door wiped everything else out of his mind.

He left his briefcase on the coffee table and walked toward the kitchen. Soft music played on the stereo. Gershwin. She must have found his CDs.

Pushing open the door, he peered inside. Fresh vegetables lay on the counter waiting for attention. Steaks marinated near the sink. His kitchen had never looked so domestic.

Dionne was there, too, in an oversize blouse and leggings that emphasized the length and shape of her legs, her hair piled loosely on her head, exposing the soft nape of her neck, the tantalizing curve of her hips visible beneath the blouse as she moved in time to the music. She looked anything but domestic, and Mark had the almost overwhelming urge to skip the apology and kiss her instead.

He stepped into the kitchen and looked around for Jared as the door swung shut behind him. "You're cooking."

She glanced back at him, and the deep scowl on her face marred the picture. "You're very observant."

Forget the kiss, better stick with the apology. "I'm sorry I'm late. I—"

She sent him an icy glare, then looked back at a bunch of scallions on the cutting board. "I'm not here to interfere in your life."

He tried again, skipping to the middle of his prepared speech. "I won't always work this late."

"Do what you need to do."

He crossed to the wine rack and reached for a bottle. "It's just that there's a lot to do to catch up."

Dionne snapped the rubber band off the scallions. "Fine."

"Fine?" He let out a harsh laugh. "If it's fine, then why are you so upset?"

She pulled a knife from the block beside her. "Do you really want to know?"

"Yes."

"Your mother called this afternoon to introduce herself. She told me about the wedding reception she's planning for this weekend. The reception you agreed to." Dionne attacked the scallions with the knife. "How could you agree to something like that without talking to me first?"

Mark sank onto a chair. "I thought you'd like something special. Our wedding wasn't anything to brag about."

She shoved the scallions into a bowl and ripped apart a head of lettuce. "Did it ever occur to you that maybe I don't *want* a huge party to celebrate our marriage?"

He tried not to show how much that hurt, especially since he didn't completely understand why it did. "I thought it would look odd if we said no."

"*We* didn't say anything," Dionne snapped. "*You* said yes without even discussing it with me." Fire flashed in her eyes, making her more beautiful than ever. "I know this isn't a real marriage. But I can't tolerate you making decisions for me."

She was right, of course. "I'm sorry. I made a mistake. Do you want me to tell her to cancel the reception?"

She stopped ripping lettuce and rested her hands on the cutting board. Her eyes traveled across his face, studying him intently. "You'd do that?"

"Yes. At least, I'll try if you want me to."

Her expression softened a little. She let out a ragged sigh, then shook her head slowly. "No. The idea of lying to all those people makes me nervous, but I don't know how we'd explain canceling to your mother."

He tried a smile. "Neither do I."

She went back to work on the lettuce, but her movements were far less agitated. "The idea of pretending to be in love has been fine when it's just you and me, but how are we going to pull it off in front of all your friends and family? I don't know very much about you."

"They all know we had a whirlwind courtship," he reminded her. "They won't expect us to know a lot about each other."

"But we should know *something*. All I really know is that you're an attorney, you live in this apartment, and you're willing to do your own laundry. I don't even know your birthday or how old you are. A wife should know those things."

"I turned thirty-one on April twenty-eighth. What about you?"

A ghost of a smile curved her lips. "I'll be thirty on October nineteenth."

He made a mental note of the date and uncorked the wine to let it breathe. "Favorite color?"

"Green. And yours?"

"Black. What else do you want to know?"

Her smile grew a little. "Where did you go to law school?"

"Harvard." He leaned back in his seat and rested an ankle on his knee. "I really am sorry, Dionne. You have to remember, I haven't ever been married before. I'm not used to this."

"But you've been in relationships."

"Not like this."

That earned a soft laugh. "Very few people have ever been in a relationship like this."

"That's certainly true," he admitted. "But most of my relationships have been pretty casual."

Her smile faded. "Even with Marianne?"

The last thing he wanted was to talk about an ex-lover—especially that one. But Dionne deserved answers. "Especially with Marianne. She was so involved with her career, she didn't care what I did. We each did our own thing and got together whenever we could. What about you and Marianne? Were you close?"

She pulled a bunch of carrots toward the chopping block. "We hardly knew each other. Our mothers were cousins."

Her gaze met his and lingered there. The fire had disappeared from her eyes, and something new lurked there. Keeping his gaze locked on hers, he gave in to temptation and crossed the room toward her. "I don't want to talk about Marianne anymore."

She swallowed convulsively but she didn't look away. "Neither do I."

Taking her gently by the shoulders, he pulled her around to face him. For one breathless moment as he looked into her eyes, Mark thought time had stopped.

He wondered what she'd do if he kissed her. Would she respond or push him away? Would their relationship turn a new corner, or would he land them back at square one?

As if she read his mind, Dionne pulled away gently and grabbed a head of fresh broccoli from the counter. "Your mother wants us to be there by noon on Saturday. I told her we have an appointment to see a house on our way up."

Well, he supposed that was his answer. He tried not to let her see his disappointment. "Are you really okay with what she has planned?"

She nodded without looking at him. "I think so."

"I can still tell her to forget it if you want me to."

This time she did look at him, and the gratitude he saw in her eyes lifted his spirits considerably. "I'm nervous," she admitted, "but I'll be fine. Your mother sounded nice on the phone. Just don't leave me alone too long."

"I won't leave you alone at all."

She laughed. "You don't have to hold my hand every minute, but if you see that someone has me cornered, I hope you'll rescue me."

"Absolutely." Desperate for something to do besides look at her, he glanced around quickly and settled on the steaks. "Since you're making the salad, why don't you let me put those on to broil?"

She blinked as if the offer surprised her. "That's fine, if you don't mind."

Mind? She had no idea how much he needed to distract himself. She'd made it clear that she didn't want their relationship to change. And Mark would do his best to honor that. But he had the distinct feeling that, for him at least, things wouldn't ever go back to the way they'd been.

CHAPTER EIGHT

SATURDAY MORNING, Dionne watched Mark turn around in front of the rock fireplace of the old farmhouse. Sunlight streamed in through the huge windows that looked out on the narrow, tree-lined street. From the corner of her eye, she could see the Realtor leaning against her car in the driveway, enjoying a cigarette while she waited for them.

Dionne had been nervous and agitated since that moment in the kitchen two nights before when she'd wanted him to kiss her. His touch had sent flames through her and the look in his eyes had nearly made her forget everything.

If reason hadn't returned, if she hadn't suddenly remembered Brent, she *would* have kissed him. And after that? She couldn't even bear to think about how close she'd come to betraying Brent's memory.

Mark had been quiet, almost withdrawn, as they made the drive from Boston north into New Hampshire to meet their Realtor. But now, standing in the middle of the broad living room, he looked happy.

His expression brought a smile to her lips. "You like the house, don't you?"

"Do *you?* You'll be spending more time here than I will."

"Yes. I like the way the kitchen catches the morning sunlight. I like the view of the pond, and the way the forest closes in around the house. And I like the flower beds in the backyard.'' Not to mention the three large bedrooms.

"I wonder about the woods," Mark said hesitantly. "Will we be able to keep Jared under control?"

"Under control?" She glanced at Jared who was racing toy trucks along the living-room floor. "Not likely. We'll probably need to fence off part of the yard for him to play in."

"We could do that." Mark ran one hand along the mantel. "So, should we make an offer?"

"I'd like that."

His pleased grin warmed her clear through. He hurried to the front door and called in the Realtor, then led Dionne into the kitchen where they spent a few minutes fine-tuning the details of the offer and earnest money agreement. Finally satisfied, Mark scrawled his signature on the documents and pushed them and the pen toward Dionne.

She signed, started to hand the agreement back to the Realtor, then caught herself and added her new last name. To lessen the confusion for Jared, she'd decided to take Mark's last name, but how long would it be before she'd remember she wasn't Dionne Black anymore? And how long before she could get rid of the twisting guilt every time she thought of Brent?

If the owner accepted their offer, this would be her home from now on. The sunny room upstairs would be her bedroom. And the man standing at the counter, writing out a check, was her husband.

She paced to the window and stared out at the deep forest and the trees, then glanced back at Mark. It was his face she'd see every morning for the rest of her life. His laugh she'd hear. They'd share meals, sit together at Jared's games and school plays. This was undeniably real.

Almost dizzy, she pushed open the door and stepped onto the deck. Gripping the railing, she gulped air and hoped it would calm her a little. She stood that way for several minutes, until the sound of footsteps behind her warned her she wasn't alone.

Before she could turn around, Mark's hand touched her shoulder. "Are you all right?"

She looked back at him, trying to ignore the sudden warmth she felt at his touch. "Yes, of course. Where's Jared?"

"In the kitchen. Don't worry, I can see him from here." The understanding in his eyes made the lump in her throat grow and tighten. To her surprise, he wrapped his arms around her and rested his chin on the top of her head. Her body tightened.

"It's going to be okay," he said quietly. "You'll see. In time, we'll both get used to this."

"I know we will. I'm not having second thoughts," she lied. She took a deep breath and added honestly, "It's just that the thought of waking up to you every morning for the rest of my life suddenly got to me."

He sent her a teasing smile. "Am I really that disgusting?"

In spite of her frayed nerves, her doubts and her reservations, she laughed. And she thanked him silently for his wonderful sense of humor. "No. You're actually quite nice."

He pulled her close again and let out an exaggerated sigh. "Well, that's a relief. I was beginning to wonder."

His lips grazed the side of her face as he spoke and the now-familiar coil of desire shot through her.

"About the other night—" She broke off when he very deliberately brushed his lips softly against her cheek. She turned to face him and rested her hands on his chest. "Please don't."

He drew back slightly and pulled his hands from her waist. "Sorry. You're just so beautiful, I'm having a hard time remembering what the rules are." He glanced at the open patio door and muttered, "Jared's climbing the stairs. I'd better get back inside. Let me know when you're ready to leave."

She nodded, keeping her eyes trained on the twisted trunk of a tree, but she didn't relax until he'd gone back inside and closed the door between them.

Only then did she allow herself to acknowledge that the bone-deep sensation that settled inside her was disappointment, not guilt, and that her feelings at the moment had nothing to do with Brent.

NEARLY TWO HOURS LATER, Dionne leaned her head against the back of the seat and watched the countryside pass by. Here in the White Mountains, the trees were already beginning to change color in some places, and she could only imagine how glorious the scenery would be in a few more weeks. But the closer they got to Sunrise Notch, the greater her apprehension about spending the weekend with Mark's family and friends.

Would they like her? Would she be able to convince them she was in love with Mark? Or would she do or say something wrong and ruin everything?

And what would she and Mark do tonight when they had to share a bedroom for the first time? Thank heaven for Jared. If nothing else, he could sleep between them.

She glanced into the back seat at Jared, who'd fallen asleep in his car seat, then at Mark who seemed relaxed and happy. Of course, he had less to worry about. He was used to being around his huge, close-knit family. He knew and loved the entire bunch.

He must have felt her watching him because he took his eyes off the road for a second. "Getting nervous?"

"A little."

"It'll be a piece of cake," he promised, steering the car off the main road onto a narrow dirt lane. "They'll adore you."

"I hope so."

He glanced at her again. "What else is wrong?"

"Nothing." She turned toward the window and hoped he'd drop the subject.

Instead, he stopped the car in the middle of the lane and shifted in the seat to look at her. "If you'd rather not do this—"

"I want to do it," she assured him, but her voice came out sharper than she'd intended. She glanced away quickly and softened her tone. "I really want to do it. I'm just a little jittery."

"I know you are." Mark touched her arm gently. "I want you to know I appreciate the effort you're making."

She smiled bravely. "Just promise me that when this weekend is over we can have some quiet time."

His thumb stroked her arm lazily and started the

familiar fire roaring through her. "Before or after we move into the house?"

She let out a groan of dismay. "After, I guess."

"Good. Because I was thinking about asking my brothers to help us move. Is that okay with you?"

She appreciated his obvious efforts to discuss things with her before making a decision. As long as they were both willing to try, they stood a chance. She let out a weak laugh. "You don't really think I'm going to say no, do you? *I* certainly don't want to do all that heavy lifting."

"Just checking." He grinned and pulled his hand away. "I might be new at this marriage stuff, but I'm learning."

His smile helped her relax a bit further. "You're doing very well," she admitted.

His grin flashed again. "Thank you, ma'am. Are you ready to go on? We're almost there."

"Yes." She laced her fingers together on her lap to keep from touching him. "Should I wake Jared?"

"Probably. It would be better to wake him now than to have him startled awake by a bunch of strangers, don't you think?"

While she reached over the seat and shook Jared gently, Mark pulled back onto the road. Jared resisted her for a minute or two, then finally awoke. But he wasn't happy. His sobs of protest filled the car and he pulled away from her hand.

"Jared, sweetheart—"

Jared pushed her hand away and dropped his head as if he intended to go back to sleep. She thought about letting him do that to avoid the scene of introducing her new in-laws to their shrieking grandson, but Jared's head popped up again and he let out another yowl.

Mark took his eyes off the road for a heartbeat and glanced into the back seat. ''What's wrong with him? Is he hurt?''

''He just wants more sleep.'' Dionne had to raise her voice to make herself heard over Jared's sobbing. She dug around in his bag of toys and pulled out his favorite plush giraffe.

But Jared wanted nothing to do with it. He tossed it, bouncing it off the back of Mark's seat.

''Maybe you should stop,'' she suggested when the giraffe landed on the floor near Mark's feet. ''Let me try to calm him down before we get to your parents' house.''

Mark rounded one last bend and drove across a narrow wooden bridge. ''Too late,'' he said, braking in front of a large white house with black shutters. ''We're here.''

While Jared screwed up his face and let out another howl of protest, Dionne glanced at the house. The front door flew open and a woman with short-cropped hair the color of Mark's and Jared's came out onto the porch. A tall man who looked almost exactly like Mark followed. His hair was shot with gray, but he still had the trim figure of a young man.

Jared drew a shuddering breath and pushed Dionne's hands away again. ''No!''

''Please, Jared. It's okay.'' She kept her voice low and soothing in spite of the heavy sinking sensation that filled her. This was *not* the first impression she wanted to make on Mark's parents, but Jared left her no choice. On the other hand, it could only get better from here.

Now all she had to do was convince them she was in love with their son.

MARK HURRIED around the car to help Dionne with Jared and watched as she took a steadying breath before she opened the car door. Before he could reach her, she'd pulled Jared from the car seat and tried to soothe him.

"You're here!" His mother ran toward them and pulled Mark into a warm embrace, then turned toward Dionne and Jared. "Oh, look at the baby, Nigel. Isn't he beautiful?"

Mark could tell her reaction soothed something in Dionne, and he was grateful beyond words.

His father clapped a hand to Mark's shoulder, smiled warmly at Dionne, then chucked Jared, whose cries were slowly subsiding, under the chin. "So this is my new grandson, eh? He's a Taylor, all right. Just listen to that voice. And I do believe he's got my nose. But he's hardly a baby, Barbara. He's already a strapping young man."

Nervous sweat pooled beneath Mark's arms. He hadn't wanted to admit it to Dionne, but he'd been dreading this moment. His parents had been skeptical about the hasty wedding. Even his continued assurances that he'd met the woman of his dreams hadn't totally convinced them.

He trusted them not to show their doubts to Dionne, and she was obviously going to keep up her end of the bargain. But he'd still feel a whole lot better once this initial meeting was behind them.

Before he could make introductions, his mother wrapped Dionne in a warm hug. "I'm Barbara, and this is my husband, Nigel. We'd love to have you call us Mom and Dad if you're comfortable with that.''

His mother's enthusiastic welcome, in spite of the misgivings she'd voiced, touched Mark. He studied Dionne's face over his mother's shoulder. She looked tiny and vulnerable.

She caught his worried frown and smiled to reassure him. He knew how much effort that took and he could've kissed her.

His father gave Dionne another friendly smile. ''So you're the woman who finally convinced my son to settle down. Welcome to the family. Glad to have you.''

Dionne hid her nervousness well. ''It's wonderful to meet you at last. Mark's told me so much about you.''

''Well, you're one step ahead of us,'' his mother said. ''We know next to nothing about you.'' She kissed Jared soundly on the cheek and smiled when the boy hid his face on Dionne's shoulder. ''But we'll soon put that right, won't we?''

''Yes,'' Dionne said softly. ''Of course.''

''We'll have lots of time to talk after the open house. We're so thrilled to have two new members of the family.''

Mark smiled at his mother and put his arm around Dionne. ''So, where's everybody else?''

''Inside,'' Barbara said, turning back toward the house. ''They didn't want to overwhelm Jared and Dionne. But they're champing at the bit to meet them both.''

He felt Dionne hesitate for a second, then straighten her shoulders. ''We're eager to meet them,'' she said as they walked behind his parents.

Mark admired Dionne's grit and her graciousness.
The worst was over, he told himself. It could only
get better from here.

DIONNE HAD SPENT two hours standing beneath an
arbor at Mark's side, clutching a bouquet of roses,
orchids and baby's breath, meeting relatives, shaking
hands, and smiling until her cheeks hurt. Her head
whirled from trying to remember so many new
names and match them to the unfamiliar faces. If
only she could slip away for a while and find a quiet
spot where she and Jared could be alone.

She took one steadying breath, then another. She
watched Jared climb onto Nigel's lap and tug on Barbara's earring. She listened to her son chortle with
delight when Barbara bubbled his cheek, and
watched him toddle away when Mark's mother put
him back on the lawn.

In spite of the warm sunshine, a chill shook her.
She closed her eyes for a moment and tried to hold
herself together. Jared was unquestionably part of
this family—in looks and in temperament—but his
resemblance to them felt like a subtle threat. If she
couldn't make her marriage to Mark work, there was
no question that any judge would place Jared with
these people.

They were all warm and friendly, and every time
one of his brothers or his sister-in-law or an aunt or
uncle drew her into a conversation, she couldn't help
feeling out of place. Her own family was so different.
She'd certainly never experienced the genuine affection she saw between members of Mark's family. She
had nothing in common with these people. Nothing.

Clutching the arms of her lawn chair, she opened

her eyes again and tried to find peace in the surround-ings. Maple, oak and other trees she couldn't identify rimmed the lawn. A few leaves drifted lazily to the ground in the slight breeze. A long table full of re-freshments stretched along the far end of the lawn. Paper lanterns hung in strategic spots near the patio, which meant the party would probably go on long after dark.

Barbara and Nigel must have spent a fortune put-ting all this together. No matter what they said, she knew they'd gone to far greater lengths than they would have for a simple gathering, and that made her feel even worse. She hated lying to them.

As she took another look around, she realized that everyone seemed to have forgotten her for a moment. Seizing the opportunity, she stood quickly. But be-fore she could take even two steps, someone put a hand on her shoulder. Holding back a sigh, she turned to find Barbara and Nigel standing behind her.

"What's wrong, dear?" Barbara took in every de-tail of her expression. "You seem awfully quiet."

"Leave the girl alone," Nigel groused, waving a celery stick in front of him. "She's just not used to us yet, are you?"

Dionne smiled at him. He really was a kind man. "I guess I'm a little tired from the trip and all the time we've spent looking for a house."

"Yes, but Mark tells us you found one in Longs Mill." Barbara glanced at Nigel. "Isn't that what he told us?"

"Nice town." Nigel bit into the celery. "You'll like it there."

"It's a lovely house." Just thinking about it made Dionne feel a little better.

Barbara pulled up a lawn chair and sat down. Nigel took up his position behind it. They looked as if they intended to settle in for a nice, long chat. "I've been wanting to tell you all day what a wonderful job you've done with Jared," Barbara said. "He's a delightful little boy, and I don't say that only because he's my grandson."

"Thank you." Dionne sank back into her own chair and clasped her hands together in her lap.

Barbara let her gaze settle on Jared, who'd found a small pile of rocks to play with. "Does he see much of your folks?"

"No. My mother passed away several years ago."

In a gesture so like one Mark would make, Barbara covered Dionne's hand with one of hers. "I'm sorry. I didn't know. What about your father?"

Dionne decided not to give Barbara and Nigel the sordid details. She was quite sure none of the Taylor men had ever deserted their wives and children. "My father's no longer with us, but Jared does see Brent's parents about once a year."

"Brent's parents?" Barbara's eyebrows knit in confusion. "Who's Brent?"

"He was my hus—" Dionne cut herself off and glanced quickly at Mark across the lawn talking to one of his brothers. Apparently, he hadn't told his family much about her.

Well, too late now. She didn't want any more secrets to worry about, and she certainly wouldn't deny Brent. "He was my first husband."

Nigel lowered the celery to his side and glanced from Dionne to Barbara and back again. "Your *first* husband? I didn't know you'd been married before, did I? Did Mark tell us that, Barbara?"

Barbara's smile faltered. "I don't remember. I don't think he did."

"Brent passed away shortly after Jared came to live with us," Dionne explained.

"A first husband," Nigel muttered. "I wonder why Mark didn't tell us."

"Well, that's all in the past, so I'm sure he didn't think it was important," Dionne assured Nigel, adding another possible lie to her list.

Barbara ticked her tongue against the roof of her mouth and scowled at her husband as if he'd had something to do with Mark's decision. "Honestly, sometimes you men can be so thoughtless." She sent Dionne a smile full of warmth and reassurance. "Mark's my son and I love him, but I don't understand how he could possibly think your first husband was unimportant. Not that it makes any difference to us," she added quickly, "but what if we'd inadvertently said something that hurt your feelings?"

Dionne couldn't imagine either of these kind people hurting anyone. "I'm sure Mark would have said something sooner or later. Things have been pretty hectic for both of us."

"Of course they have." Barbara tousled Jared's head as he came near, chasing a loose ball. "Still, I wish we'd known. I feel utterly foolish."

Dionne scooped Jared onto her lap and wrapped her arms around him. He struggled for a second, then leaned his head against her shoulder and gazed up at her with his big brown eyes. "Mama."

Relief swept through her and uncorked her other emotions, and tears filled her eyes. She blinked quickly, hoping Barbara wouldn't notice. But she was too late.

"Have I upset you, dear?"

"No." She stood quickly, still holding on to Jared for dear life. "No. I'm just a little tired."

"Then maybe you should take Jared inside for a nap. Just slip away and come back when you're ready."

Grateful for her understanding, Dionne started away but Jared squirmed in her arms. "No nap."

"Please," she whispered so softly she didn't know if he could even hear her. "Please, for Mommy?"

He pulled back and looked at her. "No nap."

"Sweetheart, I promise we'll come back and play with everybody."

Jared scowled, made one last attempt to get down, then stuck a finger in his mouth and settled himself more comfortably against her. "Jared wants a story."

She would read a hundred stories if it meant she could find a few minutes alone. Just a few minutes to pull herself together so she could make it through the rest of the day.

MARK TRIED to keep up with his uncle Bruce's story as he watched Dionne carrying Jared across the lawn and away from his parents. The sun beat down on him, as hot as mid-July instead of early September, and he longed for a glass of his mother's lemonade, or maybe something a little stronger from the liquor cabinet in his father's study.

Dionne had been wonderfully gracious to everyone, but he knew the day hadn't been easy on her. He wondered how she was holding up. Maybe she'd had enough of his friends and family.

"So," Uncle Bruce said, hooking his thumbs in

the waistband of his pants, "there we were. And what a mess it was, I tell you…"

Mark smiled but kept his gaze on Dionne. She glanced over her shoulder, as if she wanted to make sure nobody was following her.

"…Nonie threw up her hands and let out a shriek," Bruce went on with a laugh. "The woman nearly put a hole in my eardrums…"

Dionne checked behind her once more, then slipped through the kitchen door and disappeared from view. Mark started to turn back to Bruce, then glanced at the house again. *Had* she reached the end of her rope? Had the reception been one thing too many? Maybe he should have told his mother to forget it, after all.

His wife had looked secretive as she crossed the lawn—almost as if she was trying to hide something—and a knot of suspicion began to form in his stomach. Did she regret her decision to marry him? Was she thinking of leaving with Jared?

Surely she wouldn't do that. Where would she go? How would she get there?

All the logic in the world couldn't take away his sudden anxiety. He hadn't expected Marianne to disappear either. Dionne had Jared back, and Mark was involved with friends and family who wanted to wish him well. Maybe she thought she could call a cab and get away before he noticed she'd gone.

"…So I told Nonie to pull herself together. It's just a little snake, I said—"

"Excuse me, Uncle Bruce," Mark interrupted. "I need to check something."

Leaving the older man staring after him, he hurried across the lawn after her. He told himself again to give her the benefit of the doubt, but his heart raced and his mind whirled with dreadful possibilities.

He managed to sidestep three of his cousins who tried to waylay him, hurried through the kitchen, down the hall, and out the front door. There wasn't a cab in sight, but maybe she'd called earlier and it had been waiting for her.

He ran partway down the driveway, even though he knew he'd never catch a moving cab on foot. He'd have to take the car.

Wheeling around, he dug his keys from his pocket, then realized with dismay that three other cars had his blocked in. Frustrated, he ran back toward the house.

"Hey, Uncle Mark. Come with us." One of his teenage nephews made a grab for his arm. "We're going over to the hill."

Under normal circumstances, Mark might have joined them. But he couldn't relax until he found Dionne and Jared. "Not this time," he said, opening the front door. "Have any of you seen Dionne and Jared?"

Corey nodded, walking backward with the others. "I saw them going upstairs a few minutes ago."

Upstairs? Mark's step faltered. *Upstairs?* Not away in a cab? Feeling relieved—and foolish—he waved a thank-you, hurried inside, and took the stairs two at a time.

He walked quietly down the hall, hoping she'd never know he was checking up on her. As he neared the bedroom door, he heard the soft sound of her voice as she talked to Jared.

Mark ran a hand over the back of his neck, smiled to himself, and started to turn away. But an overwhelming desire to be part of Jared's naptime and the sudden need to make their family real brought him back around.

He pushed the door open an inch or two and looked inside. Dionne lay with her back to him, curled beside Jared whose little legs wriggled and whose arms flew about as he struggled to escape.

She kept up her soothing monologue. Mark felt like a voyeur, but he couldn't tear himself away.

She was like no other woman he'd ever met, not only because of the way she cared for Jared, but because of the way she treated Mark, as well. He'd never met anyone who'd been willing to go to such lengths for him. If Marianne had been in Dionne's position, she would have forced him into court to decide custody. Dionne had respected him enough to make an unbelievable compromise. And the most amazing thing was, she'd never resented him for suggesting it.

Finally, Jared yawned, put one tiny hand on the side of Dionne's face, and closed his eyes. Mark told himself he really should stop watching. But the gentle curve of her hips kept his gaze riveted, and unexpected desire kept him rooted to the spot.

He wanted to hold her, to lie down on the bed beside her, to breathe in her scent and let it surround him. He wanted more than that. He wanted to kiss her, to make love to her, and his sudden need was stronger than anything he'd ever felt for any woman.

But he couldn't do any of those things. Not only did she and Jared need time alone, but Mark knew how she'd react if he tried to seduce her. She'd made it clear from the beginning that this was nothing more than a marriage of convenience, and he'd agreed to that. Hell, he'd suggested it.

If she'd given him some sign that her feelings were changing, he might have held out some hope. But the way she'd pulled away from him that morning left no doubt that she wanted things to continue the way they were.

What bothered him most was the realization that all the time he'd been searching, while he'd been chasing the imaginary cab down the driveway, he'd had two concerns. Of course, he'd been afraid of losing Jared. But, equally important, he'd been terrified of losing his wife.

CHAPTER NINE

FOR THE THIRD TIME in less than an hour—since Dionne brought Jared back outside—Mark caught himself losing the thread of conversation with his brother, Jerry. Jerry had been talking about football, but all Mark could think about was the way Dionne had looked lying on the bed. Now visions of her in a nightgown, the way she'd be when they shared that same bed tonight, kept creeping into his mind.

Think flannel, he told himself firmly. *Long-sleeved, high-necked, hem to the floor.*

He brushed aside a mosquito and tried once again to follow what Jerry was saying. But his gaze drifted back across the lawn to where she sat, legs crossed, in a patio chair.

Her face, tilted to watch a rollicking game of badminton, caught the waning afternoon sunlight. Her fingers, long and delicate, rested on the arms of the chair. The soft blouse she wore drifted over her breasts, outlining them whenever she moved. He couldn't have looked away if he'd tried. Until she looked up and caught him watching her.

Damn. He turned away quickly. But that didn't make him any less aware of her. He still caught the sudden frown, the slight narrowing of her eyes, the stiffening that warned him she'd seen and understood exactly what was running through his mind.

"What's up with you two?" Jerry's voice near his ear caught him off guard.

Mark wheeled to face him. "What do you mean?"

"You seem jittery, and so does she." Jerry propped himself against the picnic table and stretched his legs out in front of him.

Mark forced a laugh. "Nothing's up. We were just a bit worried about the family's reaction to our marriage. After all, it was a very sudden thing."

"Yeah?" Jerry took another drink. "Well, maybe I'm just extrasensitive."

"Maybe you are." Mark knew he sounded touchy, but he didn't want Jerry to guess the truth. He couldn't let anyone shatter the illusion he and Dionne were trying to create.

"So, are you happy?" Jerry crossed one foot over the other and waited, as if he expected the answer to be no.

Mark looked him square in the eye. "Very."

Jerry nodded slowly, but Mark could tell his brother wasn't convinced. He let his gaze shift toward Dionne. "Mom and Dad seem to like her."

"Of course they do. What's not to like?"

"Nothing," Jerry said with a shrug. "She's great. But I will admit Mom sounded worried when she called to tell me you'd got married."

"*She* doesn't have to worry, either."

"Yeah?" Jerry studied Mark's face for a long moment. Too long. "Well, you know how she feels about marriage. If I had a dime for every time she told me not to get married until I'd known Alice for at least a year, I'd be a millionaire."

Mark had heard his mother's advice since David had grown old enough to notice girls. And he'd always seen the value in his mother's warning. A couple shouldn't rush into marriage. Just look at what had happened to his brother and his sister-in-law.

Jerry and Alice had been completely wrong for each other. But they'd married before they'd figured out that they'd had nothing in common except their sex life. That had quickly lost its luster, and Jerry had wound up in the arms of another woman.

When he'd confessed his indiscretion to Alice, the marriage had finally crumbled. Unfortunately for Jerry, his relationship with the other woman hadn't survived, either, and the experience had left him bitter. Mark sympathized in many ways, but he wasn't in the mood for his brother's cynicism today.

He changed the subject. "What are you doing next weekend, big brother?"

Jerry's eyes narrowed in suspicion. "Watching the football game, why?"

"Tape it. Dionne and I need you to help us move."

Jerry groaned aloud. "Move? I *hate* moving."

"Doesn't everybody? But it won't be bad. We'll only have to worry about the things I don't want to trust to the movers."

"I don't know. You want me to give up the game to move all your junk?"

"I don't own junk," Mark reminded him with mock severity. "But I'm not above offering a bribe, I'll throw pizza into the deal."

"That sounds a *little* more tempting. But I still don't think it's quite enough."

"What do you want?

"I *want* to watch the game," Jerry grumbled, then grinned and tried to sound irritated. "But if you're going to beg, I suppose I'll help.'' He nodded toward the far end of the lawn where David and Steve were playing badminton with two of the kids. "You want them to help, too?''

"Definitely.''

"Let me tell them.'' Jerry's eyes gleamed, and Mark could only imagine what he had up his sleeve. "I'll make sure they're there.'' He started away, then turned back and added, "About you and Dionne… Forget I said anything. I'm sure you're not anything like Alice and I were.''

Mark watched him cross the lawn, scoop up David's youngest son and settle him on his shoulders. Obviously, he'd put their conversation behind him. But Mark couldn't forget it quite so easily.

The truth was, he and Dionne *didn't* have anything in common. They had no shared interests. They didn't even come from the same kind of background. The only thing holding them together was Jared. And for the first time, Mark wondered if that would be enough.

DIONNE SAT on the window seat by the open window, listening to the breeze whispering through the trees while Mark said good-night to his father in the hallway. The temperature had dropped a little, but the night was still uncomfortably warm. Her body screamed for sleep, but she wondered if she'd get any with Mark in the same room.

She'd expected to have Jared sleep with her, but the entire family had joined the protest that newlyweds needed one night on their own. Barbara and Nigel had made a bed for Jared in their room, and Jared had decided the whole thing was an adventure.

He seemed to enjoy being the center of attention. In spite of her own nervousness, Dionne hadn't had the heart to spoil his fun.

Of course, the family could never know the truth about this marriage, so Dionne had smiled pleasantly and pretended to be happy with the arrangements.

Nigel smiled at her over Mark's shoulder. "You're probably getting fed up with me for keeping Mark out here, aren't you?"

"Not at all," she assured him. *Keep him as long as you want. In fact, take him with you.*

"You're sweet to an old man," Nigel said with a laugh, "but I'll get out of your hair. Good night, Dionne. Pleasant dreams."

"Thank you, Nigel. Same to you."

He turned away, and Mark stepped inside the room and closed the door behind him. The click of the latch sounded as ominous to her as prison doors shutting.

"Well." Mark propped his hands on his hips and leaned against the wall. "Here we are."

"Yes."

"You can have the bed. I'll sleep on the floor." He pulled a pillow and extra blankets from the closet and tossed them to the floor beside the bed. "If you want to change first, I'll...well, I'll look at the moon for a while. I promise I'll keep my back turned."

His apparent nervousness gave her a slight boost of confidence. She had the strangest urge to join him and lean her head against his shoulder, but she couldn't do that. "I can just slip out to the bathroom and change in there."

He glanced back at her and smiled. His almost shy expression touched her on a level she didn't want to be touched. "Good idea. But let me change in there. You can use this room."

He pulled sweatpants from his suitcase, tossed them over his shoulder, and started toward the door again. "Just leave the door open a crack when you're through so I know when it's safe to come back."

"It won't take me long," she promised. She waited until he'd closed the door behind him, then jumped off the bed and dug through her own bag. She'd brought a light pair of summer pajamas, but suddenly the thought of wearing them left her feeling defenseless. Instead, she'd follow Mark's lead and put on her baggy sweatpants and a long T-shirt.

She changed hurriedly and tucked her clothes into a drawer. After draping her robe across the foot of the bed, she opened the door an inch or two, then quickly, before he could come back, climbed under the covers and pulled them up to her neck.

He didn't return immediately, but when he did, he knocked softly before pushing open the door the rest of the way. "All clear?"

"Yes."

He tossed his jeans and T-shirt over the chair and set to work spreading the blankets.

She watched him for a moment, then asked, "Are you going to be okay on the floor?"

He looked at her. "I have to be, don't I?"

She flushed, embarrassed by the thoughtless question, shaken to the core by the look in his eyes. "We can trade places tomorrow night. I don't mind."

"We've already had this discussion once, haven't we?" He turned out the overhead light and crossed the room, illuminated now only by the dim lamp beside the bed and the glow of the moon through the paned windows. "You keep the bed, Dionne." He kept his gaze on her as he moved toward her, robbing her of breath and conscious thought. Just when she thought he might climb onto the bed, he hunkered down to the floor.

She waited until he'd covered himself with the sheet, then turned off the lamp. But sleep didn't come. Too many conflicting emotions raced through her. Too many unanswered questions and unresolved issues kept her mind jumping.

In the silence, she heard the village clock chime midnight. Eyes wide, she stared at the patterns made by the moon and trees on the ceiling. She heard Mark's breathing change as he shifted onto his side, the rustling of the sheet as he tried to make himself more comfortable, the soft groan that escaped his throat.

Did he feel it, too? This pricking of the nerves, this all-over tingly feeling? Slowly, she turned to look at him. Too late, she realized he was watching her. Her breath stopped. Her heart plummeted, then lurched into her throat.

"Can't sleep?" He kept his voice low, which didn't help. The intimate tone made her hands sweat.

She gripped the sheet and shook her head. "No."

"Thinking about Jared?"

She seized on the excuse gratefully. "Yes."

"Do you want me to get him?"

No doubt having Jared curled next to her would help, but she didn't want to disturb him. "No, I'm sure he's asleep already."

Mark sat up suddenly. The sheet fell away, exposing his shoulders and chest. The moonlight revealed dark tufts of hair and the outline of his muscles, and the suffocating feeling in the room seemed to grow. "Are you hungry?"

Dionne let out a nervous laugh. "After all that food your mother had this afternoon? I'm not sure I'll ever be hungry again."

He reached toward her, and for a second she thought he would touch her. Everything inside her stilled, waiting, anticipating, *wanting* to feel his touch. Instead, he reached for the alarm clock, checked the time, and put it back on the nightstand. "We could go down to the family room and watch TV—if you want to."

"Will we wake your parents?"

"No way." His voice caressed her. His breath brushed her cheek. "They can't hear anything from their room. When we were kids, we used to stay up half the night, and they never did figure it out."

"Oh. Good. Then, yes." Anything to get out of this room. She slid out of bed and grabbed her robe as if it were a security blanket. She walked quickly down the hall, far too aware of Mark behind her. When they reached the family room, she stopped abruptly. Someone had closed the shutters, which blocked the moonlight. The room was still unfamiliar to her, and she didn't know which way to turn.

Mark leaned in close, and again she thought he might touch her. But he only reached for the light switch on the wall.

Blinking against the sudden glare, she looked away, not wanting him to see how much she hungered for his touch. How very much she wanted him to kiss her. How bitterly disappointed she was that he didn't try.

Heat suffused her face as she hurried toward a

wingback chair and curled into it as if it might protect her. If he noticed her eagerness to get away from him, he didn't show it. He sat on the couch, found the remote on the coffee table, and turned on the television. The set came to life with a scene from *Casablanca,* and all of her earlier thoughts evaporated.

She and Brent had loved this movie and watched it often together. She'd always snuggled against his side, secure in his love, content with her life. Tonight, the music, the voices, the faces of the actors made her almost sick. Because she suddenly realized that not once all evening—while she'd been fighting her attraction for Mark, while she'd lain there and listened to his breathing, while she'd watched him move around the bedroom and wanted to feel his hands on her—

Not once had she thought of Brent.

THE NEXT AFTERNOON, Dionne sat beneath the shade of a huge oak tree that cut the temperature by several degrees. Jared played nearby with one of Mark's nieces. The heat here was different from the warmth in Boise, filled with moisture that seemed to make the air not only hot but heavy as well.

Perspiration trickled between her breasts, the humidity kept her rooted to her seat, and the sheer numbers of people milling around the backyard again today made her head spin. She'd never get used to this. Just as she'd never rid herself of the nagging guilt each time she lied to one of Mark's friends or relatives.

She closed her eyes and tilted back her head, opening them again when she felt someone touch her hand. Mark's aunt Nonie, a gray-haired woman with a pleasant round face, smiled down at her.

"Are you all right, dear?"

"Yes." Dionne struggled to sit straighter in the chair and checked on Jared, then worked up a smile. "I'm fine."

"You look tired."

"Maybe I am a little. We've had a busy week."

"Busy?" Aunt Nonie laughed and settled into a chair beside her. "I'd say it's a bit more than that, wouldn't you? You've been swept up in a whirlwind, my girl. That's what happens around these Taylor men. I know. I married one."

Dionne couldn't have described it better if she'd tried. Being around Mark *was* like being swept into a storm. Emotions buffeted her from every direction. "The whole family is full of life," she said.

"Aren't they? There's never a dull moment around this bunch, that's for sure." Nonie patted her hand almost tenderly. "Don't let it overwhelm you. You'll get used to us in time."

"For now, I'm just working on learning who everyone is," Dionne admitted with a thin laugh. "There are so many of you."

"Well, yes." Nonie let her gaze travel across the lawn, and studied her family for a moment. "But you've got years and years to get us all straight."

As always, the reality of her situation made Dionne pensive. Years and years as part of this huge, sprawling, noisy brood. She forced aside the uneasiness. "Yes, I do, don't I?"

Nonie made herself more comfortable on her chair and smoothed her hands across her lap. "We're really not so bad."

"Oh, I didn't mean—"

Nonie cut her off with a laugh. "Mark says you're from a small family."

An almost nonexistent family. "Yes. This is very different from what I'm used to."

"Then I can only imagine how overwhelming it must be to you. So let's forget about everyone else for a few minutes. Tell me how you and Mark met. That ought to put the smile back in your eyes. And don't leave anything out. I'm a sucker for a good love story."

Dionne fought the urge to pull away. She didn't want to compound the lie by embellishing it for this nice woman. "There's not much to tell, really."

Nonie laughed as if she'd said the funniest thing in the world. "Not much to tell? Mark leaves town a bachelor and comes back a devoted husband three weeks later, and you say there's nothing to tell?"

Dionne flushed and wondered what Nonie would think if she told her the truth.

Still shaking her head in disbelief, Nonie fanned a hand in front of her face. "None of that, now. I've been dying to hear the whole story. Where did you first see him?"

"In the park."

"Really?" Nonie sighed and put a hand to her breast. "Was it love at first sight?"

Dionne smiled slowly. "I wouldn't say that, but I did have some pretty strong feelings right from the first."

"Well, of course you did. Who could look at Mark and *not* feel something? If I do say so myself, he's a good-looking boy."

Dionne glanced at the "boy" who was deep in

conversation with his father on the other side of the lawn. What kind of little boy had he been? What had he looked like? There was still so much she didn't know.

"And when did you realize you were in love?" Nonie prodded.

"In love?" The afternoon heat intensified and a dull ache started in Dionne's head. "Later. I don't remember the exact moment."

"Of course you remember. Every woman remembers."

Obviously, Nonie wasn't going to give up. "I think it was when I realized how much he loves Jared."

Nonie's face wrinkled with disapproval. "That's all very well and good, my dear. But Jared won't be around forever. You can't base a marriage on a child."

Dionne floundered for a second. "No. I mean, I think that's what made me realize what sort of man he is."

"And *that's* why you fell in love with him." Nonie looked pleased at that. "Well, he does have a kind heart. Wouldn't hurt a fly, our Mark. Not if his life depended on it."

Dionne remembered the look on his face when she first saw him and knew that a good many flies could be in danger if Mark felt strongly enough about something.

"And so you married him." Nonie's voice sounded wistful. "And now here you are, part of the family."

"Yes."

"Well, we're all happy to have you, dear." Nonie

patted her hand again. "To be honest, I was beginning to think Mark would never get married."

"Really? Why?"

"When Marianne left without a word—" She broke off and her eyes grew huge. "You do know about Marianne, don't you?"

"Yes, of course."

Nonie sighed with obvious relief. "It did seem like she would be the one. And he was heartbroken when she left. Moped around for months."

Something uncomfortable darted through Dionne, but she told herself it wasn't jealousy.

"But, of course," Nonie went on, "he's over her now. He must be because here you are."

Dionne forced a smile, but her heart wasn't in it. She stole another glance at Mark and wondered if he was really over Marianne. Not that it mattered. For heaven's sake, she still loved Brent and always would. Her relationship with Mark didn't matter, as long as they gave Jared what he needed. As long as she could stay with Jared and be his mother forever.

But when she remembered the look in Mark's eyes the night before, when she caught the lilt of his laughter and deep rumble of his voice, she knew she wasn't being entirely truthful with herself. Like it or not, her relationship with Mark had begun to matter a great deal.

DIONNE STROLLED aimlessly along the gravel driveway and away from the house. A stiff wind had blown in storm clouds and dropped the temperature by several degrees. She took a deep breath of the clear mountain air and walked through a small pile of orange and yellow leaves. Autumn had always been her favorite season, and spending it in New England was a dream come true.

She'd put Jared down for a nap and then slipped out the front door instead of rejoining everyone in the living room. Sooner or later, someone would discover she'd disappeared. But until then, she had a blissful few minutes alone.

Children—nieces and nephews and cousins whose names she'd never remember—played together on the broad expanse of lawn that rolled downhill toward a grove of trees. Shouts of laughter and an occasional playful roar filled the air.

She stopped at the crest of the hill and watched them, envying them their easiness together, their shared childhood, the memories they were making. A wistfulness tinged with envy filled her heart. She'd long ago stopped wishing for something that would never be, but the noisy bunch of kids laughing and shouting together brought back all the familiar pain of childhood.

She didn't want to feel that today, so she turned her thoughts to Jared. Her son would have a different life than the one she'd had. He'd grow up loved and secure. He'd never suffer the loneliness and isolation, the sensation of being disconnected.

She smiled at the children in front of her, then turned away and started toward the house to check on Jared. But when she saw Mark standing only a few feet behind her, her step faltered.

The breeze tousled his hair, and the faint shadow of whiskers darkened his cheeks and chin. In his faded jeans and gray T-shirt, he was ruggedly handsome.

Wrapping her arms around herself for warmth, she

walked slowly toward him. "They look as if they're having fun," she said when she drew nearer, purposely keeping her tone light.

His gaze roamed her face and settled on her eyes as if he could see right through the mask she wore. "It is fun. We used to do the same thing when we were kids."

"You and your brothers?"

"And the cousins."

Another pang of envy shot through her. She forced it away, just as she had the others. "I'd better get inside and check on Jared."

"I just looked in on him. He's fine." Mark took a step closer. "And if he wakes up, someone will hear him. Mom and Kaye are in the kitchen. Dad's watching the game with the guys, and Nonie's reading in her room. Just relax and take a moment for yourself."

Dionne shook her head. "I don't want them to take on my responsibilities."

Mark laughed. "You can't honestly think any of them will mind. They all adore Jared. They wouldn't care if you and I disappeared for hours."

Dionne knew he was right. "I'm glad they love him so much. It means a lot to me."

"And to me," he admitted, his voice low. "They're all completely smitten with you, too."

Dionne smiled slowly. "They're wonderful people, Mark. They really are."

"They're a big, noisy, meddling bunch," he argued mildly. "But they mean well."

"I know they do." She shivered as the wind danced across her shoulders. And when a shout went up from the hill below them, she turned to look at the kids once more.

Boys chased girls who squealed when they got caught. One boy rolled into another, buckling the second one's knees and sending him sprawling into a small pile of leaves on one side of the lawn.

Mark grinned over at her. His dark eyes glittered with mischief. "You want to show them how it's done?"

"You mean play in the leaves?" Dionne backed a step away from him. "I'm afraid I wouldn't be a very good teacher."

"Why not?"

"I've never done it."

Mark's eyes rounded with shock. "Never?"

"Never."

"You're joking, right?"

"I'm not. I was an only child, remember? And I didn't get to play with friends often. My mother liked knowing I was safe inside while she worked."

"Well, then, I say it's time you learned."

She took another backward step. "I'm too old."

"Old?" He shook his head. "Hell, Dionne, you're not even thirty yet. Even grown-ups need to play."

His enthusiasm was infectious, but Dionne didn't give in to it right away. "I *do* play," she argued halfheartedly.

"When? *I've* never seen you play."

She propped her fists on her hips. "You haven't known me very long. And for your information, I play with Jared all the time."

He shoved aside that argument with one huge hand. "I'm not talking about that kind of play. *This* is what I'm talking about." Without giving her a chance to react, he scooped her up and barreled down the hill, letting out a shout that sounded almost like a battle cry.

Surprised, she wrapped her arms around his neck to hold on. "Stop," she squawked. "You're going to drop me."

"Me? Drop you? Never."

"I'm serious, Mark—"

He stopped suddenly and held her gaze. "That's your trouble." His cheeks burned red from the chill but his eyes were pure fire. "You need to stop being so damned serious." Before she could respond, he lowered her with a soft plop into the pile of leaves. They cushioned her fall and billowed out around her.

"That wasn't fair," she protested weakly.

"No?" Mark laughed again, a teasing rumble that sounded more like a fourteen-year-old boy than a thirty-one-year-old man. "Well, then, come and get your revenge." He backed a step away, daring her to try.

Strangely exhilarated, Dionne scrambled to her feet. "You think I can't?"

"You said you didn't know how," he reminded her, but there was nothing harsh or mean in his tone.

"Yeah? Well, it doesn't take a brain surgeon to figure it out." She scooped up an armful of leaves and tossed them straight into his face. But when the shower of red and gold stopped and she could see his face clearly again, the almost-predatory gleam in his eyes made her turn and run.

He came after her, just as she'd known he would. His laughter warmed her and the shouts of the children, some urging her to run faster and some calling for him to overtake her, filled the air.

He caught her easily and they fell back into the leaves together. He stretched along the length of her, his body hard and unyielding, his male scent slightly heady.

Mark lay there, panting, his face just inches from hers, his breath warm on her cheek and faintly scented with mint. "You didn't really think you could outrun me, did you?"

"Apparently not." She was breathless from the unaccustomed exertion but she felt wonderful, and joy bubbled up inside her. She made an attempt to get away, but he held her fast.

"Right. And don't you forget it." Their eyes locked, and the teasing light in his slowly died away. Something else, something white-hot and intense, took its place.

His eyes searched hers for answers to questions he'd never asked, and she knew what answers he found. They came from the bottom of her soul, laid bare by the moment they shared. She wanted him to kiss her, to cover her mouth with his, to hold her in his arms and never let her go. She waited, breathless, hoping, wanting, needing.

His eyes darkened and sent chills of anticipation through her. He dipped his head and brushed her lips with his, only a feather-light touch but it rocked the world beneath her and left her aching for more. She responded eagerly, savoring the feel of his lips on hers.

The kids swarmed around them, shouting, jeering, calling out encouragement. "Kiss her, kiss her," one unmistakably male voice taunted. Another hissed for the boy to be quiet.

The mood was shattered. The passion in Mark's eyes dimmed. The need inside her faded.

"Kiss her again," the boy demanded. "Whatcha waitin' for?"

Mark looked away slowly and his entire countenance changed. "I'm not going to kiss anybody with you watching," he said with a laugh. Then, growling playfully, he took off after the boy Dionne recognized as David's oldest son.

With her heart still rocketing and her head swimming, Dionne watched him. She marveled at all the different sides she'd seen in him in the short time they'd known each other. Jared was lucky to have him for a father. And she...

Well, she had to admit the truth. She was lucky to have him for a husband. Brent had been many good and fine things, and she'd always love him for his steadiness and dependability. But he hadn't kept her off balance. He hadn't embraced everything with abandon the way Mark did. If anything, Brent had been almost resistant to change.

Once, Dionne had needed that. But somehow— maybe as a result of Brent's death, *certainly* because of the upheaval over Jared—she'd grown past that need. Now she was a different person from the frightened, lonely young girl who'd fallen in love with Brent.

Rubbing her arms for warmth, she watched for another moment while the kids tackled Mark and sent him to the ground. They heaped leaves over him, nearly burying him.

Smiling, Dionne caught the eye of three young girls. Their eyes danced in anticipation of her next move, and Dionne suddenly realized they'd accepted her as one of them.

Her smile widened. Her heart began to race again. Motioning for them not to give her away, she took a deep breath and threw herself into the fray.

CHAPTER TEN

LONG AFTER DINNER was over and almost everyone else had gone home, Mark sat on the long, leather couch in his parents' living room, and gave up the pretense of reading his novel. Near the front windows, bathed in moonlight, Dionne rocked Jared in the old wooden chair that had been Mark's grandmother's. Dionne's eyes were closed, but she spoke softly to their son.

The boy snuggled close to her, his fingers alternately clutching his own hair, reaching for something on a nearby table, then settling on her arm before starting all over again. His small mouth puckered for a moment, then stretched wide as he yawned.

Barbara's laughter erupted in the kitchen followed by Aunt Nonie's a moment later. His dad and Uncle Bruce sat across the room, heads together, solving the problems of the world. Mark couldn't remember when he'd last felt so content.

It didn't get much better than this. His wife and child across the room, other family members he loved nearby. Of course, things could get a *little* better. Although he had no idea what would happen when he and Dionne closed the door to their bedroom tonight, he did know that brief kiss on the hill had left him wanting much more.

The change in her that afternoon as she'd tackled

him and stuffed leaves down his shirt had been nothing short of miraculous. And she'd been more at ease around the rest of the family all evening. He'd thought her attractive before, but she was damned near irresistible now.

Even Jared sensed the difference. He'd picked up on her mood and had seemed more settled all evening.

If Mark could have had his way, he'd spirit Dionne to the bedroom and make love to her. But doing the wrong thing now could ruin the tenuous relationship they had. He didn't want her to go back to the quiet, almost somber woman she'd been the past few weeks.

He made another unsuccessful attempt to read a few pages until his father left Uncle Bruce and came to sit beside him on the couch. Nigel propped his hands on his knees and groaned as he lowered himself into position. "What a weekend this has been."

"It's been a great weekend," Mark said, lowering his book to his lap. "And the reception you and Mom pulled together yesterday was really nice. Thanks again."

"Nothing to it, son. Nothing at all." Nigel sank back in the seat and let out a sigh of pure contentment. "Certainly made your mother happy."

Mark nodded and set the book on the couch beside him. "I think it did. She's really incredible, isn't she?"

"Your mother?" Nigel looked surprised by the question. "She's a good woman, son. But I believe you've got one, too. She's a good mother to that son of yours." His father retrieved a sailing magazine from the coffee table and propped it open on his knee. "You've done well for yourself, my boy."

"Thanks." His father's praise meant the world to him.

"Now just make sure you don't blow it."

Mark's smile faded. "I don't intend to."

"Intentions aren't everything, son." His father marked his place in the magazine and sent him a sober look. "Jerry didn't intend to cheat on Alice, but it happened anyway."

"I'm not Jerry," Mark reminded him.

Nigel chuckled softly and loosened the top button of his shirt. "No, you're not. But you can be stubborn when you want to be. And you're single-minded. Once you decide what you want, you go after it and everybody else be damned."

That hit a little too close for comfort. "I've always been that way, Dad. But you've always seemed proud of that."

"I have been proud." His father turned to face him more fully. "Damned proud. That stubborn streak of yours is what kept you in law school when the going got tough and wouldn't let you quit the football team your senior year of high school. All I'm saying is, don't turn it on your wife or you could be in trouble. Listen to the voice of experience."

"I don't intend to—" Mark broke off with a laugh and held up both hands. "I know, I know. Intentions aren't everything."

"Just be flexible." His father opened the magazine again and glanced at the page. "That's my best advice. It'll be especially tough for you. You've been on your own a long time. You're used to having things your own way. But if you want to keep that woman happy—and I'm *sure* you do—'' He accented this with lifted eyebrows.

''Of course I do.''

''Well, then, you've got to put her first and yourself second. Find out what she needs to be happy and then make sure you give it to her.'' His father propped his feet on the coffee table. ''I'm not talking about the big things, now. I'm talking about the things that are hard to do, like respecting her when you're in the mood for romance but all she wants to do is go to sleep, or pulling yourself away from the television long enough to recognize when she's too tired to cook dinner, or just listening to her when she's complaining about something even if you've had a lousy day.''

Mark nodded slowly. It sounded simple enough.

His father glanced toward the kitchen and lowered his voice before he went on. ''Nothing I do makes your mother madder than when I try to step in and fix something without her asking.'' He shook his head and sent Mark a wry smile. ''I don't understand it, but it's the way things are. So I've learned to just stand by until she asks for my help or my advice.''

Mark laughed. He'd heard a few ''discussions'' between his parents when he was younger that bore that out. ''I'll keep that in mind.''

''See that you do, son, if you love her.'' He lifted an eyebrow and looked at Mark meaningfully.

Mark felt his smile freeze, but he managed to keep it in place. He'd certainly begun to care for her, and he couldn't deny the physical attraction, but did he love her?

For some reason, he had trouble getting the words

out of his mouth. "Of course I do. I married her, didn't I?"

"People have gotten married for all sorts of reasons that didn't include love," his father said. But he turned his attention back to his magazine as if Mark's answer had pacified him.

Mark breathed a sigh of relief and picked up his book again, but the conversation left him faintly uneasy. He didn't love Dionne, he told himself firmly. He'd sworn off love after Marianne's betrayal and had vowed never to leave himself that vulnerable again.

But that had been before she'd responded briefly to his kiss. Had her reaction meant anything more than the fact that she was vulnerable right now? She'd put everything she had on the line to marry him and move here. Anyone could see her emotions were painfully raw. Only a complete jackass would take advantage of that.

A few short days ago, the idea of their living together as polite strangers had seemed not only possible but easy. Now... Now, it felt like hell.

THE FOLLOWING SUNDAY, while Dionne tried to organize her bathroom in the new house, she listened to the banter between Mark and his brothers downstairs. They were all so relaxed, they'd put her at ease almost immediately. And the boom of deep voices as they tangled over which one had to carry the heaviest boxes, over who got to drive the truck back into Boston for the last load, and over which of them had to sit in the middle made her smile.

She sat back on her heels, enjoying the sound of their good-natured bickering. Even if, God forbid, things between her and Mark didn't work out, she could never take this away from Jared.

The thought brought her up short. Of course, if things didn't work out, taking Jared away from his family wouldn't be the issue. *She* was the one who'd have to leave.

"Hey there." A deep voice cut into her thoughts and brought her around quickly. Mark's youngest brother, Steve, snagged Jared from a stack of boxes he'd climbed in the hall while she wasn't watching. "No climbing, sport. We don't want you to get hurt."

"Jared wanna climb." Jared started back toward the stack, his determined little face set in a scowl that matched his uncle's. "Jared show you."

"No you don't." Steve caught him by the waist and pulled him away from the boxes, jiggling him as he did and earning a delighted laugh. "I'm serious, Jare-Bear. No climbing." He set Jared on the floor again and looked him straight in the eye. "All right?"

"Uncle Steve is right," Dionne put in. "You might get hurt."

"No," Jared said stubbornly.

"Yes," Steve argued. "Why don't you build me a house with your blocks instead? Show me that, okay?"

Jared thought about that for a second, then scurried off. Steve turned back toward Dionne. "Sorry. I didn't think you saw him. You looked like you were a million miles away."

"I was," she admitted. "Thank you."

Steve waved a hand as if to say her thanks were unnecessary. "So what had you so far away?"

"Besides serious sleep deprivation?" she asked with a laugh. "I was just listening to the four of you downstairs together and thinking how lucky you are to have such a great family."

"It's your family now, too, you know. And your humble brother-in-law is at your service. Mark, David and Jerry took off for Boston to get the last load. They left me here to help you."

"What happened?" she teased. "Did you lose the coin toss?"

"No." He leaned against the wall. "I won."

"What a charmer," she said, grinning easily.

"It's a family trait."

It certainly was. One she noticed a little more each day. She nodded toward a stack of boxes against the far wall. "If you're supposed to help me, I suppose we ought to get started. Most of those belong in Jared's bedroom."

Steve pushed away from the wall and bowed elaborately. "Your wish is my command."

Dionne stepped over a stack of towels and checked to make sure Jared wasn't climbing something else. "With an attitude like that, how on earth have the women let you stay single?"

Steve sniffed comically and hitched the waistband of his jeans. "It's been a tough fight, but I've managed to escape the noose… Begging your pardon, ma'am. Nothing personal."

She bent to retrieve a pile of Jared's pajamas from the floor. "I'm sure it has been tough. Your resolve is commendable."

"We Taylors are famous for it," he said, starting toward the boxes. He tested a couple for weight, then hefted one with a groan. "We always get what we go after."

"Oh?"

"You're here, aren't you?" Steve waggled his eyebrows at her, disappeared with the box, and returned a minute later.

Dionne had to admit he was right. Her presence in New Hampshire on a sunny autumn afternoon *was* the result of Mark getting what he wanted—his son. But she was determined to keep the lightness between them. "Does it ever backfire?"

"Rarely." Steve's face clouded for a second, then he grinned. "Well, it did once for Jerry, but the rest of us are a lot smarter than he is."

"Poor Jerry." She stopped working and sat on the side of the bathtub. "How did the famous Taylor determination fail him?"

"He lost his wife and kids when he cheated on Alice."

"I shouldn't have asked," she said quickly.

"Why not? Jerry won't mind if you know. We're a pretty open family. Nobody has secrets."

Little did he know, Dionne thought. "Really?"

"Yeah. My parents have always been big on honesty. Drilled it into us from the time we were kids."

"It's a good trait to have."

"Yeah, it is." Steve sat on the corner of the box and wiped his forehead again. "And safe. There's nothing worse than getting caught in a lie by my parents."

That was an experience Dionne hoped to avoid. She cast about for some way to change the subject. "Is that the last of the boxes?"

Steve laughed, a warm, rich laugh that sounded

exactly like Mark's. "Are you kidding? It'll take us all day to bring in Mark's junk. But where's all your stuff?"

Dionne's gaze faltered. "I didn't bring anything with me."

"Really? Why not?"

"None of my things were as nice as Mark's," she said honestly. "Besides, it would have cost more in shipping charges than any of my furniture was worth."

Steve's eyebrows knit. "Yeah, but still— Don't you want a few familiar things around?"

More than he could possibly imagine. "The only thing I really miss is my rocking chair," she said, brushing a lock of hair off her shoulder. "And Mark already bought one of those for Jared's room, along with the new bed for mine—" She broke off and her eyes rounded when she realized her mistake.

"Yours?"

"My…study. The guest room. It's going to do double duty."

"As a study?" Steve propped one foot on a low-lying box and his chin in his hand. "I thought Mark said you weren't going to work away from home for a while."

"I'm not," she assured him, and added another lie to the list. "But I am thinking about going back to school."

"Oh yeah?" Steve looked impressed. "What will you study?"

"I've always wanted to work with disadvantaged children." At least *that* wasn't a lie.

"Good field. What school will you go to?"

Dionne picked up an armful of towels and started

into the hallway. "I don't have all the details worked out yet, and I probably won't until we're settled in here."

Steve followed her slowly. "And you won't get settled unless your lazy brother-in-law gets back to work, right? Fine. I can take a hint."

Much as she liked talking to him, it would probably be a whole lot safer to work in silence. The worst part about lying, she thought sadly, was that you couldn't ever relax.

A FEW HOURS LATER, Mark lugged another heavy box up the stairs. In spite of the chilly weekend weather, sweat ran down his forehead and dampened his shirt. His brothers had gone home, leaving him alone with Dionne at last. But the day's work had left him worn out. His knees had taken a beating running up and down the stairs, his arms ached from lifting, his back felt as if it could snap in two.

He stopped just inside the bedroom door and propped the box he carried on his knee. Dionne glanced up at him from a spot on the floor where she'd surrounded herself with towels, blankets, sheets and tablecloths. Jared had abandoned his trucks and blocks and was contentedly playing in an empty box beside her.

She lifted her hair from the back of her neck and fanned her face with her hand. She smiled, thoroughly unaware that she'd set his blood boiling just as she had so often during the week since their visit to Sunrise Notch.

Again he was reminded of that brief kiss in the leaves and again he wanted another. He remembered the way she'd looked with her lips parted slightly, her eyes dark with emotion, her face flushed, her breath labored. He remembered the feel of her lips beneath his and the thrill of her response. And, as he had every time the memory surfaced, he shoved it away firmly.

"Where do you want this?" he asked, lifting the box slightly.

His voice caught Jared's attention. The boy scrambled out of the box and raced across the room toward him. "Come see my house."

"You have a house?" Mark couldn't resist. He set his box aside and followed Jared toward his makeshift playhouse. "Can I come in?"

Jared frowned up at him. "No. You're too big."

"Well, shoot. I guess I am at that." Mark dropped to the floor in front of Jared and peered inside. When Jared seemed satisfied, he turned back toward the box he'd abandoned and realized Dionne was still watching him. Oddly self-conscious, his step faltered. "So where do you want it?"

She motioned toward the closet. Then asked, "Have you put up Jared's bed yet?"

Before answering her question, he let his gaze drift across her bedroom. It landed on the bed they'd picked out for her and stayed there. *Wrong thing to look at, old boy. You'll give yourself ideas.*

He shook his head quickly and stuffed his hands into his pockets. "Not yet. I'll do that now."

"That would be nice. Thank you." She sounded tired, and he realized she must be as exhausted as he was.

On impulse, he turned back to face her. "Come with me."

"Where?"

"We've been at this all day. I think we need a break."

"Of course. You must be tired."

"Me?" He sent her a teasing smile. "I'm too tough to get tired. I'm just thinking of you."

She laughed and stood in one fluid movement, so graceful he thought his heart would fly out of his chest. "How thoughtful. Yes, I am exhausted after folding all this linen. I'm really grateful that you and your brothers wouldn't let me carry in any of the boxes."

"Just doing our job, ma'am." He coaxed Jared from his new toy, then followed Dionne down the hall toward the stairs. "Seriously, Dionne, now that my pesky brothers are gone, let's take advantage of the peace and quiet for a minute."

She looked up at him so quickly, he wondered if she'd misinterpreted him.

He tried to set her mind at ease. "To talk."

Her expression remained wary. "About what?"

"About the weather. About movies we've seen recently, or books we've read." *About whether or not our relationship will ever change.* "You were right that night back in Boston. We *do* need to know more about each other."

He cleared a path through the boxes, found a safe spot for Jared to play and led her to the couch. When she'd made herself comfortable, he sat beside her and cocked one ankle across his knee. "Why don't you tell me more about your childhood."

Her smile faded and he knew he'd touched on a delicate subject. "What do you want to know?"

"What kind of little girl were you?"

"Pretty typical, I guess."

He doubted that. She was anything but typical now. "Did you play with dolls, or cars and trucks?"

"Whatever my mother could afford or whatever some nice neighbor's kids had outgrown." She made a visible effort to push aside her wariness. "What about you? Dolls or trucks?"

"Trucks. Cars. Bulldozers. I didn't care as long as they had wheels and made noise."

"I'm not surprised."

"Why not?"

"Because Jared's so much like you."

It was, he thought, the first time she'd acknowledged a similarity between Jared and him, and it touched him. "Do you mind?"

"That he's like you?" She shook her head slowly. "Not anymore."

Her smile, her eyes, and her scent were driving him to distraction. How was a guy supposed to be a buddy to a woman who looked and smelled like that? He tried desperately to keep up his end of the conversation and changed the subject to one he knew would cool him off. "Tell me more about your marriage."

She studied her fingers for a minute. "What do you want to know?"

"Were you happy?"

"Yes." The word fell softly between them, and he tried not to acknowledge the direct hit to his heart. She lifted her gaze again. "Were you happy with Marianne?"

He gave that some thought, then nodded. "At the time, yes." But, as always, talking about Marianne made him uneasy and brought up the worst of his emotions. "What was your husband like?"

"I guess the best word to describe Brent would be dependable. He was quiet. Reserved."

Although Mark considered himself dependable, nobody had ever accused him of being quiet and reserved. If that was the kind of man she'd fallen in love with, Mark didn't stand a chance to win her heart.

That thought pulled him up short. Did he *want* a chance? He tried to convince himself he didn't. That it was only physical attraction that held him spellbound. But the truth was, he wanted to win her heart very much, indeed.

ON THEIR THIRD NIGHT in the new house, Dionne sat up suddenly, her sleep broken by a scream of pain from Jared. Outside, the wind howled and branches scratched against the side of the house. Clouds blocked the moon, leaving the room inky black. Without thinking, she tossed back the covers and started from the room, stubbing her toe against the dresser in the process.

Biting back a cry of her own, she plowed toward the door and hit her hand against a sharp corner. When Jared screamed again, she forced the pain out of her mind, yanked open the bedroom door and hurried into the hallway...

And ran straight into someone else.

"Sorry." Mark's voice, sleep-rough and deep. Mark's chest, bare, solid, strangely comforting.

Too late, she realized she'd forgotten to grab her robe, but another cry from Jared convinced her not to go back for it. As if they were connected, she and Mark turned at the same time and started toward the third bedroom.

Mark turned on the hall light, momentarily blinding her. But she didn't stop. She ran toward her son's bed and came to a stop just half a step in front of Mark. Jared sat up, holding his blanket against his face.

"What is it, sweetheart? What's wrong?"

"Mommy?"

"Yes, sweetie. Mommy's here. What's the matter?"

"Hurt."

"Hurt?" Mark's voice came out sharp. "What happened? How did he get hurt?"

Dionne motioned for him to be quiet, then sat on the edge of the bed. "What hurts, sweetheart?"

Drawing in a shuddering breath, Jared covered his ears with his hands. "Hurt."

Mark moved closer, his face pinched with worry. "What's wrong with him?"

Dionne pulled Jared onto her lap and attempted to cradle him, but he tried to get away and covered his ears again. "I think he has an earache," she said to Mark. "He has them occasionally."

"What do we do? Should I call the doctor? There's a hospital about twenty miles away—"

A mixture of gratitude and relief filled her. It had been a long time since she'd had anyone with her when she faced a crisis in the middle of the night. "He'll need to see a doctor," she said. "The infection won't clear up without an antibiotic."

"Then, let's get him one." Mark turned and started across the room. When Jared's howls increased, Mark turned back again. "Is there anything we can do for him now?"

Still holding Jared, she stood. "We could give him some children's pain reliever."

"Are you sure? Is it safe?"

"That's what the doctor in Boise had me do."

Mark didn't look at all relieved. In fact, he looked downright skeptical. "Do we have any?"

"I always keep some on hand."

Like a windup toy, he changed direction once more, raking his fingers through his hair as he walked. "Where is it?"

She held back a laugh. "Calm down, Mark. It's in my purse."

His step faltered and hesitation flickered across his face. "Maybe you should get it."

"All right." She settled Jared into his arms and smoothed his hair again. "Stay with Daddy, okay?"

Jared nodded solemnly and another sob shook him, but he snuggled up to Mark.

"Daddy?" Mark's eyes softened in the dim light. "I think that's the first time you've called me that since we got married." He touched her gently with his free hand and his fingers trailed up the side of her arm. As if someone had yanked a veil away, she became acutely aware that he wore nothing but a pair of boxers, while she wore only a thin nightgown.

"I'll be back in a second," she said and rushed from the room. She dug the baby Tylenol from her purse and threw on a robe before she rejoined her husband and their son.

Jared's cries drove everything else from her mind until they'd seen the doctor. But when Jared was finally able to sleep again on the return drive from the hospital, she thought about Mark's earlier comment and realized just how much she'd changed over the past few weeks.

Mark *was* Jared's father, but even more—he was a daddy in all ways. He was a kind and gentle man who'd given up his own chance at love and happiness for his son. He'd been as concerned about Jared that night as any father would be for his child.

Sudden, unexpected love for him surged into her heart and tears blurred her eyes. She looked out the window to keep Mark from seeing them, but she couldn't turn away from the emotion.

She didn't delude herself into thinking he loved her. He'd made that very clear. But he did care for her in some way. She'd have to be senseless not to know that. And he was certainly capable of loving. She only had to watch him with Jared and his family to know that.

Maybe one day he'd begin to love her. In the meantime, she'd be wise to keep her feelings to herself. The days would be easier that way.

And the nights far safer.

CHAPTER ELEVEN

COMFORTED BY THE FACT that Jared seemed a little better this morning, Mark had gone to work. But he'd made Dionne promise to call if Jared took a turn for the worse.

Now, checking the signs on each building as she walked, Dionne pushed Jared's stroller slowly along the Front Street sidewalk and looked for the pharmacy. Quaint buildings lined the narrow road. Shade from an occasional tree covered the sidewalk and half a block away a dog lazed in the autumn sunshine.

To her, the village of Longs Mill looked like something out of a movie or a Norman Rockwell painting. It was utterly charming. Exactly the kind of town she'd dreamed of living in as a young girl.

When the sign she'd been looking for caught her eye, she stopped walking. "Looks like we've found it, sweetheart. After we get your medicine, you'll feel better in no time." She maneuvered the stroller into the recessed doorway, skimming a bright orange piece of paper taped to the glass announcing the Longs Mill Autumn Festival the following weekend.

She smiled softly and let her imagination run for a second or two, picturing the scene. But when Jared shifted fitfully, she forced her attention back to the present, propped open the door with one foot, and worked the stroller up the single step and inside the building.

It took only a moment to get her bearings. Three narrow aisles flanked by packed shelves ran the length of the building to the pharmacy in back where a woman of about Dionne's age, with softly curling shoulder-length brown hair finished a telephone call.

Dionne pushed the stroller toward her and waited until the woman replaced the receiver. "Dr. Miller said he'd call in a prescription for my son this morning. It's for Jared Taylor."

The woman smiled, her warm brown eyes friendly and welcoming. "So *you're* Mrs. Taylor. I was wondering when I'd finally get to meet you."

"Really?"

"We've all heard that you bought the old Preece place, of course. Someone new moving in is always big news." She turned away to speak over her shoulder to the pharmacist, then smiled again at Dionne. "I'm Patsy Wagner. We live out on the Old Post Road not far from you. I've been meaning to stop by and say hello, but I've had a houseful of sick kids. Looks like you're in the same boat."

When Jared reached for something on the shelf in front of him, Dionne took it from him and moved the stroller back a few inches. "My son has an ear infection."

"Same with two of mine. The others have regular colds. It's that time of year. My kids always get sick when the seasons change." Patsy straightened some papers in front of her and leaned both arms on the counter. "I just hope they're all well by next weekend."

Dionne glanced over her shoulder at the door. "For the autumn festival?"

"Yes. I love the festival and I don't want to miss it. You'll be there, won't you?"

"Oh, I—" Irritated by the response that rose automatically to her lips, Dionne cut herself off. Why did she immediately think "no"? She longed for friends and family, yet she instinctively held back from both. "I didn't know about it," she finished lamely.

Patsy waved one hand toward the street. "You really should come. It's not a big deal. Just a party we hold every year in the square. But it would give you a chance to meet everyone."

"It sounds wonderful," she said tentatively. "But we wouldn't want to intrude."

"But you wouldn't be intruding," Patsy assured her. "You're a part of Longs Mill now. You're *supposed* to be there."

The sense of belonging warmed her clear through. "In that case," she said with a smile, "I'll mention it to Mark. If Jared's feeling better, we may come."

"Hopefully, he'll be better, and so will all of mine." Patsy checked behind her to see if Jared's prescription was ready, then leaned over the counter to smile down at Jared.

To Dionne's surprise, Jared sent her a toothy grin and tried to climb out of his stroller. Though he'd never been shy, he'd always been slightly wary of strangers. But he'd lost even that since becoming part of the Taylor clan.

"If you do come," Patsy said, "bring something with you for the potluck dinner. And there's dancing afterward."

"It really does sound like fun," Dionne said.

"It is," Patsy said, laughing. "And you'll be doing yourself a disservice if you don't have some of Hazel White's crab cakes or Nancy Wiggs's blueberry cobbler. And there are always lots of people around," Patsy went on, "so there'll be someone to watch this cute little bundle while you and your husband dance."

Dionne glanced down at Jared, who'd lost interest in his surroundings and had started fussing quietly. She found his toy giraffe on the seat where he'd dropped it and offered it to him. He clutched the toy tightly, then rested his head on its plush body.

The idea of skimming across a dance floor in Mark's arms certainly had appeal, she thought, suppressing a delicious shiver of anticipation. "The party sounds perfect," she said to Patsy.

"Then you'll be there?"

"I hope so," Dionne said, a little surprised by how deeply she meant it.

After paying for the antibiotic, Dionne pushed the stroller back into the warm September morning. She found herself hoping she and Patsy would become friends. Losing Cicely was the one deep void still left in her life.

She drank in the sight of the quaint little town, the shops, the narrow road, the weathered buildings. She and Mark had been right to buy the house here. This was a perfect place to raise a family.

That thought caught her by surprise. She pondered it for a moment, testing the idea of giving Jared brothers and sisters. Did she really want that?

Yes, she realized with a start. She did. But she

couldn't give him brothers and sisters unless her relationship with Mark changed drastically.

What she wanted, what she *longed* for, was to be loved again. And she couldn't help wondering if she'd locked herself into a life without any hope of that happening.

EXHAUSTED AFTER a lengthy deposition that had left him frustrated, Mark put the last file he needed in his briefcase and took another long look at his desk to make sure he hadn't forgotten anything. Through the open door, he could hear Anna moving around in her office, closing file cabinets, locking her desk, getting ready to call it a day.

Usually, Mark stayed long after Anna went home. His most productive hours were those spent after the phones stopped ringing and the support staff disappeared. But tonight, he was leaving on time.

He'd been worried about Jared all day, in spite of Dionne's promise to call and the doctor's diagnosis. Even talking to his son for a minute on the phone that afternoon hadn't made him feel much better and he'd been watching the clock, just waiting for five o'clock to roll around.

To be honest, concern for Jared wasn't the only thing drawing him home. More and more, he found himself wanting to be with Dionne.

He was still thinking about his family as he reached for his jacket. But before he could put it on, the door to his office opened wider and Royal Spritzer poked his head inside. "Got a minute?"

Mark bit back a groan of dismay and nodded. Royal's "minutes" were notoriously long. But he couldn't very well refuse the boss. "Sure. What is it?"

"I need to talk to you about the Young Technologies case." Royal closed the door behind him and settled his long, lanky frame into one of Mark's client chairs. He cocked an ankle across one knee and made himself comfortable.

Obviously, Mark wasn't going anywhere soon. He dropped his suit jacket to the second chair again and sat on his own. "Is something wrong?"

"Not at all." Royal smoothed his silk tie across his stomach and sent Mark a smug smile. "As a matter of fact, everything's right as rain."

"Great. What's up?"

"We lined up a witness this afternoon who's willing to talk to us."

"No kidding?" They'd been floundering so far, trying to find someone who could give them evidence that Young had filtered money from the employee pension plan. "Who is it? How did we find him?"

Royal's smile grew larger by the minute. Mark couldn't remember ever seeing him so pleased. "He's a former employee who worked directly with the pension plan at Young's national office in New York."

Mark grinned. "Chalk one up for our side. Why is he willing to talk?"

"I don't have all the details, but apparently Young fired him under some pretty questionable circumstances. He's what you'd call disgruntled."

"And he's willing to talk to us?" No wonder Royal looked so pleased. "That's the best news I've heard all day. Do you need me to pull something together for Oscar before the meeting?'' Mark glanced at the clock on his desk, calculating the time it would take to get what Oscar needed and make the drive home. It was still doable.

''Oscar's not handling this witness.'' Royal leaned back in his chair and linked his fingers together on his stomach. ''You are.''

''Me?'' Mark stared at him, dumbfounded. ''Why?''

''Because you've been doing a good job for the firm. Oscar tells me you've given your all on the cases he's worked on with you. And I think it's about time to give you a leg up. You've earned it.''

''Thank you, sir.'' Mark made a mental note to also thank Oscar next time he talked to him.

Royal waved away his gratitude. ''You have a sharp legal mind, Mark. We value that. You're loyal. Dependable. Devoted to your career.''

Mark tried to look appropriately humble, but it wasn't easy. He wanted to punch his fist into the air and shout, ''Yes!''

''And now you're also a family man. A wife *and* a son in one fell swoop.'' Royal smiled again, rested his elbows on the arms of the chair, and linked his hands together in front of him. ''That's what we like to hear, Mark. Stability has always been at the core of Jamison and Spritzer's success. It's an image we like to promote.''

Mark wasn't sure how to take that. He'd always considered himself stable, even when he wasn't married. But he wasn't about to argue. He'd been waiting a long time for Royal to give some sign that Mark's efforts hadn't gone unnoticed.

''Things are going well at home?'' Royal sounded

casually interested, but Mark suspected there was a reason behind the question.

"Very well."

"Glad to hear that, too. A family can be a real asset. Makes a man look successful."

They could make a man *feel* successful, Mark thought with a smile. "I appreciate you letting me get more involved in the case, sir."

"Nonsense. It's well deserved. Just have your secretary book you a room. The firm will pick up the tab, of course. The meeting's scheduled for eight o'clock."

"Tonight?" Mark couldn't keep the dismay from his voice.

Royal's close-set eyes narrowed slightly. "What's the matter? Do you have a conflict?"

"Sort of."

"Well, whatever it is, cancel. This witness can give us everything we need to prove our case at trial. We could blow the other side right out of the water." He leaned forward slightly and held Mark's gaze. "We can't afford to lose him."

"I know that. It's just—"

"Your wife will just have to understand that this sort of thing comes with the territory." Royal's thin lips curved into a smile as he spoke, but Mark heard the warning in his words.

"Dionne will understand," Mark assured him, knowing she would. He was the one who was disappointed at not being able to be with his family.

"Well, then, what's the problem?"

"No problem," Mark said. "Which hotel?"

"We'll put you up at the Seaport." Royal's eyes gleamed with satisfaction, and Mark knew he'd passed the test. "We want to make sure the firm looks good."

Mark had never stayed in the five-star hotel, but he tried to find some pleasure in knowing that if he had to be lonely, at least he'd be doing it in style.

"You'll have to handle the witness with kid gloves," Royal warned. "He's agreed to talk to us, but he's still pretty skittish."

"Don't worry. I'll get what we need."

Royal's smile widened. "I know you will."

The vote of confidence pleased him. "I won't let you down."

He watched Royal stand and stride across the office, waited until the door clicked shut behind him, then picked up the phone and dialed. Though he liked knowing that Royal's confidence in him was increasing, he hated having to make the choice between his career and his family. And he wondered how many times he'd be asked to make a similar choice in the future.

DIONNE GAVE the kitchen counter a final sweep with the cloth and stepped back to survey her handiwork. Dinner was over. Dishes were done. The kitchen was spotless. Jared had already drifted off to sleep, Mark was probably already settled in at the hotel in Boston, and she had absolutely nothing to do.

She sighed softly and wandered into the living room. She'd already put away Jared's toys, the furniture gleamed from polishing, and the carpet still bore tracks from vacuuming. She'd never been this efficient with housework. But then, she'd never had so many hours to get it done before.

Curling onto one end of the couch, she turned on

the television and watched for a few minutes, flicking between channels and trying to find something that would hold her interest. Unfortunately, her only choices seemed to be mindless sitcoms, a shoot-'em-up police drama and a melodramatic movie of the week.

She turned off the television and looked out the window at the sunset. The sun hovered on the horizon. Streaks of orange and deep red tinted the clouds. The sunset was beautiful, but she couldn't find any satisfaction in watching it.

With a sigh, she picked up a magazine and leafed through it. When none of the articles looked even slightly interesting, she tossed it onto the coffee table again.

What was wrong with her? She'd been in the strangest mood since Mark called to let her know he wasn't coming home. But why did that bother her? She'd only been living with him for a month. It wasn't as if her entire life revolved around him.

Or did it?

What else did she have? In Boise, she'd had work and her friendship with Cicely to fill the hours and keep her connected to the adult world. Here, she had Mark. No friends. No job. Nothing.

Not good, she told herself. Not good at all.

Without thinking twice, she picked up the cordless phone and dialed Cicely's number as she walked back into the kitchen. When Cicely answered, she lost herself for a moment in the excitement of hearing her friend's voice again and catching up on all that had happened during the past few weeks.

But it didn't take long for Cicely to drop the social

niceties and zero in. "Tell me the truth," Cicely demanded. "How are you doing?"

"I'm doing fine," Dionne assured her. "You really should see this place. It's like something from a Christmas card. There's a covered bridge just outside of town and everything."

"That sounds great," Cicely said patiently. "But what I'm interested in is how things are going between you and Mark."

"Things are going well. We've stopped arguing all the time and we're even becoming friends."

"Seriously?"

Dionne laughed. "Seriously."

"No trouble yet?"

"No trouble." Dionne put the kettle on to boil and pulled a tea bag from the cupboard. "Honestly, Cicely. You sound as if you *want* us to have trouble."

"Don't be silly. Of course I don't. I just want you to be happy. So...*are* you?"

"I'm not delirious," Dionne admitted as she lowered a mug to the counter. "But I'm certainly not miserable. You really can stop worrying about me."

"Right." She could almost see Cicely rolling her eyes in frustration. "You could be living a million miles away for all I ever hear from you. And you want me to stop worrying. It's not going to happen, girl."

Dionne sat at the table where she could look out into the backyard. "Well, then, try not to worry so much. Mark is terrific with Jared. And his family— Well, they've welcomed us both with open arms."

Cicely was quiet for a moment, then asked, "What are you doing? Falling for Mr. I'm-Taking-My-Son-Away-and-You-Can't-Stop-Me?"

"I'm getting to know him," Dionne hedged. "He really is a great guy."

Cicely humphed in disbelief.

"Wouldn't you rather hear that I like him than to find out he's beating me or something?"

"Of course." Cicely's voice softened considerably. "You know I would. But I still don't trust him."

"Well, I do," Dionne assured her. "And I'd rather talk about something else."

"Okay," Cicely said. "Are you working yet?"

"No."

"Are you looking for work?"

"No."

"You're staying home and playing housemaid, then?"

"I'm not playing housemaid," Dionne said firmly as the kettle began to whistle. She turned off the burner and poured hot water over the tea bag. "I'm raising my son. *Our* son."

"And doing dishes. And cleaning house. And keeping the home fires burning while he goes to work every day. Is that enough for you?"

That was a tough question. "For now."

"I don't believe you." Cicely's voice took on a sharp edge. "What about all those dreams you once had?"

"I still have them. In fact, Mark offered to loan me the money so I can get my degree."

"Really?" Cicely didn't sound impressed, but that came as no surprise. "Are you going to take him up on it?"

"I don't know." Dionne sipped and wrapped both

hands around the mug. "I feel funny accepting money from him."

Cicely let out a harsh laugh. "You can't be serious. You're already accepting money from him— rent money, food money, utility money. Why not tuition, too?"

"That's different," Dionne argued, though she couldn't explain how. She sighed. "I didn't call you so we could bicker, Cicely. I called because I miss you."

Cicely's voice softened. "I miss you, too. You know that. But I'm worried...and maybe just the tiniest bit jealous."

"Jealous? Why should you be jealous?"

"Because I feel as if I've lost you as my friend. I feel as if Mark has taken you away from me."

Dionne smiled. She'd always valued Cicely's honesty, even though it sometimes felt brutal. "I'm still your friend. I'll always be your friend. And I miss getting together as much as you do. I miss shopping and having lunch and hanging out on Saturdays." Just talking about the things they used to do brought tears to her eyes. "I wish you could come for a visit."

"So do I. But I don't have vacation scheduled until Christmas, and I've already promised to spend that with my parents."

Dionne's heart sank. She hadn't realized until that moment how much she'd been hoping to see Cicely again.

The conversation drifted on to other topics until Cicely finally pleaded fatigue and an early-morning meeting the next day. Hanging up reluctantly, Dionne battled an odd sense of disquiet as she walked through the kitchen and climbed the stairs to her bedroom. But as she undressed for the night, she put a name to it at last.

She was bored.

Yes, she loved being home with Jared, but Cicely was right. She did want more out of life than cooking meals and straightening the house while Mark pursued his career. If she wanted to be truly happy, she'd either have to go back to work or accept Mark's offer.

Cicely was right about another thing, too. Accepting a loan—and Dionne still couldn't justify taking Mark's money any other way—was no different than accepting everything else he'd been providing. That he did so without complaint only endeared him to her more. And his encouragement seemed genuine. He wanted her to follow her dream.

She pulled on her thin cotton nightgown and sank onto the foot of the bed. If she moved quickly, maybe she could still enroll in classes for the fall semester.

Excitement began as little more than a tingle close to her heart, then worked its way up to an almost electric charge. If only she could talk to Mark immediately, but she'd have to wait until tomorrow.

Too worked up to sleep, she descended the stairs again, poured a glass of wine, and carried it to the living room. She didn't bother with a robe. It was a warm night, and except for Jared she had the house to herself. Nor did she bother turning on the light.

Instead, she curled in a corner of the couch and looked out at the night. She thought about Cicely's question and whispered, "Happy? Yes, Cicely, I really think I am."

CHAPTER TWELVE

AT A LITTLE PAST MIDNIGHT, Mark pulled into the
driveway and turned off the engine. Clouds hid the
moon, and a breeze brushed the tops of the trees. In
the distance, a dog barked. He smiled and reached
for his briefcase. Home, sweet home.

Maybe he'd been foolish to drive for more than an
hour after his meeting instead of staying at the hotel
overnight. But after getting what he needed from the
witness, the idea of celebrating alone in a lonely
room—even in the posh hotel—hadn't appealed to
him. He'd rather stumble over toys than sit alone in
an elegant hotel room any day.

He was, of course, too late to see either his wife
or his son tonight. Jared had been in bed for hours,
and Dionne rarely stayed up this late. But if he got
up early, he could spend a few minutes with them in
the morning.

Giving in to a huge yawn, he grabbed his suit
jacket from the seat beside him and hurried up the
front walk. He let himself in and flipped the light
switch, then froze at the sight that greeted him.

Dionne, wearing only a thin white nightgown that
left little to the imagination, lay curled on the couch.
A glass of wine, nearly untouched, sat on the floor
beside her. The gown had twisted slightly, and its
hem skimmed the tops of her thighs.

His breath caught at the same time his pulse began to race. He turned away quickly, closed and locked the door, then looked back at her. He could just leave her there, but she looked uncomfortable.

And that's how he justified his next move.

Slowly, cautiously, he crossed the room and touched her shoulder. Her skin felt warm—too warm, and far too soft. He should have pulled his hand away, but he didn't want to. He let it rest there for a moment, then shook her gently. "Dionne?" He shook her again. "Dionne? Wake up."

She mumbled something and curled closer to the cushions, and he had to fight the sudden craving to have her snuggle against him that way.

"Dionne?" He leaned a little closer, catching the scent of her hair.

This time, she opened her eyes. But she seemed disoriented, unaware of him for a second. In the next breath, she lurched upright and tugged at her gown. "What's wrong?"

"Nothing. I just thought you'd be more comfortable in bed." He held out a hand toward her, only half-convinced he could touch her again and still maintain control. "Come on. I'll help you up."

She took it warily. "What are you doing here? I thought you were staying in Boston."

"I was. I decided to come home instead. I was worried about Jared. Is he okay?"

"He's fine."

Mark helped her stand, which brought her to her feet mere inches from him. Light traces of her scent floated toward him, but more enticing was the scent of her skin he caught beneath it. He released her hand quickly. After all, he could only resist so much temptation. "Maybe I should have let you sleep, but you, uh…" He ran his hand over his face and backed a step away. "You looked uncomfortable."

Her eyes clouded for a moment. She rubbed the back of her neck, testing for kinks. "I guess I must have drifted off. I didn't plan to fall asleep there."

With the dim light behind her, the nightgown seemed to vaporize. Mark told himself to look away, but he couldn't. It had been a long time since he'd been with a woman and this one had gotten completely under his skin.

He cleared his throat and tried to pull himself together. "Why don't you go up to bed. I'll double-check the doors and windows." Anything to get away from her before he did something they'd both regret.

Obviously unaware of her effect on him, she started past him, then stopped and smiled. "I made a decision tonight."

"Oh? What kind of decision?" *Please, let it be that she wants a real marriage—starting now.*

"If your offer to loan me tuition still stands, I've decided to take you up on it."

He did his best not to look disappointed. "Yes, of course. But what brought about this change?"

"A lot of things." She ran a hand through her hair, tousling it even more, making him want to work his hands into the curls and do it for her. "Mostly I realized that I can't teach Jared to reach his fullest capacity if I don't even try to meet my own. Actions say more than words ever can. I need to teach by example."

Mark dropped onto the couch to put some distance

between them. "I'm so glad," he said honestly. "I'd like to see you doing something you enjoy."

"I enjoy being home with Jared." She sat beside him, and Mark couldn't decide if the distance between them was too little or too great. "But I also need to do something more personally challenging than housework."

"I think that's great," he said. "Just find out how much you'll need for tuition and books, and let me know. I'll have the money for you by the next day."

Dionne smiled, and the room brightened. "Thank you. You know I'll pay back every penny."

He shook his head emphatically. "I don't want you to pay back anything."

"But I do." Her smile faded for an instant. "You're already doing so much—"

"I'm doing nothing." The words came from the deepest, most honest part of himself. "You're the one who's making all the sacrifices in this marriage."

Something flitted through her eyes too quickly for him to read it. "We're both making sacrifices, Mark. And I need you to know how much I appreciate what you've done."

Were those tears glinting in her eyes? Mark's heart sank. He didn't want her to cry. He didn't handle tears well. They made him feel inadequate, rough, coarse.

He did the only thing he could think of. He put a comforting arm around her. But the instant he touched her again, desire overtook him. Pulling her closer, he lowered his mouth to hers and brushed it softly. When she didn't move away, he let the last remnants of control disappear and deepened the kiss.

Her mouth felt warm and soft, and he lost himself in it.

This was right. So very right. He didn't want to stop. When he realized she wasn't going to pull away, he tugged her onto his lap and wrapped his arms around her waist, exploring her mouth with his tongue, running his hands along her back, her thighs, her hips.

He told himself to hold back, to stay in control, but some logical piece of his brain reminded him that they were husband and wife, that there was nothing wrong with what they were doing, that everything he'd done for the past two months had been leading up to this moment.

When she whimpered softly, waves of fresh yearning rolled through him and his thoughts jumbled again. "You feel so good," he whispered when he could finally drag his mouth from hers. "So very good."

"So do you." Her breath caressed his neck and sent another surge of need through him. He ran his hands along her sides and slipped them beneath the top of her nightgown. She was beautiful. Sexy. Desirable. And he was more alive than he'd been in a long time.

He half expected her to pull away from his touch. When she didn't, he grew braver. Groaning softly, he cupped her breasts with both hands and closed his eyes. She moaned, responding to his touch. Every nerve in his body flamed. "I want you," he muttered as he claimed her mouth again.

It seemed to take forever before she could catch her breath enough to whisper, "Yes."

He pulled away slightly. "Are you sure?"

"Yes."

Groaning again, he caressed her one more time. Then, holding himself in check, wanting to make the moment special for both of them, he carried her up the stairs to his bedroom.

He kicked the door shut behind them and lowered her onto the bed. And he slowly, patiently, lovingly took them both over the crest into paradise.

DIONNE WOKE before the sun came up, before Mark's alarm went off, before Jared stirred. She lay tangled in the sheets, cradled in Mark's arms.

Rolling onto her side, she watched him for a moment. His mouth was parted slightly. His dark lashes fanned on his cheek. He looked young and defenseless.

She touched his hand with her fingertips, but when she remembered everything they'd done, when she realized the extent of their intimacy, she blushed furiously and pulled her hand away.

She'd never been so uninhibited during lovemaking before, not even with Brent. She realized, in the soft gray of sunrise, that though she'd loved Brent and enjoyed his lovemaking, it had never been like this.

Slowly, without disturbing Mark, she inched out of bed, pulled on her nightgown, and stepped out into the hall. She needed to think, to decide exactly how she felt about this change between them, and she didn't want to wake him.

Padding softly across the hall to her own bedroom, she checked on the sleeping Jared, changed quickly into jeans and a T-shirt, then hurried downstairs and slipped out onto the deck where she could enjoy the solitude of the morning.

The air felt clean and cool against her still-fevered skin. The scent of earth and trees and water soothed her. Maybe, she thought with a wry smile, she should have felt guilty. But she didn't. She felt alive and achingly feminine and surprisingly hungry for more. But there was one thing missing.

Mark hadn't said he loved her.

He'd said a thousand wonderful things last night, but he hadn't used the word *love*. And she'd held back her own confession, afraid to let go of that one last piece of herself, afraid he'd answer with silence. She could have borne many things, but she didn't think she could bear that.

So what was she going to do now?

She could continue the physical relationship with Mark and hope he'd fall in love with her. But what if he didn't? What then? Would her love alone be enough? Or would the pain of knowing Mark didn't love her eventually drive a wedge between them?

They couldn't afford that. Neither of them could. They'd be right back where they'd started—battling each other for Jared. She didn't want to go through that again, and she wouldn't put Jared through it. And she knew Mark would feel exactly the same way. That's why they'd gotten married in the first place.

Sighing, she walked to the edge of the lawn, tilted back her head, and let the silence wrap itself around her. She'd like to think she could still protect her heart, but the truth was, she'd already moved far beyond that point. The only choice left to her was to protect Jared from the pain that adults could impose on their children.

WHEN THE ALARM WENT OFF, Mark stretched and reached across the bed for Dionne, but his arm encountered only the pillow and rumpled sheets. He sat up, blinked, and looked around the room. The sky had just begun to lighten but he could see she wasn't there.

Wondering if Jared had woken her, Mark pulled on his briefs and a pair of jeans and hurried into the hall. But Jared's bedroom door stood open, and Mark could see the small mound of his son under the sheet on his bed.

Next he checked Dionne's room. To his relief, her bed was empty and unrumpled. At least she hadn't had second thoughts about this new phase in their relationship and gone back to her own bed.

Yearning to hold her again, to taste her sweet lips and feel her against him, if only for a moment, he looked for her in the kitchen, the living room and the bathroom. Each time he left an empty room, his uneasiness grew.

Finally, he caught sight of her through the patio door. She stood on the far edge of the lawn, her face tilted to catch the rising sun, her hair the color of ripe wheat where the sun touched it. She was heartbreakingly beautiful.

Smiling, he slipped outside and watched her for a moment. The need he'd thought they'd satisfied last night twisted through him again, stronger than ever now that he knew the absolute joy of making love to her.

More than anything, he wanted to take her back

to bed so they could spend the rest of the morning discovering each other all over again. But Jared would be up soon. And Royal and Oscar would be waiting for him. Clients needed him. He couldn't stay.

More irritated than he'd ever been with the demands of his job, he crossed the lawn and came to a stop behind her. If she heard him approaching she gave no sign, but kept her face turned toward the sky.

He wrapped his arms loosely around her waist and pressed a kiss to the back of her neck. "Good morning."

She must have heard him because she didn't seem surprised by his touch. Neither did she turn toward him. "Good morning."

"How long have you been up?"

"Only a few minutes."

He wanted her to snuggle against him, to turn and kiss him, to wrap her arms around his neck and hold him close. But she did none of those things. He moved his hands to her shoulders and turned her around. Her eyes were shuttered, as if she had something to hide from him, and his mood took a nosedive.

"What's wrong?" he asked gently.

Her gaze lifted to his almost reluctantly. "I've been thinking about last night."

"Not having second thoughts about what we did, are you?" he said lightly. A joke. And he longed for a denial.

Instead, she met his gaze slowly. "Are you?"

"No. Not at all." He brushed a tentative kiss to her lips, but she didn't respond as she had last night.

He struggled to keep his tone light in spite of the heaviness that settled around his heart. "So, what's wrong? Did I hog the blankets? Keep you awake with my snoring?"

She laughed softly. "No. And no. You're an absolute gentleman in bed." Her cheeks reddened and she lowered her gaze again. "In all ways."

That helped, but he could still sense her withdrawal. "Then what is it? You seem distant this morning." When she didn't respond immediately, he said, "We didn't do anything wrong, you know. We *are* married."

"Married, yes." She glanced at him, and her eyes clouded with some emotion Mark couldn't name. "But what is our relationship, really?"

"I think it's better than ever," he said. "I'd much rather take you to bed than argue with you."

She stepped away from him and folded her arms across her chest. "Is it really better? Or have we made it more complicated?"

The question stunned him. "Complicated? How?"

"Everything's changed now. There's more at stake. There's a greater risk." She studied his face for a moment, searching for something, sighing when she didn't find it. "And yet nothing's changed, has it?"

A strange sort of dread began to churn in his stomach. What was she asking? What did she want him to say? If he knew, he'd say it in a heartbeat. "Like what?"

"We don't love each other, Mark."

Until that moment, he hadn't realized how much he wanted to believe she felt differently about him— about them. And realizing that she didn't, hit him like a fist in the gut. "What we have is a good start," he argued. "It might turn into love in time."

She shook her head and looked away, speaking so quietly he could hardly hear her. "That's not how you start a relationship. Not if you want it to last. You don't make love first and then try to fall in love afterward."

He shivered, more from the chill between them than the morning breeze. "Is that what you think we did?"

"Isn't it?" When he didn't answer, she prodded. "Do you love me, Mark?"

One part of him believed he did love her, but what was love, really? He'd loved Marianne, but what he felt for her now was anything *but* love. She'd claimed to love him, yet she'd betrayed him. Jerry had loved Alice, but he'd hurt her and destroyed their marriage. Mark said none of this to Dionne. Instead, he spoke softly. "I thought we'd agreed to this marriage because neither of us had any delusions about love. But I care about you, Dionne. A great deal."

"I see." She turned away and rubbed her arms. "I guess that tells me everything I need to know."

The knot in Mark's stomach grew. "You could have stopped me at any time last night. You could have pulled away and locked yourself in your own room. But if memory serves, you were pretty damned willing."

"I was. I won't deny it."

"Are you saying *you* love *me?*"

She hesitated long enough to make him wonder. Long enough to make his pulse slow and his fingers grow numb.

"I don't know," she said after a long pause. "But

I do know that just because we have a piece of paper that says it's legal for us to make love, that doesn't make it morally right if our hearts aren't involved. And it wouldn't be fair to Jared to put our relationship at such risk.''

Mark clenched his jaw and worked hard not to let her see his disappointment. ''So, you're saying you don't want what happened last night to happen again?'' He could hear the defensive coolness in his voice, but he made no effort to change it.

Something flashed across her face too quickly for him to identify. ''It *can't* happen again. Wonderful as it was—and it was great—I don't want a relationship with you that's only physical.''

He laughed bitterly to hide the pain. ''Well, you don't have to worry about it. I'll control myself in the future.''

Without giving her a chance to make things worse, he pivoted and strode across the lawn toward the house. She was right about one thing—it would have been much easier to take the rejection if they hadn't shared last night.

FOR TWO DAYS, Mark tried to keep his anger and disappointment under control. He left in the mornings before Dionne came downstairs and he didn't come home again until he knew she'd be in bed. That meant he also missed seeing Jared, but he didn't trust himself to be near Dionne and not tell her everything that was boiling inside him. He couldn't go on this way for long. He'd fought to have Jared with him, and he wasn't going to let this come between them. He and Dionne had to work through this.

Mark was torn between the rational argument that

people had sex all the time without love, and the painful knowledge that that's exactly what ruined so many relationships. The bottom line was, he had only himself to blame. In one thoughtless, hormone-driven moment, he'd ruined everything.

He ran his hand across his chin and glanced at Anna, who stood in front of his desk holding a stack of legal books he'd asked her to find an hour earlier. Normally, he'd have gone to the firm's library himself, but he'd snapped unnecessarily at one of the interns the previous afternoon and he'd decided not to risk a repeat performance today.

He tried to shake off his frustration and focus instead on his job. Logic. Law. Rules. Regulations. At least they made sense to him. "So, did you find them all?" he asked.

"No, unfortunately." Anna lowered the heavy books to his desk along with the list he'd given her. "But I found most of the cases you wanted."

He could feel the scowl forming and tried to wipe it away. Anna shouldn't have to pay for his mistake. "Just tell me you've got Fed Second 367."

Anna shook her head and flashed an apologetic smile. "Don't get mad, but it wasn't in the library."

That figured. His bad luck was holding. "Can you find out who has it?"

"I can E-mail everyone, but we still may not find it in time. Lots of people are out of the office."

"Great." The word came out unnecessarily harsh. Even he knew that.

Anna matched his scowl. "You want to tell me what's wrong with you?"

That was the last thing he wanted to do. "Nothing's wrong."

"Right. You're always this pleasant."

"I'm fine. I just have a lot of work to do."

"We all do," Anna reminded him and swept an arm toward her desk. "I'm not exactly partying out there. This new case has put us all in a bind."

The reminder brought him back down to earth with a jolt. He sent her an apologetic smile. "I know you're busy. I didn't mean to imply that you weren't."

"Good." Anna looked slightly mollified. "Then tell me what's really bugging you."

He looked away from her and opened one of the books. "Nothing important."

As usual, Anna wouldn't take no for an answer. "Money trouble?"

Mark shook his head.

"Has Royal done something?"

"No."

"Shoes too tight?"

He flicked a smile at her. "No."

"Then it must be something to do with your new bride."

Mark's smile faded. "I said I don't want to talk about it."

Anna sat in the chair facing his. "I heard you, but *I* don't want to put up with this foul mood you've been in for the past two days."

"If you go back to your desk," he pointed out, "you won't have to."

"That's not true." Anna made herself even more comfortable and crossed her legs. "You're so cranky, it's seeping out from under the door. I can't escape."

He glanced at her, caught her smile, and relented

a little. "I appreciate your concern, but it's personal."

That didn't faze her. "It's not as if we've never talked about anything personal before. I thought we were friends."

"We are." He closed the book slowly. "Of course we are."

"Then tell me what's wrong."

He sighed heavily, ran a hand along the back of his neck, and leaned back in his chair. "I did something stupid, okay? And I'm not exactly proud of it. So, if you don't mind…"

"*You* did something *stupid?*" Anna's eyebrows rose. "I find that hard to believe."

He let out a thin laugh. "Okay, so it's not such a rare occurrence."

"You'll feel better if you talk about it."

"I don't think so."

He reached for the book again, but she leaned across the desk and put a hand over his to stop him. "All kidding aside, Mark, I hate to see you like this. You know that whatever you tell me won't go out of this room."

"I know."

Her lips twitched, a sure sign that she was about to wallop him with one of her one-liners. "I'll just bring everyone in here when I tell them."

The joke broke through the last thin wall of his reserve. He pulled his hand away, stood, and paced to the window. "I think I've ruined everything."

"With Dionne?"

"Yes."

"How?"

He turned to face her, feeling as sheepish as a

twelve-year-old who'd been caught necking on the school playground. "I made love to her."

Disbelief and amusement darted across Anna's face. "Excuse me?"

"I said, I made love to her."

"How did that ruin everything? She's your wife, isn't she?"

"You don't understand." He shoved his hands into his pockets and turned back toward the window. "We got married so that we could share Jared. I promised I wouldn't take advantage of her. But when I got home the other night..." He shuddered just thinking about it. But the shudder wasn't entirely self-loathing.

"Did she mind?"

"Yes. Of course she minded."

"Of course?" Anna stood and came behind him. "You didn't force her, did you?"

"No." He shook his head quickly. "I wouldn't do that."

"You had me worried for a minute. So, explain, please. You made love to her, and she minded."

"Not at the time," he said with a bitter smile. "But she sure as hell minded the next morning."

"What happened? Did you shout out another woman's name or something?"

"Of course not. She just doesn't want it to happen again."

Anna scowled. "Why not? Has it escaped her notice that you're a fairly good-looking guy?"

"It's not about that," he said sharply, then tempered his voice again. "It's about trust. It's about breaking a promise—an *important* promise."

"Okay." Anna lifted a hand as if she intended to

put it on his shoulder, then dropped it to her side. "I understand that. But if she didn't resist, if she didn't tell you no, if she didn't belt you in the nose and tell you to stop—"

"She didn't."

"Did she…" Anna blushed slightly. "Did she respond?"

"At the time." He looked down at the windowsill.

Anna folded her arms and stood beside him. "Maybe the important question is why you made love to her in the first place."

"Because." He glanced up at her quickly. "Because she was just so damned beautiful lying there, and because she was wearing a thin cotton nightgown, and because—" He broke off, uncertain what else to say.

"So, did you make love to *her?* Or did you just have sex with a beautiful woman?"

"Both."

Anna sighed with impatience. "If you'd walked in and found some other beautiful woman there, would you have come on to her?" She moved a step closer and held his gaze. "Were you just horny, or was it Dionne?"

"It wasn't just physical."

"Do you love her?"

He frowned at her. "That's what she asked, but I don't know."

Anna smiled knowingly. "Then I suggest you figure that out. And when you do, make sure she's the first person you tell."

She pivoted and crossed to the door. And with one last, silent glance, she stepped through and pulled the door shut behind her, leaving him alone and utterly confused.

CHAPTER THIRTEEN

EXCITED AND APPREHENSIVE at the same time, Dionne clutched her purse and followed a group of students into the crowded room being used for registration. The sheer volume of students—all at least ten years younger than she was—left her feeling slightly dazed.

Taking a deep breath, she squared her shoulders and tried to orient herself. She'd made the decision to come back to school, and she'd do her best to succeed. Looking around for the first instructor she wanted to see, she finally settled on a tall, good-looking man about her own age near a long table. He didn't look like an instructor. No suit. No tie. Just Dockers and a pale blue shirt. But several students flanked him, and he had the confident air of someone in charge.

She took her place in line and checked the cell phone in her purse once more to make sure the baby-sitter Patsy had recommended could reach her in an emergency. Within minutes, a young girl of about twenty joined her in line and let out a sigh. "Have they started the waiting list yet or is there still room to get into this course?"

"Waiting list?" Dionne hadn't anticipated that. "Does that happen often?"

"It happens a lot, especially with Eskelson's

classes.'' The girl shifted her purse to her other shoulder. "You look nervous. Are you new here?"

"Very," Dionne admitted with a smile. "I haven't had to study anything for years. I'm afraid I'm out of the habit."

"Well, you picked the wrong class to start with," the girl told her. "Eskelson's famous for being tough even in a first-level course like Introductory Psych."

Dionne could have gone all day without hearing that. "Is that Eskelson up there in the blue shirt?"

"That's him." The girl folded a piece of gum and wedged it into her mouth. "One of my roommates, Trish, took this course from him spring semester. She said it was really hard." The girl dug something else from the depths of her backpack. "I think it's because of the amount of homework he assigns."

"Great."

The girl laughed, but she sobered again immediately. "If I could have gotten this credit any other way, I would have done it. But this is the only time it's offered, and if I don't get it this semester, I can't take Applied Psych next semester." She waved a pair of glasses in the space between them as she talked. "It'll throw my whole schedule off and I'll end up having to wait a couple of semesters to graduate." She started to put on the glasses, then smiled at Dionne again. "I'm Heidi, by the way."

"It's nice to meet you. I'm Dionne." She stole another glance at Mr. Eskelson. "What kind of homework are you talking about?"

"Trish said she had to read fifty pages a night just to keep up. *And* he doesn't go over the reading material in class."

Fifty pages? Dionne's heart thudded to the floor

and landed between her feet. How would she find time to read fifty pages a night? The last time she'd tried to read a novel, she'd fallen asleep long before the end of the first chapter.

"And Trish says there's a lot of writing," Heidi added with a frown. "Like, a paper due every other week or so."

Dionne took a steadying breath and tried to force away the sudden feelings of inadequacy. She'd find a way. If she ever had to support Jared on her own again, she wanted to do it right.

Thinking about Jared reminded her of Mark, and the familiar ache in her heart worsened. She hadn't expected Mark to be happy about her decision not to continue the physical part of their relationship, but she hadn't expected him to pull away so completely.

Very often, when she let herself dwell on it, she found herself remembering her father. He'd turned to another woman when a second difficult pregnancy for her mother interfered with his sex life. Mark's mistress might be his career but the effect was the same.

He'd kept his word and left a blank check for tuition and another for books on the dining-room table one morning. But what did his money matter? What she wanted was his heart.

Today wasn't the time to think about that, she reminded herself.

She lifted her chin and asked Heidi, "Is there anything else I should know?"

The young woman thought for a moment, then shook her head. "I don't think so. Don't worry. You'll be fine as long as you keep up—that's what Trish says, anyway."

Sighing softly, Dionne looked around at the others in the room. They were all so young and full of energy, they looked as if they could conquer the world. Dionne doubted she had the stamina to conquer the piles of laundry waiting for her at home.

When she realized that the line had inched forward, she moved with it. She could do this. She'd just have to make a few adjustments, that's all.

Mark or no Mark, she could do this. No more self-pity. No more self-doubt. She had the chance to fulfill her dream, and that's exactly what she was going to do…come hell or high water.

OUT OF HABIT, Dionne checked for oncoming traffic before pushing Jared's stroller into the deserted intersection of Front and Sycamore Streets. She had plenty to do at home, but she'd deserted it all to take a walk. She needed the exercise and she wanted to play with Jared. But she'd also needed to get out of the house, away from her never-ending homework, and away from the nagging discontent she felt whenever she thought of Mark.

She wasn't sure which of them was avoiding the other, but one by one the days ticked past and nothing seemed to be getting better. For three days he'd left early in the morning and come home late at night—when he came home at all.

When they did see each other—always briefly in passing—his eyes were unreadable. His muttered excuses about a big trial that was demanding all his time didn't make her feel any better.

She could forgive him for not loving her. That had never been part of their bargain. But she couldn't forgive the confusion she saw in her son's eyes when

Jared asked for his daddy at breakfast and dinner, or when Mark wasn't there to tuck the little boy in at the end of the day.

Jared twisted in the stroller to look at her. "Jared wants juice, Mommy."

She smiled down at him and bent to smooth a lock of hair from his forehead. "I'm thirsty, too, sweetheart. Let's see if we can find something to drink, shall we?"

Jared nodded solemnly, twisted back in his seat, and reached toward one of the concrete planters on the edge of the sidewalk. The summer flowers had been removed and the planters stood stark and empty, but bunting draped the fronts of the buildings and reminded her that the autumn festival was that night.

The town still made her think of the movies she'd watched as a young girl. The ones where parents loved each other and children didn't have to question their parents' devotion to one another.

Such a fantasy. Such a foolish dream.

And such a foolish dreamer.

Biting back a self-mocking laugh, she stopped in front of a narrow building with a carved wooden sign and peered in through a picture window at a cluster of old-fashioned tables and a long, gleaming counter.

"Well look at this," she said to Jared. "It's called Mabel's. Shall we go inside?"

Jared started to climb from the stroller, but the safety strap held him in place.

"Hold on a minute. Mommy'll get you out." She hunkered down to undo the belt and glanced up when a shadow fell over the sidewalk and a friendly voice said, "Hi, there. Out for a walk?"

It took her only a second to recognize Patsy. "We're exploring the town."

"You picked a good day for it." Patsy glanced up at the sun overhead, then at the shaded doorway. "Are you going inside?"

"Yes, for a few minutes."

"Then I'll join you...if you don't mind."

"I'd enjoy the company," Dionne said, realizing she sounded almost desperate for a friendly face. Determined to put Mark out of her mind, she chose a table near the front window and situated Jared away from the aisle so he'd have to get past her if he wanted to take off exploring on his own.

While they placed their orders, she dug the tiny trucks and cars she always carried from her purse and gave them to Jared, then turned back to Patsy. "You're not working today?"

"I have the day off to get ready for the festival. You're still planning to come, aren't you? Jared's obviously healthy again."

Much as Dionne wanted to go, she didn't want to face all her new neighbors without Mark. She didn't want to face them *with* him, either, she realized. She swallowed hard and said, "I don't think we can make it."

"Oh, but you have to come," Patsy insisted. "I've already told everyone you'll be there, and they're all looking forward to meeting you."

"I'd like to meet them, too," Dionne assured her. "But Mark's been putting in so many extra hours at work, he doesn't get home until late."

"Then come by yourself."

Dionne waited while their waitress settled their

drinks on the table, then helped Jared onto his booster seat. "Another time, maybe. Next year."

Patsy's dark eyes filled with concern. "But I hate to think of you staying home alone tonight."

"I don't mind. I have plenty to do."

"Is everything all right? You sound kind of sad."

The temptation to confide in her was almost overwhelming, but Dionne didn't give in to it. She didn't know Patsy well enough to share confidences. "Everything's fine. I'm still adjusting to the move, to living in a new house and strange town, *and* to going back to school."

"Not to mention having a new husband," Patsy interjected.

"And that." Dionne looked away and let her gaze travel down the street, hoping to keep Patsy from seeing the truth in her eyes. "Actually, I've still got a few boxes from the move left to unpack."

"Do you want some help?"

Dionne looked back at her quickly. While the offer sounded tempting, she couldn't risk Patsy finding out that she and Mark didn't sleep in the same room. Nor did she want Mark to come home while Patsy was there. Patsy would immediately sense the strain between them. "No, thanks. I can manage. It's just a matter of making myself do it."

"I'd be glad to help. I love organizing things," Patsy said with an easy, infectious laugh that helped to lift Dionne's spirits. "Especially when they're other people's things."

"What I'd really like," Dionne said, trying to change the subject, "is to find out more about the town. Tell me what I should see."

Patsy shrugged. "There isn't much *to* see, really. It's a perfectly ordinary town."

"You only say that because you're used to it. There's nothing ordinary about it. It's fascinating."

Patsy looked out the window, as if seeing the town for the first time. "Do you really think so?"

"I really do. It's very different from what I'm used to. Even the countryside is different." She picked up a stray car for Jared. "I'm used to a place where trees are an import and water might as well be on the endangered species list."

Patsy laughed again. "I guess what we find fascinating is relative, isn't it? I've never been out west, and I'd love to go. The pictures I see are so raw and wild, and this all seems rather boring by comparison." She sighed and reached across the table to touch Jared's cheek. "So is my life when I get right down to it. I envy you."

"Me?" Dionne's hand froze just as she reached for a truck that teetered near the edge of the table. "Why?"

"Why not?" Patsy waved a hand toward her as if to take in everything. "You're having a grand adventure and you're living that thrill of new love. George and I have spent our entire lives within fifty miles of Longs Mill, and we've been married so long, we've lost the magic."

Dionne handed the truck back to Jared. "There's something to be said for being together a long time. You become comfortable with the other person, you know how they think, and what they like and dislike."

"True." Patsy frowned thoughtfully. "But it was so exciting to *discover* all that about George when we first got together. And to watch our love grow as we did.'' She toyed with her napkin for a moment. ''I miss it, but I didn't realize how much until you came to town.''

Just as Dionne missed being at ease, the way she'd been with Brent. ''How long have you been married?''

''Ten years.''

''That's a long time.''

''It's forever.''

As long as Dionne would have been married to Brent if he'd lived. She wondered if they'd have eventually reached the same point in their marriage, if she'd have been bored and yearning for adventure. But that was one question that would never be answered.

Unexpectedly, Mark's image took the place of Brent's, and she had the uncomfortable notion that life with him would never be boring. He had too much electricity and the emotions she felt around him were too sharp-edged to ever become dulled.

Slowly, she became aware of Patsy watching her. She fidgeted with her napkin, and laughed softly. ''Sorry. I was thinking about something else for a moment.''

''You don't have to apologize to me. I just can't wait to meet the man who puts that look in your eyes.'' Patsy smiled mischievously. ''In fact, I'm looking forward to introducing him to George. Maybe some of it will rub off.''

Dionne laughed. ''Maybe.'' But the yearning she saw in Patsy's eyes made her wonder if she'd been overlooking the positive things about her relationship with Mark.

She'd loved Brent the first time they made love, but not fully and completely. And she hadn't been absolutely certain that he loved her. That kind of love took time to grow. So why hadn't she been willing to give Mark a chance? Was she afraid he'd leave one day like her father had? Or was she afraid of living through another horrible loss like Brent's death? Had she been holding Mark at arm's length to protect herself?

With brutal honesty, she admitted the answer was yes. She also had to admit she'd failed miserably. Pushing Mark away, and convincing herself it was all *his* fault, hadn't protected her at all. With him around or without him, she still felt everything. And if she lost this time, the loss would be of her own making.

"HERE COME the peas. See?" While Dionne's dinner cooled on her plate, she swooped the spoonful of vegetables in front of Jared, hoping to tease him into eating.

He clamped his mouth shut and pulled away. "No," he said through tightened lips.

"Peas are yummy," Dionne argued gently. "Mommy loves peas, Jared. Try some."

"No." Jared folded his arms and scowled at her.

A miniature Mark, she thought, and her heart gave one of its familiar skips. She didn't know when she'd see him next. Nor did she know what she'd say when she did. She only knew she had to try to explain what she'd been afraid of and then pray that he'd understand.

She urged the spoon at Jared again. "Come on, sweetheart. For Mommy?"

"No. Jared want ice cream."

"You can have ice cream when you've finished your peas."

Jared's scowl deepened and wariness flashed in his dark eyes. But before he could argue again, the sound of a car in the driveway had him squirming frantically to get out of his high chair and knocking the spoon from her hand. "Daddy."

Dionne glanced at the clock. It seemed early for Mark, but she hoped Jared was right.

She didn't have to wonder long. Her body gave her the answer almost before she heard his key turning the lock. Her heart began to pound, she couldn't draw a breath, and her knees felt wobbly. But she tried to look normal when she lifted Jared from his chair. "You're right, sweetie. Let's go say hello."

Jared didn't have to be told twice. The instant she set him on the floor, he took off at a dead run. Dionne followed more slowly, reaching the middle of the living room just as Mark opened the door.

When he saw them, he froze for a moment, and all Dionne's insecurities come rushing back. In the next breath, he dropped his briefcase and suit jacket and scooped Jared from the floor.

"Hey there, big boy." Mark pulled back, noticed the bib, and added, "I'm late for dinner again, aren't I?" He turned his gaze toward Dionne slowly, hesitantly. "Am I too late?"

Dionne shook her head. "Not at all. We just started."

"Do you mind if I join you?"

"Of course not." She stopped, then forced herself to add, "We've missed having you around."

He met her gaze over the top of Jared's head. "I've missed *being* around."

Time slowed, then stopped altogether while he held her gaze. She could almost hear her pulse as her heart tapped out a staccato rhythm.

Mark kissed Jared's cheek, then lowered him to the floor and took his hand, all without taking his eyes from hers. "We need to talk about the other night."

"All right." She forced away the dread that had replaced the anticipation.

"I acted like a jerk. I promised I wouldn't take advantage of you, but that's exactly what I did. I know you're angry with me and you have every right to be, but I've been miserable this week. I'd like to put it behind us so I can come home again."

"You can come home whenever you want," she said quietly. "I never asked you not to."

"I know, but I was afraid to look in your eyes and see how much you hated me."

"I wasn't angry with you."

"You sure avoided me as if you were."

"Well, yes. But only because you made it pretty clear nothing had changed for you."

"Are you kidding?" He looked shocked. "*Everything* changed for me that night." He reached a tentative hand toward her and touched her cheek, sending flames to every extremity. "I've done a lot of thinking since then."

"So have I."

"Maybe what we have isn't exactly what you had with Brent—"

She touched her fingertips to his lips to stop him.

"This isn't about Brent," she said softly. "This is about us."

"But it is about him," Mark insisted. "I know I can't give you the kind of love you had with him, but I do love you, in my own clumsy way."

Tears filled her eyes and her heart threatened to jump out of her chest. "I don't want the kind of love I had with him," she said honestly. "I want something new. I want what *you* can give me."

His eyes turned a soft golden brown. "Do you think you can learn to love me?"

She laughed, nearly choking on her tears. "I already do."

He kissed her briefly, gently, but she knew his entire heart was in it. Before he could deepen the kiss or she could respond, Jared tugged on his hand. Mark pulled away, smiling. "I guess we can stop avoiding each other then, can't we?"

"I guess we can. But I wasn't the only one who missed you this week, Mark. It's been hard on Jared, too."

His gaze faltered. "I'm sorry."

"Just promise me that whatever happens between us, you won't let it affect your relationship with him."

"I won't. He'll always be my son. Just as I hope you'll always be my wife."

"That's what I want, too," she told him gently.

He responded to another impatient tug from Jared by taking a couple of unsteady steps toward the kitchen. "What's going on in town tonight? Everyone seems to be going somewhere."

"It's the autumn festival." Dionne reached for

Jared, to put him back in his high chair. "It's a big deal around here, I guess."

"Why aren't you there?"

"Because I don't really know anyone, and I didn't want to show up alone and have to answer a bunch of questions."

He sent her a rueful smile. "Because your husband's a jerk and a coward who won't come home before you're in bed?"

"Not exactly. I'm the one who created this rift between us."

He shook his head quickly. "Wrong. But we can work all that out later when Jared's not listening. The question of the moment is, would you like to go?"

She turned to face him. "I would. But what about you? Aren't you tired? You haven't had much sleep all week."

He waved away the question. "Sleep? Who needs sleep? I'm in such a good mood right now, I could go another three or four hours without it." He met her gaze again. "Seriously, if you'd like to go, let's do it…unless you're too tired after being in class all day."

His willingness to please her and his concern touched her deeply. "I'm not tired, and I think it would be fun. I'd like to get to know the people in town. I've only met a few of them."

"Then you're a few up on me." He loosened his tie, then stopped and made a face. "Is it casual, or do I have to stay dressed?"

"Patsy told me it's casual."

"Great. I'll change after dinner."

"Maybe I should change, too," she said with a glance at her own faded jeans and T-shirt.

His eyes traveled slowly, appreciatively, over her. "You look great just the way you are."

Everything felt different and wonderful between them. "Thank you," she said with an embarrassed smile, "but I could look better."

His gaze settled on her again, took her in almost hungrily and left her tingling with anticipation. "Maybe," he drawled, "but you'll have to prove it to me before I'll believe it."

Amazed at how right this new mood between them felt, she grinned. "Okay, I will."

She fixed Mark a plate and gave it to him. "I should warn you," she said as put the plate in front of him, "everyone in town knows we're newly-weds."

"Then I say we give them what they're waiting for." He trailed a finger down her cheek and used it to tilt her chin. He kissed her thoroughly and left her nearly breathless. "What do you say we show them a pair of newlyweds so in love they can't see straight?"

She grinned, feeling mischievous and excited, desirable and wanted all at once.

He kissed her again, quickly. "Are you ready?"

"Yes." For that and a whole lot more.

CHAPTER FOURTEEN

THE EVENING WAS PERFECT. Outdoor lanterns cast a magical glow over everything, white-clothed tables holding refreshments lined one end of the square, music from an unseen stereo wafted through the crowd and blended with the laughter and conversation.

Patsy had found them immediately, guiding them from one knot of people to another, introducing them to everyone in town. A few faces looked familiar— Mrs. Wiggs from the post office, Arlen Harris from the small village grocery store, a tall blond man with a rugged face Dionne had seen outside the hardware store, who turned out to be Patsy's husband, George.

To Dionne's delight, Mark and George hit it off immediately, and the Wagner children took to Jared as if he'd always been one of them. Visions of family outings and shared barbecues filled her head and left her floating. And the food— It was everything Patsy had promised and more. Dionne gathered promises of shared recipes with every dish she tasted.

"I forgot to tell you," Patsy said as the music started and people began to gather around the temporary dance floor in the center of the square. "You two are supposed to lead off the dancing."

"We're what?" Dionne glanced up at Mark, but he didn't look at all surprised. She'd been anticipating a dance with him, but not with the whole town watching.

"The dancing," Patsy said, taking Jared from her. "The newest and oldest couples always lead off. That'll be Hattie and Arlen Harris—they've been married sixty-two years last May—and the two of you since you're the newlyweds."

The background music stopped for a moment, then began again, louder now. Dionne recognized the tune. A waltz, of course. The most romantic dance in the world.

"Well, I'm sure not going to flout tradition," Mark said, holding out his hand. "Shall we?"

Dionne put her hand in his, relishing the thrill of his touch. He led her onto the dance floor, and though she was vaguely aware of everyone's eyes following them, she no longer cared. She would have danced on hot coals at that moment, as long as she could do it in Mark's arms.

A few feet away, an elderly couple moved into the spotlight and began to dance. Arlen held his wife as if she were a new bride, smiling into her eyes with such love and devotion, Dionne's heart stilled for a moment.

Mark pulled her close, wrapping an arm around her waist and holding her hand as if they'd done this a thousand times before. Dionne closed her eyes and submerged herself in the nearness of him. He tightened his arm to hold her more securely and whirled her in time to the music, for all the world to see. The soft gleam of the lanterns and the dim hum of conversation faded and there was nothing else in her world but Mark. Mark and the music.

He nestled his cheek against the top of her head. "You dance divinely, Mrs. Taylor."

She smiled up into his eyes. "So do you, Mr. Taylor."

"Every man in this place is seething with jealousy. They're wishing they could hold you like this."

She laughed, as he'd intended her to. "It's the women who are jealous."

His delighted smile warmed her clear through. "Poor things. We could really make them suffer."

"How?"

"Like this." Without warning, he dipped her so low she couldn't hold back the tiny scream that escaped her lips. While she lay back, vulnerable and completely dependent upon him to hold her, he waggled his eyebrows comically. "I think we got 'em."

Dionne glanced at the people watching, at the staid, respectable couples standing on the sidelines, the eager young ones, and at Patsy and George a few feet away. Someone laughed aloud, and other couples moved onto the floor with them.

Mark pulled her upright and cradled her against him. "They're *all* jealous."

Dionne laughed again and pushed playfully at his chest. "I thought you were going to drop me."

"Never." He tightened his arm on her waist again, but the teasing light left his eyes. "You can trust me, Dionne."

It was impossible to keep grinning at him when he looked so earnest. "I believe you."

"Do you? I'm glad." The light in his eyes returned, and he whirled her until she lost her breath.

Somehow, she managed to match his footwork and keep up with him. No one but Cicely knew how many hours she'd spent watching old musicals and fantasizing about dancing this way. The only thing missing was a swirling ball gown and heels. But even jeans and tennis shoes couldn't spoil the mood.

Mark slowed, then stopped completely. His chest heaved as he panted slightly, his eyes narrowed with concern. "What's wrong?"

"I was just trying to remember if I've ever had a moment that felt so absolutely perfect before."

The worry left his eyes and a twinkle replaced it. "You haven't."

She scowled at him playfully. "Well, now, how would you know?"

"*I've* never had one," he said, running a fingertip along her cheek and sending delicious shivers of anticipation through her. "So it wouldn't be fair if you had."

He let his gaze travel from her eyes to her lips and linger there. She waited, breathless, knowing he was going to kiss her again, and wanting it with every fiber of her being.

"Mommy? Daddy?" Jared worked his way between them and held up his arms.

Mark laughed, released her for a moment, and settled Jared between them.

"Jared, sweetheart—" Patsy tried to intervene. "Come with me, okay?"

"He's fine," Dionne assured her. "He belongs right here."

"You two were incredible," Patsy said. "Where did you learn to dance like that?"

Mark put an arm around Dionne's waist and they turned together to face Patsy and George. Grinning, she said the first words that came to mind. "From the movies."

"Believe it or not," Mark added, "this is the first time we've ever danced together."

"You're kidding," Patsy argued. "You must have taken lessons."

George let out a deep groan. "Please don't say yes, or she'll have me signed up for the damned things before the end of the week."

"Don't worry," Mark said with a laugh and shared a grin with Dionne. "It's just chemistry."

"And magic," Dionne added.

"Yes." Mark met her gaze again and held it. "And magic."

THE MOOD STAYED with them as they walked home. A million stars shone in the clear night sky, but a soft breeze had dropped the temperature enough to make Dionne wish she had a jacket in addition to her sweater. One by one, other couples and families turned up sidewalks toward their homes and left Dionne feeling as if she, Mark and Jared were the only people on earth.

Mark carried a sleeping Jared high against one shoulder, leaving her free to touch trees, fences, anything and everything that invited contact. And, it seemed, everything did.

She stopped to inhale the fragrance of the night air and turned back to find Mark watching her with an expression that made her heart skip a beat.

He put his free hand on the small of her back. "Did you have a good time tonight?"

"I had a wonderful time," she admitted. "What about you?"

"Perfect." His hand brushed her back lazily, stirring the embers of the passion that had ignited when he'd held her in his arms to dance.

"I've only seen parties like that in the movies," she said.

"They're pretty common fare in small towns. But it wasn't just the party that I enjoyed." He looked deep into her eyes again, the rest of his message as clear as if he'd spoken aloud.

"It wasn't just the party for me, either," she admitted.

They walked on in silence for a moment before Mark spoke again. "We're going to be okay, aren't we? This is going to work."

"Yes." She smiled at him. "I think it is."

He stopped walking and stepped in front of her. "Thank you."

"For what?"

"For agreeing to marry me."

"Thank you for asking."

He laughed softly, a delighted laugh that started deep inside his chest and rolled outward to wrap itself around her. A second later, his laughter stopped and he dipped his head to kiss her.

She relaxed, leaned into the kiss, breathing him in. When his tongue brushed her lips, she opened her mouth and invited him in. The kiss grew more demanding, as if neither of them could get enough, until Jared stirred fitfully.

They broke apart guiltily, and Mark took her hand again. "I guess we should get this guy home to bed."

Dionne laced her fingers with his and leaned her head on his shoulder, wondering if they'd pick up where they'd left off when they got home.

Correction, she thought with a silent laugh. She *hoped* they'd pick up where they left off. She knew exactly where they were headed, and she wanted to race toward their inevitable destination.

MARK CAUGHT HIMSELF whistling as he strolled down the corridor toward his office. And why not? Life was damned good at the moment. Perfect, in fact. He was in love with the most remarkable woman in the world. And even better, she was in love with him.

Making love to her all weekend had made him feel powerful. As if there was nothing that could stop him and no one who would dare get in his way. As if he alone was responsible for the brilliant autumn sunshine outside and the changing leaves that lined the highway of his morning commute.

Still whistling, he stopped in front of Anna's empty desk and checked his box for messages, then turned toward his office. But when he saw her standing in the doorway wearing a knowing grin, he checked his step and let his song die away.

"You're certainly in a good mood today," she teased. "I wonder why."

"Nice weather," he said with an innocent shrug.

"Yes. Very." She stepped aside to let him enter and followed him inside. "It must have been warm at your house this weekend."

"Like a tropical island." He took off his suit jacket and set his briefcase on the desk. "And I have you to thank."

"Not having to put up with your bad moods is thanks enough." She rested her hands on the back of a chair. "I hate to burst your bubble, but Royal said to send you to his office as soon as you got in."

"Fine."

"He said he's got another new case for you."

"Great."

"On top of all the others? Aren't you even going to get upset?"

Mark laughed and put on his suit jacket again. "Nope. Nothing could spoil my mood today, not even Royal."

He left her sitting in his office and whistled all the way to Royal's huge corner office. He listened without batting an eye to the details of the case Royal wanted to dump in his lap. He even smiled all the way through his first court case of the morning and stopped at the florist shop on the corner to order roses for Dionne and buy a small bouquet to thank Anna.

But when he settled the flowers amidst the files, documents and other clutter on Anna's desk and caught the look in her eyes, his smile faded. "What's wrong?"

She stood and motioned toward his door. "I'll tell you in your office."

Praying that nothing had happened to Dionne or Jared, he followed her inside and closed the door. "What is it?"

"Marianne called while you were in court."

Mark tried not to acknowledge the apprehension that curled in his stomach. "Marianne who?"

"Your ex-girlfriend. Jared's mother."

"What the hell did she want?"

"She wouldn't tell me," Anna said with a bitter smile. "And believe me, I tried to find out. She just said to have you call her."

He took the message slip she offered with Marianne's name and number scrawled across it, barely resisting the urge to crumple it into a ball and toss it away. Whatever she wanted, it couldn't be good.

Anna obviously shared his opinion. "Be careful. She's up to something."

Nodding grimly, he crossed to his desk and yanked the receiver from the hook. Anna watched him in silence, then let herself out and shut the door behind her with a soft click.

He punched in the long-distance number, taking out his nervousness on the dial pad, clenching his jaw so tightly it hurt. When she answered, he barely kept his fear under control. "What do you want?"

"Mark?"

"Who else?"

"Thank you for calling me back."

"What do you want, Marianne?"

"I've been doing a lot of thinking in the past couple of months."

"If you're calling to say you want Jared back, you can go straight to hell."

"Is that what you think?"

"What else should I think?"

She must have realized that he was in no mood to chat because her voice changed subtly. "All right. I'll get to the point." She took a deep breath, as if she needed courage for what came next. "I have to come back to Boston later this week, and I'd like to see you."

"We have no reason to see each other."

"I think we do. Seeing you again during the summer made me realize that I need to see the baby again, too."

It was his worst nightmare and Dionne's biggest fear come true. "Over my dead body."

Marianne sighed again. "You really do hate me, don't you?"

"Hate is a weak word for what I'm feeling right now."

"For what it's worth, I'm sorry for what happened between us."

"I don't give a damn about what happened between us," he assured her. "It's what you're trying to do now that matters."

"I'm not trying to do anything. I'd just like to see you and the baby."

"Forget it."

She took her time before she responded to that. "Obviously, you're upset. Why don't you think about it? I'll be at the Oyster House at noon on Wednesday. If you change your mind, you can find me there." And without giving him another chance to refuse, she disconnected.

THE WEATHER THAT EVENING matched Mark's mood perfectly. Wind howled and tossed tree branches against the house. Windows rattled, and leaves skittered across the patio. He sat back in his seat and watched Jared playing with building blocks in one corner of the kitchen. And the anger he'd been nursing all afternoon surged again.

Marianne had wreaked havoc on his life once. Now she threatened it again. Worse, she threatened his family. The urge to protect Dionne and Jared swelled within him, and he made a solemn vow not to let her hurt either of them.

Unfortunately, the more he thought about Marianne, the more convinced he became that the only way to stop her was to meet her. If he didn't, there was no telling what she'd do next.

Dionne poured another cup of coffee and raised the pot in silent question. He knew she could sense that something was bothering him, and he tried to hide his churning emotions. Nodding, he pushed his cup closer for a refill.

She filled his cup and poured one for herself. "You really don't mind watching Jared while I study again tonight?"

"Of course not," he told her. "I'm his father, not his sitter. You don't have to make arrangements with me to take care of him. I love the time he and I spend together."

She sat on the seat beside his and her thigh brushed against his. "I know you do. Maybe I'm just looking for an excuse not to study."

He tried to smile, but he knew it probably came out looking more like a grimace. "Why don't you want to study? Don't you like your classes?"

"I love them," she said quickly. "They're fascinating. But between your job and my school, it feels as if we never get time together. And now Patsy wants me to go shopping with her in Boston on Saturday—"

"You're going, aren't you?"

"I don't know." She watched Jared pull some plastic bowls from a cupboard, then added, "I'd rather spend time with you."

She wouldn't want to be around him if she could see the darkness inside. He wasn't fit company tonight. He took a sip of coffee before he responded.

"You should go. It will do you good to go out with a friend."

"You'd have to stay with him," she warned.

"That's fine. I told you already I don't mind."

Her gaze traveled over his face and her eyebrows knit as if she could see right through him. "What's wrong?"

He had to be more careful if he didn't want to frighten her. He took another long sip and lowered his cup to the table carefully. "What makes you think there's something wrong?"

"You seem distracted."

He stood and started clearing the dinner dishes away. "I had a hard day at work. Big case."

"Do you want to talk about it?"

"There's nothing to talk about."

"I wish you would." Dionne stepped in front of him. "I know almost nothing about what you do all day."

"It would only bore you."

"Not if it interests you." She smiled softly. "I'll admit, the law isn't exactly the most fascinating subject to me, but it would help me understand you better if I knew how you felt about the cases you're working on. Or are they all top secret?"

"No, not really. I can't divulge names, but issues of law are fair game for conversation."

"Then tell me about an issue of law."

He tried to think of one, but Marianne's call wiped all the details from his mind. "Maybe later," he said, sidestepping her and stacking the dishes by the sink.

He could see Dionne's reflection in the window, the slight narrowing of her eyes. "I don't like it when you pull away like this."

"I'm not pulling away." He forced himself to face her again, though it was hard to do with the lie between them. "I just have a lot on my mind and I'd rather talk about something else."

She searched his face for a moment, and her eyes looked so sad he wanted to kick himself. "Is this how it's going to be every time something bothers you? Are you going to pull away and shut me out?"

"No." And it wouldn't be, he assured himself. He argued with himself for a moment more, then reluctantly realized he owed Dionne the truth—no matter how frightening it might be, no matter how hard it was for him to tell her. "It's not a case that has me worried," he admitted at last.

"I didn't think so."

He motioned for her to sit and took the seat across from hers. "It's Marianne."

Dionne's eyes widened and the blood drained from her face. "What about her?"

"She called me today at the office. She wants to see Jared."

"No!" The word exploded between them and that same panic that had been so much a part of her when they first met filled her eyes. "Why?"

"I don't know."

Dionne shook her head quickly. "Tell me the truth. She wants him back, doesn't she?"

Mark covered one of her hands with his, trying to comfort her.

She jerked it away and stood. "Don't say anything more. Let me get Jared into the other room. I don't want him to hear any of this."

"You stay. I'll do it."

"No. No, I need to. I want to." Her voice trembled. Her eyes darted frantically around the room as if she expected Marianne to materialize before her eyes.

He waited for her to come back, too agitated to sit still, too angry with Marianne to think clearly. When Dionne returned, he tried again to comfort her. "Don't worry, sweetheart. I'm not going to let her barge in here and start telling us what to do."

"You can't let her see him, Mark." Dionne kept her voice low and put one trembling hand on his chest. "You can't. If she does, she'll want him back."

He covered her hand and tried to calm her. "I'll take care of it, I promise."

Her eyes strayed to the doorway where she could see Jared playing. "Promise me you won't let her see him."

The legalities of Marianne's position rose up in front of him and kept him from making a vow he might not be able to keep. "I'll handle her."

Dionne paced away from him and stared out the patio door into the night. Mark watched her, wishing he could guarantee that Marianne wouldn't be a problem.

He had no idea what he was going to do or say. He only knew his happiness and his family's depended on him.

MARK STOOD just inside the dimly lit lounge and looked for Marianne. The building had been a tavern in colonial times, and the low-beamed ceilings and huge fireplace in the center of the room, the pewter trays and pitchers lining the dark brick and wood walls, all gave the place atmosphere.

Dionne would love it here, though she'd raise her eyebrows at the prices. And he'd love to bring her.

Later.

Today, more important things demanded his attention. The past two days of watching Dionne worry had been pure hell. This morning at the office had dragged by so slowly, he'd started wondering if he'd go stark, raving mad waiting for noon to roll around.

Now that it had, his nerves were shot. The conversation and laughter of the other diners irritated him and his palms were sweat-slick from dread. Just as he began to suspect that Marianne had changed her mind, he spied her at a corner table nursing a drink.

He tried to affect the cool, unruffled look he used in court and made his way through the crowded restaurant to her table. "I want you to stay the hell away from me and my family."

Her smile faltered and died. "That's a nice greeting. Didn't your mother even teach you to say hello before you attack?"

"Hello."

"That's better. Now, I'm here because I want to see the baby."

"No."

"He's my son."

"You gave up that right," Mark said, his voice low. "You gave it up when you gave *him* up."

Marianne's jaw set in the stubborn lines he knew so well. "I haven't given anything up—not legally. Why are you always so quick to assume the worst of me?"

"Maybe because that's the side I've seen most."

She laughed harshly. "And you've always been a paragon of virtue, I suppose."

"I have my faults," he admitted, "but I didn't run away when the going got tough. I didn't hide Jared from you. And I sure as hell didn't abandon him."

She flushed slightly and tilted her head to one side. "We're butting heads again, you know. This is exactly what went wrong between us in the first place." She trailed her finger along the rim of her glass. "I didn't ask to meet you so we could argue, Mark. And I don't want to take the baby away from you and Dionne, if that's what you're worried about. I just want closure on that episode in my life."

"Episode?"

"You know what I mean."

He eyed her suspiciously and tried not to get his hopes up. "You'd better be telling me the truth, because there's no way in hell I'll ever let you take him."

She smiled. "He's really gotten to you, hasn't he?"

"He's my son."

"And mine."

"And *Dionne's*."

"I gave birth to him."

"She's been raising him."

"I know she has." Marianne turned her glass slowly. "What is he like?"

"Do you care?"

"I'm curious."

Touching. Again, he tried to rein in his irritation and hoped she'd get what she needed and go away for good. "He's a good boy. Stubborn."

"Like you?"

"Worse." In spite of his apprehension, he smiled.

"And he's totally bonded with Dionne?"

The question chilled him. "She's his mother. The only mother he'll ever know."

Her eyes traveled over his face and to his surprise, he saw nothing but mild curiosity there. "You've really fallen for her, haven't you?"

"Yes, I have."

"Are you in love with her?"

"Yes."

"It's written all over your face." Marianne looked almost wistful. "I'm happy for you, Mark. And for her." She brushed a lock of hair from her cheek and crossed her legs. "And all this hostility I'm getting is because you're worried that I'm going to hurt her?"

"Something like that."

She took a drink and carefully lowered her glass to the table. "I don't want to take Jared away from her, Mark. Truly, I don't. I just need to see him, that's all. I want to see how he's turned out so far. Then I'll go away and leave you alone."

"What about later? Will you want to see him again in two years, or ten, or fifteen?"

"Maybe." She pulled her hand away and shrugged. "I don't know. But even if I do, what can it hurt?"

"It can hurt a lot, Marianne. I won't ask Dionne to live with that kind of uncertainty."

"But you're willing to let me live with it?"

"You can't reject a child one day and then decide you want him back the next. You can't place a baby in a mother's arms and then rip him away again." His voice tightened. "It was your choice, Marianne.

And the rest of us have been paying the price for it. If you have to pay one now, that seems only fair.''

Her gaze faltered and some of her certainty vanished. ''I wouldn't have been a good mother, you know. I never was as big on family as you were.''

He didn't respond to that. He forced himself to wait as he would have if he'd been facing opposing counsel across a conference table.

''Will you ever tell him about me?''

He hid his elation and said, ''Probably.''

''He'll have questions.''

''Dionne and I will answer them.''

''Maybe he'll want to meet me. Have you thought about that?''

''If he does, we'll find you. But I'm not leaving this open-ended so you can come and go whenever you please. It wouldn't be fair to Jared or to Dionne.''

She linked her hands together on the table. ''You're quite the papa bear, aren't you?''

''Call it what you want. I take care of the people I love. I'm not going to ask Dionne to live with you lurking in the background, and I'm not going to confuse Jared.''

''You're still as hard-nosed as ever, aren't you? No compromises. No prisoners.''

''I'll compromise,'' he said, feeling the familiar rush of imminent success begin to move through him. ''If you'll sign the consent-for-adoption forms, I'll let you see him once. But you'll have to promise in return that you'll go away and not come back unless we contact you when he's older. You can't come and go whenever it's convenient for you, Marianne. That's pure selfishness.''

"I've already agreed to give you custody," she reminded him, "and the court has approved it. Why do you still need a consent form?"

"It's not for me," he told her. "It's for Dionne and Jared. She needs to know he's really hers. He needs the stability of having a mother around forever."

Marianne thought about it for so long, he began to worry. But she finally conceded. "All right. You have a deal."

"Good." He struggled to keep his face impassive, but the thought of Dionne's reaction to the news made him light-headed.

"I guess the only things we still need to work out are where and when."

"Saturday," he said without hesitation. "Dionne's going shopping with a friend, so I can get away easily."

Marianne's eyes widened. "You're not going to tell her?"

"Not until everything's signed, sealed and delivered."

She laughed and tossed her head to see him better. "So, it's okay for *you* to keep secrets."

The last thing he needed was a lecture on ethics from Marianne. He stood and glared down at her. "I'm not bringing Jared all the way to Boston, but I'll meet you halfway. Riverside Park in Welby's Landing at two o'clock. I'll bring the documents for you to sign."

She laughed again. "You're not taking any chances, are you?"

"No."

"Okay. I'll bring a pen." And when he turned away, she added, "Until Saturday, then."

He left the restaurant quickly, anxious to leave Marianne behind, equally anxious to escape the guilt made worse by her observation. He *was* keeping a secret from Dionne, he told himself as he strode back to his office. But after the way she'd reacted to the idea of Marianne seeing Jared, how could he tell her he'd compromised? Once she saw why he'd agreed, she'd understand. And he fully intended to tell her the truth as soon as he could offer her some peace of mind to go with it.

That made all the difference.

CHAPTER FIFTEEN

NEARLY DEAD on her feet, Dionne trailed Patsy along the sidewalk. The bags she carried—full of pants and shirts for Jared and a fisherman sweater she hadn't been able to resist for Mark—dug into her fingers and dragged at her arms. Thinking about Marianne dragged at her heart.

Mark had promised to think of a solution that would protect them all, but Dionne still hadn't slept well all week. She'd suggested that she talk to Marianne, hoping she could appeal to her cousin, but Mark had discouraged her. He and Marianne had issues to resolve, and Dionne had agreed to let him handle it—for now. But if he wasn't successful, she'd confront Marianne herself. She'd had trouble concentrating at school and she'd started the day exhausted and nearly a week behind in her homework. If she hadn't agreed to come shopping with Patsy, if Mark hadn't encouraged her to do something to take her mind off things, she would have stayed home.

She'd left home hoping he was right—that spending the day with Patsy would help push Marianne to the back of her mind, that some quality time with a friend would help her relax. But it hadn't helped. Instead, the exhaustion had grown so overwhelming, she wondered if she might be coming down with something.

On the plus side, Patsy had changed her mind about driving all the way to the city and had suggested instead that they stop at the outlet stores midway between Longs Mill and Boston. Dionne hadn't argued. The drive through the woods, now deep in the change of seasons, had been breathtaking, but she'd been more than ready to stop when Patsy pulled into the parking lot.

Now, on the sidewalk in front of her, Patsy slowed her step and sniffed the air. "Can you smell that?"

Dionne barely managed to stop before she plowed into Patsy's back. She could smell something, but the aroma made her stomach pitch. "What is it?"

"Food, silly." Patsy grinned back at her. "I don't know about you, but I'm starving. Let's grab something to eat and take it to the park."

Dionne checked her watch and noted with surprise that it was already past two o'clock. She should be hungry after the meager breakfast she'd forced herself to eat, but she wasn't. Worry and her constant state of exhaustion were even starting to affect her appetite.

"And afterward," Patsy said, picking up the pace and heading toward a hamburger stand, "we're going to buy something for you."

"I told you," Dionne said, huffing a little as she hurried after her friend. "I don't want anything."

"Don't be silly." Patsy drew up in front of the building and pushed open the door. "You've completely spoiled the men in your house. Now it's your turn. What do you need?"

For Marianne to disappear and leave us alone, she thought. But she said only, "About ten more hours every day and a long nap every afternoon."

"Can't help you there. What else?"

"A clone. I love the courses I'm taking, but school's wearing me out. I'm exhausted all the time. I feel as if I could fall asleep right here."

Patsy laughed and moved to the end of a line leading to the counter. "Maybe you're doing too much."

"Maybe," Dionne said skeptically. "But this shouldn't be harder than working full-time and being a single mother. Mark's been getting Jared to bed every night while I'm supposed to be studying. Instead, I fall asleep."

"All the more reason to relax in the park while we eat." Patsy moved up in line. "What do you want for lunch?"

Dionne studied the menu, but nothing sounded even remotely appetizing. "Maybe just a salad."

"You should try one of their Philly sandwiches. They're positively wicked. Cheese and onion and peppers, and beef this thick." Patsy held up her fingers to illustrate.

Just the sound of it made Dionne nauseated. She shook her head quickly. "I'll stick with the salad. I don't think my stomach could handle the sandwich."

Patsy eyed her suspiciously. "Are you sick?"

"I'm not sure. I don't feel bad all the time. The queasiness comes and goes. I'm probably just over-tired."

Patsy turned to face her. "Is it worse when you're hungry?"

Dionne thought back over the past few days. "Yes, but then I have no appetite."

A slow smile stretched Patsy's mouth. "And in the mornings?"

"I think so."

"As in *morning sickness?*"

The suggestion stunned Dionne and made her take a step back. She'd never been able to get pregnant with Brent. She *couldn't* be pregnant now. "No, it's not that. It can't be."

"Why not?"

"Because..." Dionne shook her head frantically. "It's impossible."

Patsy tucked her hand under Dionne's arm and gave her a gentle squeeze. "Correct me if I'm wrong, but you are a married woman. And I'm assuming that you and Mark have a healthy relationship...if you know what I mean."

"Well, yes. But—" Dionne's thoughts flew in a thousand directions at once. She and Mark had taken precautions after the first couple of nights together, but there *had* been those two nights.

Patsy leaned a little closer and whispered, "Are you late?"

Dionne had stopped keeping track of her monthly cycle after Brent's death, and it took her a few seconds to calculate it now. When she realized she was overdue by several days, her knees grew weak. "I think I might be," she whispered.

Part of her wanted to be pregnant and experience the miracle of creating another life. She longed to carry Mark's child and to give Jared a brother or sister. But she also knew that a pregnancy would complicate everything just when their relationship was beginning to work. And she didn't even want to think about how it would affect school.

Patsy laughed softly. "Now we know what to buy for you. We'll stop somewhere and pick up a home pregnancy test."

Dionne managed to nod. "Thanks. I think that would be a good idea." If she *was* pregnant, how would Mark take the news? Knowing how he felt about Jared, she couldn't imagine him being anything less than ecstatic. Of course, he'd be thrilled. And having a baby would forge another link between them and maybe make Marianne think twice about trying to take Jared back...unless it encouraged her because she figured they'd have someone to take Jared's place.

While she stood by and struggled with her conflicting emotions, Patsy placed their orders and collected their food. Dionne followed her across the street to the park, still too stunned to do much more than listen to Patsy's running monologue about her own pregnancies.

With every passing minute, the idea of being pregnant grew on her. But she told herself not to get her hopes up. She didn't want to be disappointed if the test came back negative.

MARK HELD ON TO Jared with one hand and his briefcase with the other as they walked slowly through the park. Marianne was nearly half an hour late, but Mark wasn't ready to give up and go home. If she didn't show, he'd track her down. One way or another, he'd have her signature on the consent for adoption before the sun set tonight.

Jared stopped to pick up a pebble and held it out to him. "See, Daddy?"

"For me? Thank you, son." Mark slipped the pebble into his pocket and smiled when Jared picked up another for himself. Today, with the threat Marianne posed looming in front of him, Mark understood

Dionne better than he ever had. She had countless memories of time spent alone with Jared, but they would never be enough. The more time Mark spent with his son, the more time he wanted.

It was hard for him to believe that such a short time ago he hadn't even known Dionne and Jared existed. Now, his world revolved around them.

When a man walking a dog caught Jared's attention, Mark let him watch for a moment, then urged him forward again. "Come on, sport. Let's go around the loop again."

When Jared held back, Mark set his briefcase on the ground and lifted the boy onto his hip. "How about a piggyback ride? Would you like that?"

Jared nodded and Mark settled the boy on his shoulders. "Hang on tight and don't let go, okay?"

"Okay." Jared laced his fingers through Mark's hair. "Run, Daddy."

Mark didn't want to go too fast, so he set off at a gentle trot, holding Jared's legs tightly. He circled the briefcase twice, delighting in his son's laughter. On the third circle, he caught sight of Marianne on the edge of the lawn watching them.

He slowed from a trot to a walk, then stopped completely and steeled himself while she hurried across the grass toward them.

"Sorry I'm late," she said when she drew closer. "I got caught in a last-minute meeting about this case I'm working on and couldn't get away."

"No harm done." Mark tilted his head to look at Jared. "Ready to get down?"

"No. Again."

Even with Marianne watching, Mark wasn't going to deny his son. He trotted twice more around the briefcase, then helped Jared down. "Let's get your trucks out, okay? You can play with those for a few minutes."

Jared looked disappointed, but not for long. Laughing mischievously, he set off at a run toward the other side of the lawn.

Mark raced after him, scooped him up again, and carried him back toward Marianne. "I need to talk to this lady for a minute, son. Will you play with your trucks while I do?"

Jared thought about that for a second, then nodded. "Okay."

Mark led them both toward a park bench, spent a few minutes settling Jared on the grass nearby with his trucks, and left the briefcase open on the bench beside him.

"So," Marianne said when he turned his attention to her again, "this is Jared. He looks like you."

"Thank you."

"He seems happy."

"He is."

"I'm glad." Marianne ran a finger along the chain of her necklace and sighed softly. "That's what I wanted for him."

Mark watched Jared for a few minutes in silence. "I haven't thanked you for him, and I need to. He's the most incredible person I've ever met."

Jared chose that moment to drive a truck across Mark's foot and chortle with glee.

"It's hard to believe I had anything to do with bringing him into the world," Marianne said with a sad smile. "I didn't want to see him when he was born, so he's always seemed a little unreal to me. I think that's why I needed to see him now. Just once," she added quickly, "before he's really not mine anymore."

Mark's heart skipped a beat. "Then you're still willing to sign the consent?"

She looked back at Jared, then nodded. "I gave my word."

Her word had never meant much between them, but Mark had to trust her now.

"I suppose you brought it with you," she said.

"I did."

Marianne leaned against the bench to see him better. "You know, in one way you haven't changed a bit. But in another, you've become a completely different person. When I saw you running around on the grass with Jared on your shoulders, I thought I was seeing things."

He laughed softly and ran his hand along the back of his neck. "I am a different person," he admitted. "But I'll still do anything to protect my family."

She held up both hands to ward off the warning. "You don't need to protect them from me. I'm fully prepared to sign. I just needed to see him." She trailed her gaze back to Jared and a fond smile curved her lips. "I was right to give him to Dionne and so wrong to keep him from you. Can you ever forgive me?"

The question wiped away the rest of his wariness. "Yes, I can," he said, touching her arm gently. "Because everything worked out for the best, just the way you did it."

MARK'S CAR wasn't in the driveway when Patsy dropped her off, but Dionne thought that might be just as well. This way, she wouldn't have to disappoint him if Patsy was wrong.

After promising at least a dozen times to call with the test results, Dionne watched her new friend drive away. Inside the house, she dropped her bags to the floor and let out a sigh. She kicked off her shoes, resisted the impulse to stretch out on the couch for a few minutes, and started toward the stairs.

First, the pregnancy test, she told herself. Then she could relax and plan how to tell Mark if the results were positive. She hugged the idea to herself as she walked past the telephone table, but the blinking light on the answering machine stopped her.

Wondering if Mark had left a message about where he'd gone, she pressed the button and listened.

"Mark? Mark, are you there?"

Dionne recognized Marianne's voice immediately and she had to clutch the table for support.

"Mark, if you're there, pick up."

Fear slammed her like a fist in the stomach. She covered her mouth and listened, every nerve taut.

"Well, I hope you get this before you leave. I'm going to be about an hour late to meet you and Jared—"

There was more, but Dionne's body reacted so violently she barely heard the rest. She retched, covered her stomach with one hand, and ran up the stairs toward the bathroom. It was a false alarm, but she wondered if she might have felt better if the urge had been real.

Why was Mark meeting Marianne? Obviously, he'd agreed to let her see Jared, in spite of Dionne's objections. But why? If there'd been a good reason, a valid reason, surely he would have told her. So why was he sneaking around behind her back?

The only possible reason snaked through her, making her nausea return even more strongly. Why did any man sneak around to meet a woman? There was only one reason. Only one.

Now she understood why he'd discouraged *her* from talking with Marianne. With a dreadful certainty, she knew that the past six weeks had been a lie. Mark had used her to get Jared. He'd deceived her. He'd made her think he loved her. And like a fool, she'd believed him.

He was planning to leave, just as her father had. The only difference was, Mark planned to take *his* child with him.

She pushed back to her feet, knees wobbling, head throbbing, stomach still rolling. Fear filled her, so strong she could almost taste it. She moved as quickly as she could, and crossed the hall to Jared's room. Praying silently, she threw open the door to his closet. When she saw his tiny clothes still hanging there, tears of relief filled her eyes.

She checked his drawers next and made sure all his favorite toys were still scattered around the room. Yes. Everything was still here. Leaning against the wall to steady herself, she took several deep breaths to restore calm and get her mind working again.

Instinct told her to pack her things and run. But she wouldn't go anywhere without Jared. And she couldn't grab him and walk out the door while Mark was here or he'd stop her. She'd just have to bide her time and wait for the opportunity to get away safely.

Still trembling, she made her way to her bedroom,

sank onto the foot of the bed, and tried to formulate a plan. She had no cash except the leftover grocery money, and that wasn't enough to get them very far. She had Mark's credit cards, but he could track her too easily if she used them.

Maybe running wasn't the answer. Mark had found her once. He could easily find her again. As Jared's legal father, the law would be on his side. No matter how frightened she was, she couldn't do anything illegal or she could lose Jared forever.

And what if she was pregnant?

Her stomach lurched again. The knowledge that Mark would be able to do this again if he wanted to brought on a wave of helplessness.

She stood abruptly and paced to the window. Maybe she should find an attorney. One who believed in her case. But who? And where?

Boston was full of attorneys, but any of them might be friends of Mark's. How would she ever know which of them she could trust?

Dashing away tears with the back of her hand, she pivoted from the window and told herself to be strong. Mark might have connections, he might know his way around the court system, he might have more money than she did and the law on his side, but surely she had rights as well.

First things first, she decided. She'd do the pregnancy test and plan her next move after she saw the results. As she started toward the living room where she'd left her bags, the shrill ringing of the telephone stopped her in her tracks. She stared at it, suddenly unable to move.

Who could it be?

Patsy? She might have some suggestions about where Dionne could find legal help.

What if it was Mark? What would she say to him? How would she hide her fear? Clutching her hands in front of her, she listened while it rang twice more, then forced herself to answer just before the answering machine clicked on.

"Hello, Dionne. Am I interrupting something important?"

Mark's mother. Of all people. Dionne sank onto the couch, fought another wave of tears, and tried desperately to keep her voice sounding normal. "No. I'm just waiting for Mark and Jared to get home."

"Oh? Well, I'm glad to hear Mark is giving you a day off. I'm sure you could use some time to yourself." Barbara's voice sounded oddly strained, but Dionne told herself she was just imagining it. "What have you done with yourself while they've been gone?"

Had my heart broken, she thought. *Had my world destroyed.* But she said only, "I went shopping with a friend."

"Wonderful. You've been so busy, I'm glad to hear you're doing something for yourself."

Dionne closed her eyes and tried to control the tears she felt threatening. This woman had accepted her into the family without question. Barbara had given Dionne a place to belong, and Dionne would miss her horribly.

"Listen, dear, I'm calling because I need to ask you a favor. But if this is an imposition, I want you to say so..."

Dionne refused to let Mark's behavior affect the

way she treated his parents. "Of course, Barbara. What is it?"

"Nigel has to have some tests done at a hospital in Boston starting early Monday morning. We need to check him in tomorrow, and he may need to stay for a few days."

Dionne held her breath. "It's nothing serious, I hope."

"His doctor says it's not." Barbara sounded so sad, Dionne's heart broke for her. "Anyway, I'm calling to ask if we could impose on you for a day or two."

"You want to stay here with us?" How could she face them now? But how could she say no?

"If you don't mind. I wouldn't even ask, but the drive between here and Boston is so long. And I remember Mark saying that your house has a third bedroom." She must have hesitated too long because Barbara's voice changed subtly. "If it's a problem, we can just stay in a hotel."

"It's no problem at all, Barbara." The words came out slowly, hesitantly. She forced herself to sound more certain. "Of course you can stay here."

"If you're sure. We don't want to intrude."

"I'm positive. Mark will be thrilled when I tell him."

Barbara sighed. "We were thinking of driving down this evening. We thought it would be nice to spend some more time getting to know you. And, of course, we'd love a chance to see Jared again."

"That's fine." Maybe having them around would actually help. It might create a buffer between her and Mark and give her time to firm up her plans.

"What time will you get here? Will you join us for dinner?"

"That would be lovely. But don't go to any trouble. Something simple will be fine." Barbara's voice went soft as she spoke to Nigel, then said, "We're leaving now, so we should be there around six."

"Wonderful." Dionne rubbed her forehead and tried to still the sudden pounding there. "I'll have the room ready for you."

When she replaced the receiver a moment later, she rested her forehead on her knees and let out a soul-wrenching sigh. The last thing she wanted was to spend another night in Mark's bed, but she couldn't think of any way to avoid it without tipping her hand.

Slowly, she lifted her head again and stood. She crossed to the door and gathered the bags she'd dropped there. Taking a steadying breath, she pulled out the pregnancy test and carried it up the stairs.

DIONNE STARED at the test-result window in horror while two deep pink stripes formed in front of her eyes. Positive. She was pregnant. It should have been the happiest moment of her life. But it was one of the worst she could remember.

She touched the plastic case with one trembling finger, then drew her hand away quickly as if it might contaminate her. As if she needed more proof, her stomach gave a sickening lurch. She dropped to the floor and leaned her head against the cool porcelain.

What was she going to do?

She couldn't tell Mark. She couldn't tell Barbara and Nigel. She couldn't even call Cicely. Cicely would confront Mark, which would be the *worst* thing she could do. And Patsy would no doubt react exactly the same way.

She couldn't confide in anyone.

It wasn't the first time she'd had to face something difficult on her own. But she'd started getting used to having people in her corner, to feeling as if she belonged somewhere. And having that security yanked out from underneath her made everything worse.

Tears threatened again, but she forced them away. Crying wouldn't help. She had to remain strong.

But when she heard Mark's car pull into the driveway a few minutes later, her resolve weakened. Heart racing, she gathered all the evidence of the pregnancy test and stuffed it into a garbage bag.

Working quickly, before he could come inside and find her, she searched for a hiding place. In desperation, she shoved the bag into her drawer in the bathroom behind her makeup and toiletries. Then she squared her shoulders and slowly walked down the stairs to face the man who'd betrayed her.

WHISTLING UNDER his breath, Mark put his key in the lock and turned it. After his meeting with Marianne, he'd spent a pleasant afternoon celebrating with Jared in the park. Unfortunately, he'd stayed longer than he'd planned at the petting zoo, but Jared had been so entranced by the animals, Mark hadn't had the heart to pull him away.

While he drove and Jared slept in his car seat, he'd planned the best way to give Dionne the signed consent for adoption. Simply handing it to her seemed almost anticlimactic. He wanted to do something special.

Maybe he'd take her out for a romantic candlelight dinner—without Jared—and give it to her there. Or maybe he'd talk to Patsy and make arrangements for Jared to spend the night with her and George. Or he could wrap it in a box and give it to her for her birthday…except he didn't want to wait that long.

He couldn't wait to see the look on her face. And he took great pleasure in the knowledge that he could finally give her the one thing she wanted most—security. He'd finally make her as happy as she'd made him in the past few weeks.

In all the years he'd dreamed about having a home and family, he'd never imagined it this good. The house had become a haven to him, a place where he could escape the pressures of the office, the demands of clients, and the worries of real life.

And Dionne was the main reason their home felt like such a sanctuary.

She managed to soothe him and drive him to distraction at the same time. Her eyes, her lips, the soft curve of her neck. Her inner strength, her courage and that incredible determination, all housed in one deliciously sexy body.

Still whistling, he unlocked the door and stepped inside. But when he saw Dionne standing in the middle of the room, his step faltered. She wore a form-fitting sweater and jeans that hugged every curve. But her eyes looked wild, and he could almost feel the tension radiating from her.

He shifted Jared to his other arm, pocketed the keys, and pushed the door shut with his foot. "What's wrong?"

Her eyes widened with surprise. "What makes you think something's wrong?"

"Because it's written all over your face."

She turned away and folded her arms as if she needed to protect herself from him. He'd seen clients use the same defense mechanism when they faced something unpleasant, and it made all his senses leap to the alert.

"Your parents called earlier," she said. "Your dad has to have some tests run at the hospital over the next couple of days."

Concern immediately replaced his wariness. "What kind of tests?"

Her expression softened slightly. "Your mother didn't give me any details, but she assured me they're nothing serious."

"But you don't believe her?"

"I don't know. She sounded worried."

"I'm sure she did. My dad's never sick." Mark put Jared on the floor beside his blocks and studied her cool expression. "What else?"

Her shoulders stiffened, but she forced a smile. "They want to stay here with us so your mother can be close to the hospital. Nigel has to check in tomorrow."

He let out a relieved laugh and closed some of the distance between them. "I'm glad that's the only problem. I was beginning to think I'd done something wrong."

Her eyes flew to his face, then away just as quickly.

"I know you're not used to having people around all the time," he said, sliding his arms around her waist. "But my parents won't be any bother. And we do have an extra bedroom now, you know."

He expected her to relax. Instead, she grew even

more rigid and stepped away from his embrace. "I know."

Her reaction confused him. He took a step back and studied her face for a long moment. "Do you want to tell me what you're really upset about?"

"I'm tired," she said, picking up Jared and holding him to her. "I've just spent the last hour getting the bedroom ready for your parents."

"You should have waited. I would have helped you."

"If you'd come home earlier, I would have let you."

He still had the unsettled feeling that she wasn't telling him everything. "I didn't plan to be so late. I took Jared to the petting zoo and lost track of time."

She smiled, but there was no warmth in it. "How nice."

For the life of him, he couldn't figure out why she was behaving so coldly toward him. He hadn't done anything wrong. He hadn't even been around. A few hours ago, she'd been looking forward to shopping with Patsy, and she'd kissed him so thoroughly before she left, he'd been tempted to try coaxing her to stay.

Now, the inexplicable chill brought back vivid memories of his last few weeks with Marianne. "I know you had a lot to do, but this isn't my fault."

She leveled him with a glance, but she didn't say a word.

Confusion made his next words come out a little too harsh. "Why are you angry with me? *I* didn't tell my parents they could come."

"*You* weren't here to take their call."

"Is that what you're upset about? That I went somewhere with Jared?"

She took another deep breath and let it out slowly. "No."

"Well, you can't possibly blame me because my dad needs to have some medical tests done."

"Of course not."

"Maybe you should have told my parents not to come."

She rounded on him, eyes blazing. "Are you telling me I should have sent them to a hotel?"

"If having them here is going to upset you—and obviously it is—then maybe you should have."

She laughed bitterly. Obviously affected by the anger and harsh words, Jared squirmed to get back onto the floor. She put him down, but she seemed reluctant to let him go. "Of course, your parents aren't a problem, Mark. I'm just tired."

He wanted desperately to believe her, but the truth glared out at him from her icy blue eyes. He pressed a little harder. "I don't want to be arguing when my parents get here, so why don't you just spit it out— whatever it is."

"We won't be arguing." She turned away from him, making it clear she didn't want to talk about it anymore.

Mark bit back his frustration. For one desperate second he thought about showing her the papers Marianne had signed in the park. But he wanted that to be a happy moment, not a last-ditch attempt to coax her out of a bad mood.

It was pretty damned clear to him, though, as he watched her leave the room without a backward glance, that home wouldn't be much of a sanctuary tonight.

AT LONG LAST, Mark closed the bedroom door to shut out the rest of the world. His parents were settled in Dionne's old room and Jared was sound asleep across the hall. Mark could finally have some time alone with her and, hopefully, get to the bottom of whatever it was that had her so edgy.

He turned slowly and looked at her. She sat on the foot of the bed, hands linked on her lap, gaze averted.

After their initial argument, she'd put up a convincing front all evening. But he could tell by the set of her shoulders and the grim look on her face that she was still upset with him.

And he still had no clue why.

He turned out the overhead light, leaving only the soft glow of a bedside lamp to illuminate the room. And he tried not to notice how beautiful she looked, or how intimate the setting was. It was obvious she wasn't interested in romance tonight.

Mark could live without it, even though he wouldn't have turned down a chance to explore that new facet of their relationship. Right now, it was far more important that they clear the air between them. And to do that, he needed her to talk to him.

He took his loose change from his pocket and put it on the dresser. "Are you still upset?"

She glanced at him, just a flick of the eyes. "I'm not upset."

He took off his watch and tried to act as if he believed her. "So how was your shopping trip today? Did you and Patsy have fun?"

"Fun?" She sent another contemptuous glance in his direction. "Not especially."

The look on her face gave him an idea and a tiny bit of hope that maybe this wasn't about him, after all. "Did something happen between you and Patsy?"

"No. She's a good friend," Dionne said evenly. "And don't worry. I didn't spent much money."

"I don't care about how much money you spent. I've already told you that." Frustration was making him tense and he resented having to beg for an explanation when something was so obviously wrong. He unbuttoned his shirt slowly, letting that latest clue sink in for a moment. "Is that what's bothering you? The money?"

She stood quickly and turned her back on him. "It's not the money. It's not anything. What will it take to make you drop this?"

"How about the truth?"

"I'm telling you the truth."

He closed the distance between them and took her gently by the shoulders. "Are you? I don't think so."

She shrugged away from his touch and glared at him. "When did *you* become so interested in telling the truth?"

The question—the accusation—set him back a pace and he wondered if she could possibly know how he'd spent his afternoon.

No. Impossible. She *couldn't* know.

But that didn't stop the guilt from churning in the pit of his stomach. "Is that what this is about? You think I'm lying to you about something?"

"Are you?"

Again he resisted the urge to tell her the truth. He

really wanted it to be a special moment when he handed her the consent for adoption Marianne had signed. "What do I have to lie about?"

Her eyes narrowed, and for an instant he thought she might actually tell him. Instead, she took a step away. "I'm tired, Mark. I have a ton of homework to do for class tomorrow. And this discussion is getting us nowhere."

That was certainly true. He tossed his shirt over the back of a chair and stripped off his pants. She averted her gaze as if they were still strangers.

Increasingly frustrated, he tried to decide whether to let the conversation drop, or if he should push a little harder. He'd been oblivious with Marianne, and look where that had gotten him. He loved Dionne enough to try again.

He walked slowly toward her and touched her again. "Come on. Let's go to bed. Whatever it is, you can talk to me. I love you, Dionne. Trust me."

She jerked away and climbed into bed, turning her back toward his side. And a flash of memory, of Marianne turning away from him exactly the same way, taunted him.

Was this a sign that Dionne was changing her mind? Was she having second thoughts? But if so, why? He was as clueless as he'd been when Marianne left. But this time, he had far more at stake. His son. His dreams. His heart.

CHAPTER SIXTEEN

MARK LAY on his side of the bed watching shadows drift across the ceiling. Noises—an occasional passing car, a dog barking, the soft sound of Dionne sleeping next to him—were magnified by the stillness of the night air and kept him awake. Or maybe it was the fear that once again he was failing at love, and he didn't know how or why.

Too agitated to relax, he climbed carefully out of bed and walked to the window. Shadows from the moon pooled beneath the trees and undergrowth rimming the backyard. He rested one hand on the wall and rubbed his eyes with the other.

Dionne shifted in the bed behind him and let out a breath soft as a baby's sigh. His heart constricted, and he wondered when she'd become so necessary to him. He'd gone into this marriage for Jared's sake; and though keeping Jared happy was still important, somehow everything had shifted and the relationship with Dionne had become his top priority.

He couldn't lose her. No matter what it took, no matter what price he had to pay, he wouldn't screw up again.

Dionne stirred and rolled over in bed. She'd been so exhausted lately, he didn't want to wake her so he padded across the room, let himself out into the darkened hallway, and closed the door behind him almost soundlessly. Using both hands to feel his way, he stumbled down the stairs toward the kitchen.

Inside, the neon light over the range was on, a sure sign that his mother was prowling as she often did when something worried her. He searched for her in the shadowy room. "Mom?"

"Over here, son." Her voice came from somewhere near the patio doors.

Squinting to make out the furniture between them, he crossed the room and stood beside her. There, in the glow of the moonlight, he could see her at last. The tattered bathrobe she'd been wearing as long as he could remember, the slightly tousled hair, the face scrubbed of makeup.

He put an arm around her shoulders, taking comfort from the familiar scent of her face cream. "What are you doing up?"

"I couldn't sleep."

"And why not?"

"I'm worried about your father."

"I thought you said the tests were nothing to worry about. Is there something you're not telling me?"

She flapped a hand at him as if to wave away the suggestion. "Of course not. Unless the doctor's lying to me."

He drew back and looked down at her. "You don't believe him?"

A sad smile curved her lips. "I'm trying to."

Mark gave her a gentle squeeze. "I'm sure he'd tell you if there was anything to worry about."

"You're probably right. I'm just not used to anything being wrong with your father. You know he's always had the constitution of an ox."

Mark finished the family joke for her. "And the disposition of a mule."

His mother laughed, then sobered again. "We've been married nearly forty years, and suddenly I find myself staring mortality right in the eye. For the first time, I'm facing the possibility that he could go before me, and I don't know what I'd do without him."

And for the first time in his life, Mark understood how she felt. "Do you want me to go with you tomorrow and talk to the doctor myself?"

"I'd like that very much. But you know your father. He'd think we were trying to baby him, or that I was keeping something from him."

"You're right. He would." Mark let his gaze trail away again.

His mother took a deep breath and smiled at him. "We'll be fine. It's you I'm really worried about."

"Me?" He laughed nervously. "Why me?"

"Because something's wrong between you and Dionne. I can sense it."

She didn't need his burdens added to her own, nor did Mark want to make them real by voicing them. "Everything's fine," he said quietly.

He could see her scowl in the moonlight. "Don't lie to me, Mark Taylor. I know when something's wrong with my children."

"We had a little disagreement earlier," he admitted. "But everything's fine now."

"Every couple has disagreements. Heaven knows, your father and I have had our share. But it's not one minor disagreement I'm talking about. It's something more substantial. I felt it the first time I saw you together."

Mark tried to laugh away the suggestion. "What did you feel?"

"If I knew that, I wouldn't have to ask. It's just an uneasy feeling I experience at times. Don't get me wrong, I adore Dionne, and I don't think you could have picked a better wife. And she's a wonderful mother to Jared. But there's something…" Her scowl deepened. "Do you love her?"

"You can't even imagine how much," he said truthfully.

That seemed to relax her a little. "And she loves you. I can see that whenever you two are together. But I've been worried. I had doubts about whether you truly loved her, or if you only married her because of Jared."

Mark kept his face impassive, his body from reacting in any way. "What made you think that?"

"You have to admit, it's a bit of a coincidence that you'd go in search of your son and then fall madly in love with the woman who's been raising him."

Mark kept his gaze riveted on a lawn chair on the patio. "Coincidences do happen."

"Well, I'm glad to know you two *are* in love. Marriage is tough enough between two people who love each other. And trying to keep a marriage together when there's not love involved isn't only foolish, it's dangerous. Look at Jerry."

He laughed sharply. "Jerry had an affair, Mom."

"It's not *what* he did as much as *why* he did it. You know as well as I do that he and Alice never did really love each other. They got married for the wrong reasons." She sighed softly. "I'm not condoning what he did by any means. I'm just saying that the affair didn't cause their problems. It was a symptom of what was wrong between them. If that hadn't ended their marriage, something else would have eventually.''

Mark believed that, but he sure as hell didn't like thinking that his marriage to Dionne was headed toward the same fate.

''The saddest part,'' his mother went on, ''is what it's done to the girls. Children are always the victims when a marriage goes bad.''

That made him feel even worse. Were he and Dionne setting Jared up for disappointment and heartache? ''You don't have to worry, Mom. That's not going to happen to us.''

''I'm glad, sweetheart.'' She leaned up and kissed his cheek, then patted it gently. ''Maybe now I can get some sleep. Are you coming upstairs?''

''Not yet. I don't want to wake Dionne.''

''Well, don't stay up too late. You need your sleep.''

He forced a laugh. ''I'm thirty-one years old, and you're telling me when to go to bed.''

''I'm still your mother,'' she said, and patted his cheek again. ''And I still care.''

He smiled in spite of the ache in his heart and watched her cross the room. But when she disappeared, his smile faded. And the new doubts she'd raised began to tear holes in his resolve.

He wanted desperately to believe he could hold his marriage together, but he wondered if he could do it on his own.

THE NEXT MORNING, Dionne felt as if she were walking on a tightrope. She'd slept fitfully all night, waking in the middle of the night to find Mark gone. She had no idea where he'd gone or if he'd ever come back to bed. His side of the bed had been empty when she woke again and finally got up.

He'd been thoughtful all morning, stepping in to help with breakfast and Jared. At least he'd stopped pressuring her to confide in him. But she kept waiting for him to do or say something about last night, and her emotions were so close to the surface, anything might push her over the edge.

She filled a plate with scrambled eggs and tried not to let the smell make her sick. As she turned to carry them to the table, Mark stepped in front of her and took the plate from her hand.

Nigel was hidden behind a section of the newspaper. Barbara sang softly to Jared as she fed him cereal. The realization that she'd have to leave them soon brought tears to Dionne's eyes, but she forced them away.

Barbara glanced at her with a bright smile. "Are you sure I can't help you with something?"

"You're already helping," Dionne assured her.

Barbara lowered the spoon to the table slowly. "You look pale this morning. Are you feeling all right?"

Dionne sat at the table. She could feel Mark watching her, but she didn't let herself look at him. "I'm fine," she said, trying not to look queasy when the breakfast aromas hit her full force. "Just a little tired." She stood quickly to get away from the eggs and bacon and mumbled something about making more toast.

Barbara helped Jared with his apple juice. "Why don't you let Mark do that." She sent him a pointed glance that would have made Dionne laugh under other circumstances.

And when he popped up again like a puppet and hurried to do his mother's bidding, she had to force away a rush of affection.

Nigel lowered his newspaper and peered at them over the top. "If you ask me, you ought to get this wife of yours some help around the house. Can't expect her to keep up with school and the house and Jared, too." He ruffled Jared's hair and chucked him under the chin. "We want Mommy to be happy, don't we?"

Jared giggled and reached for his apple juice again.

"I want Mommy to be happy, too." Mark pulled two slices of bread from the bag, but he kept his gaze riveted on Dionne. "Would you like that?"

"You mean, a maid?" The offer surprised her. Mark had always been generous with his money, but why was he talking about the future when he was planning to desert her? Or was he just putting up a front for his parents? She shook her head slowly. "I don't think so. It's terribly extravagant."

"Money's not the issue," Mark said firmly. "If we found someone who could come in a couple of days a week, maybe you wouldn't be so tired all the time."

If Patsy's stories about pregnancy were anything to go by, nothing would help that for a few months. Dionne started to nod, then stopped herself. She couldn't let Mark hire someone to help her when she didn't intend to stay.

Out of nowhere, tears filled her eyes. She blinked them away and shook her head. "No, I..." She pushed aside the coffee that was making the nausea worse and tried to still the rolling of her stomach, the swaying of the room.

Mark dropped the bread into the toaster, still without looking away. Barbara stopped feeding Jared to watch her. Even Nigel had lost interest in his newspaper.

Barbara put a hand on hers. "Dionne, dear, what is it?"

"Nothing." She nudged herself back from the table and tried to take a deep breath, but she could feel sweat beading on her forehead and knew she had to get away—and fast.

Jumping up, she rushed from the room, ran up the stairs, and shut herself in the bathroom. She didn't have time to lock the door before she had to give in to the nausea that had taken over her entire body.

Just as she began to feel a little better, someone knocked softly on the door. Barbara's voice followed a second later. "Dionne? Are you all right?"

She closed her eyes and leaned her head against the wall. "I'm fine," she lied.

The door opened a crack and Barbara looked inside. "You're most definitely *not* fine. Is there something I can do?"

"No." Dionne forced herself to stand, even though her knees barely held her. "Thanks, but I'll be all right if I can just lie down for a while."

"Let me help you get to bed, then."

Dionne backed a step away, her eyes brimmed with tears, her throat thickened with emotion. Why did Barbara have to be so nice to her? It only made everything harder.

The concern on Barbara's face deepened. "Do you want me to get Mark?"

"No." The word fell between them, the desperation behind it obvious. She tried to smile it away. "He has enough on his mind, and so do you. Go ahead and have breakfast without me. I don't want you to be late getting to the hospital."

Barbara didn't turn away, but studied her for a long moment. Slowly, Dionne saw recognition dawn in her eyes and a knowing smile curve her lips. "Does Mark know?"

"Know what?"

"Why you're so tired and nauseated all the time?"

"There's nothing *to* know." Dionne turned to the faucet and splashed her face with water. "Nothing at all."

Barbara's smile died but the light in her eyes didn't dim. "If you say so, dear. Don't worry, I won't say anything. This is your surprise to give him. But if you're worried about how he'll react, don't. He'll be thrilled."

Dionne kept her face impassive as she patted it dry with a towel. "There's nothing to be thrilled about, Barbara. I'm sure it's just a reaction to stress."

Barbara stood there, watching her for a few long, agonizing seconds. "All right," she said at last. "I guess I was mistaken."

After what felt like forever, she closed the door and walked away. And Dionne sank onto the edge of the bathtub and buried her face in her hands.

Of course Mark would be thrilled. No matter how he felt about her, he loved his son. And she knew with unwavering certainty he'd feel the same way about the baby she carried. That's what frightened her most.

Her time had run out. Like it or not, she had to leave. She couldn't stay here and keep the pregnancy a secret from Mark. Barbara had already figured it out. He wouldn't be far behind.

MARK DROVE quickly along the winding road leading home. Late-afternoon sunshine spilled in through the car window. Leaves drifted lazily from the huge old trees lining the highway to the pavement in front of him. It was a perfect autumn day and he was in a good mood.

His mother's call earlier that afternoon telling him that his father's tests were going well and that the doctor had ruled out the more serious conditions he'd suspected had been a good start. Drawing up the petition for adoption so Dionne could sign it had only made things better. And when Royal left the office early, Mark took advantage of the opportunity to sneak out, as well.

Smiling, he glanced at the box of roses beside him on the front seat. He drove through the center of town and was pleased when he passed the green. He wanted the rest of his and Dionne's lives to feel as magical as the night of the autumn festival. And he had the means to a very good start in his suit pocket.

Tonight was the night. He'd talk his mother into staying with Jared for the evening. Over dinner in some wonderfully romantic restaurant, he'd tell Dionne everything. He couldn't wait to watch the stress vanish from her face and the clouds leave her eyes.

When he saw Patsy coming out of the drugstore,

he honked lightly and waved. To his surprise, she didn't return the greeting, but propped her hands on her hips and glared at him. Her reaction bothered him for a moment, but by the time he turned off Front Street toward home, he'd decided she probably hadn't recognized him.

Feeling like a kid on Christmas morning, he pulled into the driveway, gathered the roses and his brief-case, and jogged up the walk. But when he let himself into the house, unexpected silence greeted him.

"Dionne?" He left his briefcase by the door and the roses on the end of the couch. "Jared?"

Still nothing.

Maybe she was putting Jared down for a nap. He took the stairs two at a time and peeked inside Jared's room. It was empty.

Great. The one day he got away from the office at a reasonable hour, and she wasn't here. Trying hard not to be disappointed, he hurried into their bedroom to change. Before he could do more than take off his jacket and tie, he heard someone come in the front door.

He raced down the stairs again, hoping to reach Dionne before she could look inside the florist's box. "You're home," he said as he rounded the corner into the living room.

"Yes." His mother dropped onto the empty end of the couch and leaned her head back. "And exhausted. What are you doing here so early?"

Mark tried not to let her see his disappointment. "I snuck out. I was hoping to surprise Dionne, but she's not here. Have you talked to her today?"

His mother shook her head and closed her eyes.

"I didn't even try to call. I assumed she'd be in classes all day."

He stole a glance at his watch and scowled. "She was, but she should be home by now."

"Maybe she's gone to the grocery store. Or maybe she's studying late at the library."

"That's probably it." He sank into a chair and propped his feet on the ottoman. "I was thinking of asking if you'd watch Jared so I could take her out to dinner tonight. But if you're too tired I'll do it another night."

Barbara opened her eyes again and smiled. "What a lovely idea. I think the two of you could use some time alone, and I'm never too tired to watch Jared."

He grinned and stood again. "Thanks, Mom. You're the greatest." He hurried upstairs, took off his suit pants and opened the closet to grab a hanger. When he realized that Dionne's clothes weren't on the other side of the closet, his hand froze in midair.

As if in slow motion, he pushed the closet door open the rest of the way and stared at the empty hangers and the bare space on the floor where her shoes had been that morning. But it wasn't until he crossed the hall into Jared's room and found his son's favorite toys gone, his drawers empty, and his closet bare, that the realization finally hit him.

Moving on autopilot, he walked back to his bedroom and dressed in jeans and a sweatshirt. His mind still refused to take it in, but his heart screamed the truth with every beat. He sank onto the foot of the bed and buried his face in his hands.

He had no idea how long he sat there before he heard his mother's tread coming up the stairs and moving down the hall toward the guest room.

"Mark?" She paused with her hand on the doorknob. "What's wrong?"

Slowly, painfully, he lifted his gaze to meet hers. "She's gone."

"Gone? What do you mean, gone?"

"I mean gone." The pain was too intense. He couldn't bear to feel it. In the blink of an eye, it turned into anger. He stood and threw open the closet door again. "Gone. Her clothes are gone, and so are Jared's. Apparently, I've failed again."

"Mark—" His mother's dark eyes filled with sympathy.

He looked away. He couldn't bear her sorrow or her pity.

"Mark, sweetheart—" Barbara moved into the room to stand behind him and put her hands on his shoulders.

He jerked away and mopped his face with his hand. He fought tears and tried to hold on to the anger. It was, he thought bitterly, much easier to handle.

"Do you know why she left?"

"If I did, I'd know how to fix it. Maybe I work too much. Maybe I'm just an insensitive jerk. Who the hell knows?" He paced toward the window and glared out at the lawn. "I tried my best this time, Mom. I really did."

"I don't know Dionne well," Barbara said quietly, "but I find it hard to believe that she'd leave without telling you why."

He thought back over the last few conversations they'd had. Once again, he had the uncomfortable suspicion that she'd found out he was hiding something from her. But how?

He turned to face his mother again and slowly, hesitantly, told her the whole story.

MARK PACED in front of the drugstore, watching the sun set, rubbing his hands together for warmth while he waited for Patsy to get off work. Dionne and Jared had been gone for nearly a week. He'd given his anger free rein for the first day or two and tried like hell to convince himself he was better off without her.

But every time he came home to that empty house, his heart broke all over again.

For the last few days, he'd tried everything he could think of—short of hiring a private detective again—to find her. He'd even called Cicely, who'd insisted in a cold, flat, unemotional voice that she hadn't seen Dionne.

He didn't believe her, of course. And tomorrow, he'd fly to Boise and begin his search in person. But he had one last step to take before he did.

Patsy had been with Dionne the day everything turned sour. If anyone knew what had suddenly made Dionne change, Patsy would. And he wouldn't undertake the most important argument of his life without preparing for it.

He glanced through the window and paced to the corner, then turned back toward the door again. The last customer had left at least fifteen minutes ago. Surely, she'd come outside soon.

Maybe he should have gone inside, but he didn't want to have this conversation in front of anyone else. It was bad enough that he had to beg a relative stranger to tell him why his wife had left.

At long last, the front door opened and light spilled

onto the sidewalk. A moment later, the light extinguished and Patsy stepped outside.

As she turned to lock the door behind her, Mark closed the distance between them. "Patsy?"

She whirled to face him. "Hello, Mark." Her voice was cool and brittle. She knew, he thought with a surge of hope. Whatever it was, she knew.

Now, if he could just convince her to share it with him. "Do you have a minute?"

She glanced up the sidewalk, then shrugged casually. "I suppose. What do you need?"

"Have you talked to Dionne lately?"

Her eyes flashed, but she managed to keep the rest of her face emotionless. "Not since the day after we went shopping."

"She hasn't called you?"

"No."

He stepped more fully in front of her. "Did something happen to upset her that day?"

Patsy's shoulders tensed and she looked again toward the end of the street, as if she was searching for an escape route. "Dionne is my friend. I don't think I should talk about her with you."

"And she's my wife." His shoulders sagged and he raked his fingers through his hair. He abandoned the few ragged bits that remained of his pride. "She's gone, Patsy. She left me."

"Yes, I know."

A flash of anger tore through him, but he tried not to show it. He couldn't afford to alienate her. "Do you know why?"

Patsy's mouth settled into a thin line. "I can't believe you need to ask."

He took a steadying breath and tried to keep his

tone level. "I do need to ask. I have no idea why she'd leave."

Patsy laughed bitterly. "Just think about it, Mark."

"That's all I have thought about," he assured her. A gust of wind swirled around them. Cold, savage wind that matched the icy dread in his heart. "I can't eat. I can't sleep. I think back over the last few days she was here again and again, but I don't know what happened. You're my last hope. She seemed fine when she left with you that morning. By the time I got home again, everything had changed."

"You really have no idea?"

"None." He took a ragged breath and let it out again slowly. "I love her, Patsy. If I did something wrong, I'd like to know what it was."

She studied him for a moment and her hostility appeared to fade slightly. She tugged the collar of her sweater closer and shivered in another blast of wind.

"Patsy, please."

She turned her gaze back on him. "Where did you go that day, Mark? Who did you meet?"

Mark's stomach knotted and his mouth dried. "How—" He broke off, then tried again. "How did she find out?"

"Apparently, there was a message from what's-her-name on the answering machine when Dionne got home that day."

That took the wind out of him as surely as if she'd punched him in the stomach. "From Marianne?"

He thought he might be sick. No wonder Dionne had been so cold. No wonder she'd held him at arm's length. He said the only words he could manage. "It was nothing. Why didn't she ask me about it?"

Patsy's smile turned bitter again. "Maybe because she didn't trust you."

"But—"

"And I don't blame her," Patsy said, cutting him off. "You took Jared to meet Marianne without telling her. Why *should* she trust you?"

He looked deep into Patsy's eyes. "It wasn't what you're thinking. Believe me. Marianne agreed to sign the consent for adoption if I let her see Jared one last time. That's *all* it was."

"If it was so innocent, why didn't you tell Dionne?"

"I didn't want to worry her. I thought she'd get frightened if I told her, and I wanted to spare her that. Obviously, I have a lot to learn."

"Yes, you do." Patsy studied him again before she allowed herself a thin smile. "I suppose you look sincere."

"I am," he assured her. "More than you can imagine. And I need to explain everything to Dionne."

"I agree with you," Patsy said, hitching her purse onto her shoulder.

"Then you'll tell me where she is?"

"I would if I could. But I don't have any idea. I haven't heard from her." She patted his shoulder gently and turned away. "For what it's worth, I hope you find her."

"Oh, I will." Now that he knew why she'd run, he knew exactly what to say to get her back. And he knew right where to look.

"YOU'RE GOING to wear a hole in my carpet if you keep pacing like that."

Dionne stopped in her tracks and glanced over her shoulder at Cicely who sat at the kitchen table cradling a cup of cocoa in both hands. She'd only been home from work a few minutes, and she hadn't changed out of her work clothes yet. In her suit, nylons and pumps, she made a stark contrast to Dionne, who hadn't been able to work up much interest in her appearance since she left Longs Mill.

"Sorry," Dionne said, forcing a weak smile. "I'm just restless, I guess."

Cicely's eyes narrowed. "You're still thinking about him, aren't you?"

Every waking minute, Dionne admitted silently. She missed him terribly. She heard his laugh everywhere she went. A dozen times she'd thought she glimpsed him in a crowd, only to discover it wasn't him after all. Every time she closed her eyes, she saw him.

She'd expected the longing to fade. Instead, it seemed to be getting worse. "I'm waiting for the bomb to drop," she said. "It's been almost a week already, and he hasn't done anything."

"Maybe he won't. After all, I told him I hadn't seen you."

She laughed harshly. "Oh, he will. I'm absolutely certain of it."

Cicely sipped cocoa and carefully settled the cup on the table. "Maybe he really is in love with you."

"I'd give anything for that to be true," Dionne admitted. "But if he is, why did he take Jared to Marianne without telling me? He knew how I'd feel about it.'' She shook her head and started to pace again.

"There may be a perfectly good explanation for that,'' Cicely said quietly. "But you never gave him the chance to explain. I think you should talk to him.''

Dionne turned to glare at her. "I can't believe you're even suggesting that. If I call him, he'll know where we are.''

Cicely made a face at her and sipped again. "I hate to break it to you, girl, but I don't believe you're really trying to hide from him. This will be the first place he looks, and you know it.'' She leaned back in her chair and crossed her legs. "You came here because you want him to find you.''

Dionne rested her hand on the stomach of her oversize sweatshirt, trying to feel the new life she carried. She glanced at Jared, who drove a fleet of toy trucks across the floor. He'd been unusually quiet since they'd left Longs Mill, and each time she noticed the difference, guilt overwhelmed her.

"I *don't* want him to find us,'' she argued without conviction. "I just didn't have anywhere else to go.''

"Uh-huh.'' Cicely rolled her eyes and kicked her foot gently. "I don't believe you.''

"It's true,'' Dionne insisted. "Where else was I supposed to go?''

Cicely rolled her eyes again. "All I'm saying is, if you really don't want him to find you, you'd have thought of something else. Admit it, Dionne. You're hoping he comes after you.''

Dionne wanted to deny it again, but she couldn't. "Maybe you're right,'' she said. "I've tried over and over again to make myself hate him, but I just can't stop loving him.''

''Then, talk to him.''

''I can't.''

''Why not?''

''Because.'' She sat across from Cicely and rested her chin in her hand. ''I know he'd come after us if he knew about the baby. Maybe he'd even stay with me. But it would be out of obligation, not love, and I don't think I could bear that.''

''So what are you going to do?''

''Find a job. Get an apartment. Get on with my life.''

''Dionne, listen to me.'' Cicely rested her hands on the table and faced her squarely. ''You're carrying that man's child. Do you really think it's fair not to tell him?''

''And let him take both of my children away?'' Dionne shot to her feet and put some distance between them. ''Never. Why are you suddenly on his side?''

''I'm not on his side.'' Cicely shook her head sadly. ''I'm on your side, whether you know it or not. You love him, Dionne. You're miserable without him. And if he was the heartless creature you're trying to make him out to be, you never would have fallen in love with him in the first place.''

''I made a mistake.''

''I agree with you. But your mistake was leaving without giving him a chance to explain.''

Dionne studied her friend's face for a long moment. ''Why the sudden change of heart?''

Cicely shrugged innocently. Too innocently.

It sent a rush of apprehension through her. "You know something, don't you?"

"I know you're in love with him," Cicely said firmly. "And I know you're dying inside being away from him."

"So, what do you want me to do? Take Jared back to Longs Mill and hand him over to Mark and Marianne?"

"No. I just want you to talk to him." Cicely took a deep breath and turned away. "He's here in Boise."

Dionne's heart dropped. Her stomach lurched. Her mouth dried and her hands grew moist. And in the midst of it all, her spirits soared. "He's here? How do you know?"

"He came by to see me this afternoon."

"And you didn't tell me? Does he know I'm staying with you?"

"I told you, girl. This is the first place he looked."

She dropped into a chair and held on. "What did he say?"

"Just that he wants a chance to explain."

"Explain what?"

Cicely turned back to her with a smile. "I think you'd better let him tell you that."

"How do you know he's not trying to set me up so he can take Jared away?"

"I recognized the look in his eyes. Pure misery, exactly what I see in yours. Dionne, that man is in love with you and he wants you back."

"What about Marianne?"

"I'll let him tell you."

"What about—"

Cicely cut her off with a wave of her hand. "I'll

let him tell you," she said again. "I'm not getting any more involved than I already am."

Dionne took a deep breath and tried to still the trembling of her hands. "Did you tell him about the baby?"

"Nope. I figure that's for you to tell. I told you, girl, I'm not getting involved."

Dionne managed a weak smile. "Where is he?"

"Outside."

"Outside?" She lurched to her feet and ran into the bathroom. She checked her reflection and noted with dismay that she looked like a corpse. Her cheeks were pale, her hair tousled, her face gaunt and shadowed from lack of sleep. "I look horrible," she moaned softly. "I can't see him looking like this."

"I think you look wonderful."

The deep male voice brought her around sharply. He stood there, blocking the bathroom door, his face creased with worry, his eyes dark with concern. Soft spikes in his hair told her he'd been raking his fingers through it the way he always did when he was worried.

Torn between the urge to rush into his arms and the need to protect herself, she gripped the sink for support. "Where's Jared?"

"In the hall with Cicely. She wanted to give us some time alone." He shifted uncomfortably but he didn't look away. "I talked to Patsy last night. She told me about the message Marianne left on the answering machine."

She nodded, too numb to do anything else.

"It wasn't what you thought, Dionne."

"Wasn't it?" The words came out little more than

a whisper. She willed herself to be strong. "What was it, then?"

"I met Marianne so I could get this." He reached into his coat pocket, pulled out a document, and handed it to her.

Scarcely breathing, she took it. But she couldn't make herself open it.

"It's a consent for adoption," he said softly. He took a tentative step toward her, as if he was as afraid of this moment as she was. As if he had as much at stake. "I wanted to surprise you with it."

She unfolded it quickly, scanned the document, and checked for Marianne's signature. Then slowly, she lowered it to her side and let the relief sweep through her. "Is it real?"

"One hundred percent real." He handed her another document. "And here's the petition for adoption I had drawn up. All it needs is your signature."

"You—" She gulped back tears and met his gaze. "This is what you were doing?"

"This is it."

"I thought you and Marianne were planning to take Jared away from me."

"I know." He moved toward her, but stopped short of taking her into his arms. "I'm sorry, Dionne. I should have told you, but I didn't want to worry you." He laughed at the absurdity of it and touched her gently. "I love you, Dionne. I want you with me always. I need you with me. I didn't even realize how much until you left. If you'll come back to me, I promise I'll always be honest with you."

She dashed tears away with the back of her hand and resisted the urge to throw herself into his arms. There was still one piece of unfinished business.

"Mark, I—" She broke off and studied his face, memorizing the details, loving him more than she could have ever imagined loving anyone. "I haven't been completely honest with you, either."

His dark eyes narrowed. His smile faltered. "What is it?"

"Well, I—" The words wouldn't come. She gripped his hands for strength and forced herself to say it. "I'm pregnant."

For one heart-stopping moment, time stood still. His eyes registered shock and she waited. Then he threw back his head and let out a whoop loud enough for everyone in Cicely's building to hear. "Pregnant?"

"Yes."

He pulled her into a bear hug and held on as if his life depended on it. "You've made me the happiest man in the world."

"But—"

He touched her lips with his fingertips, then pulled them away and replaced them with his lips. He kissed her gently, thoroughly, putting his entire heart into it. When he let her go again, he smiled into her eyes.

The last of the reserve between them vanished as if it had never been. He kissed her until she was gasping for breath, then released her quickly and dropped to one knee on the cold tile floor. "Mrs. Taylor, will you do me the honor of marrying me…again?"

The tears came freely now. She couldn't have stopped them if she'd tried. "Oh, Mark—"

"I'm serious." He took her hand in his and held it. His eyes danced with joy that matched hers.

"You've got to admit, that first wedding was nothing to write home about."

"I don't need a big, fancy wedding," she whispered around the lump in her throat. "I just need you and my children, forever."

He stood slowly and wrapped her in his arms again. "Then that's exactly what you'll have." He kissed the top of her hair, trailed his lips to her temple and down the line of her jaw.

Nothing had ever felt so right, so wonderful, so much like heaven on earth. "I've missed you so much."

"And I've missed you." He gathered her close. "I love you, Dionne. You hold my heart in your hand. Please, say you'll come back to me."

She buried her face in his shoulder and sighed. She belonged with him, in good times and in bad. "Can we tell everyone the truth? I hate lying."

"Absolutely. No more lies. Not to anyone."

She took a ragged breath and smiled up at him. "Take us home, Mark. All of us."

HARLEQUIN®
SUPERROMANCE®

*Pregnant…and on
her own?*

HER BEST FRIEND'S BABY by **C.J. Carmichael**
(Superromance #891)
Mallory and Drew are best friends—and then they share an unexpected
night of passion. With an unexpected result. Mallory's pregnant….
Being "just friends" again is impossible. Which leaves being lovers—
or getting married.
On sale January 2000

EXPECTATIONS by **Brenda Novak**
(Superromance #899)
Jenna's pregnant by her abusive ex-husband, although the marriage is
definitely over. Then her first love, Adam, comes back on the scene,
wanting to reconcile. Will he still want her when he learns she's
pregnant with another man's child?
On sale February 2000

BECAUSE OF THE BABY by **Anne Haven**
(Superromance #905)
They're friends and colleagues. One hot summer night, Melissa and Kyle
give in to the secret attraction they've never acknowledged. It wasn't
supposed to happen, but it's changed their lives forever—because
Melissa is pregnant. Their solution is a shotgun-style wedding…and
love's not supposed to be part of the bargain.
On sale March 2000

Available at your favorite retail outlet.

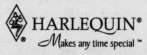

HARLEQUIN®
Makes any time special™

HSR9ML00

Come escape with Harlequin's new

Series Sampler

Four great full-length Harlequin novels bound together in one fabulous volume and at an unbelievable price.

Be transported back in time with a Harlequin Historical® novel, get caught up in a mystery with **Intrigue®**, be tempted by a hot, sizzling romance with **Harlequin Temptation®**, or just enjoy a down-home all-American read with **American Romance®**.

You won't be able to put this collection down!

On sale February 2000 at your favorite retail outlet.

HARLEQUIN®
Makes any time special ™

Visit us at www.romance.net

PHESC

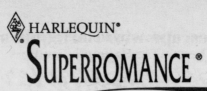

Welcome to cowboy country!

MONTANA LEGACY by **Roxanne Rustand**
(Superromance #895)
Minneapolis cop Kate Rawlins has her own reasons
for wanting to sell her inheritance—half of the
Lone Tree Ranch, Montana. Then she meets
co-owner Seth Hayward and suddenly splitting the property
doesn't seem like a good idea....
On sale February 2000

COWBOY COME HOME by **Eve Gaddy**
(Superromance #903)
After years on the saddle circuit, champion bronco
rider Jake Rollins returns home—determined to find
out whether his ex-lover's daughter is *his* child.
On sale March 2000

Available at your favorite retail outlet.

3 Stories of Holiday Romance from three bestselling Harlequin® authors

Valentine Babies

by

ANNE STUART

TARA TAYLOR QUINN

JULE McBRIDE

Goddess in Waiting by Anne Stuart
Edward walks into Marika's funky maternity shop to pick up some things for his sister. He doesn't expect to assist in the delivery of a baby and fall for outrageous Marika.

Gabe's Special Delivery by Tara Taylor Quinn
On February 14, Gabe Stone finds a living, breathing valentine on his doorstep—his daughter. Her mother has given Gabe four hours to adjust to fatherhood, resolve custody and win back his ex-wife?

My Man Valentine by Jule McBride
Everyone knows Eloise Hunter and C. D. Valentine are in love. Except Eloise and C. D. Then, one of Eloise's baby-sitting clients leaves her with a baby to mind, and C. D. swings into protector mode.

VALENTINE BABIES

On sale January 2000 at your favorite retail outlet.

HARLEQUIN®
Makes any time special ™